A CATASTROPHIC THEFT

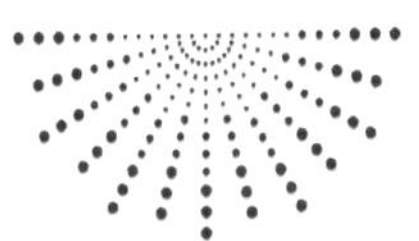

A CATASTROPHIC THEFT

REG RAWLINS, PSYCHIC INVESTIGATOR #3

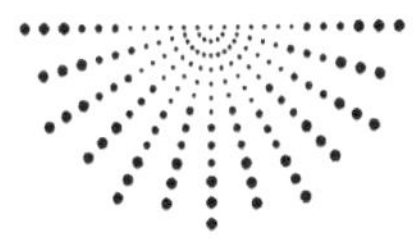

P.D. WORKMAN

ISBN: 9781989080696 (IS Hardcover)

ISBN: 9781989080689 (IS Paperback)

ISBN: 9781989080658 (KDP Paperback)

ISBN: 9781989080665 (Kindle)

ISBN: 9781989080672 (ePub)

pdworkman

Vegan Baked Alaska

Muffins Masks Murder

Tai Chi and Chai Tea

Santa Shortbread

Cold as Ice Cream

Changing Fortune Cookies

Hot on the Trail Mix

Recipes from Auntie Clem's Bakery

Zachary Goldman Mysteries

She Wore Mourning

His Hands Were Quiet

She Was Dying Anyway

He Was Walking Alone

They Thought He was Safe

He Was Not There

Her Work Was Everything

She Told a Lie

He Never Forgot

She Was At Risk

Kenzie Kirsch Medical Thrillers

Unlawful Harvest

Doctored Death (Coming soon)

Dosed to Death (Coming soon)

Gentle Angel (Coming soon)

AND MORE AT PDWORKMAN.COM

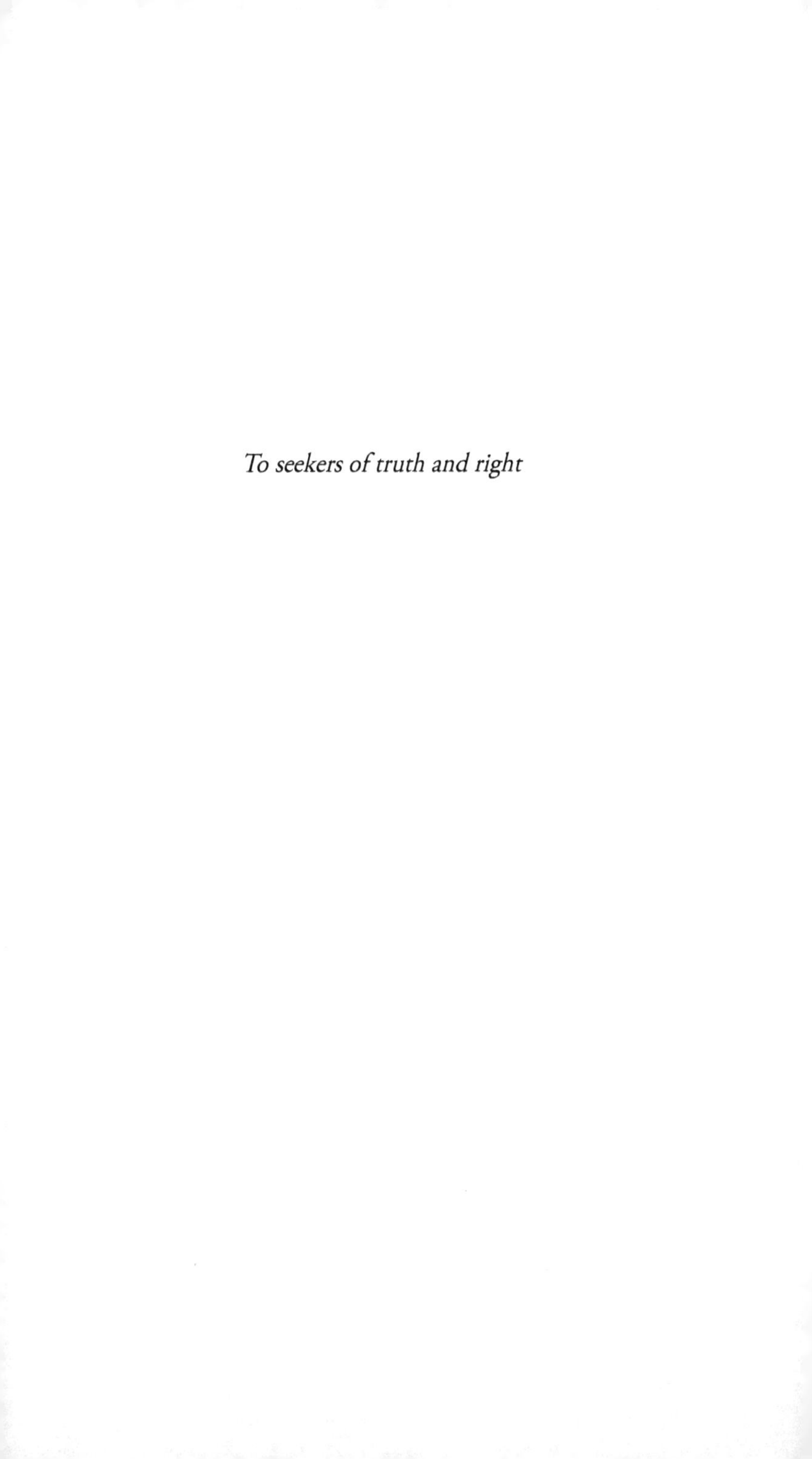

To seekers of truth and right

CHAPTER ONE

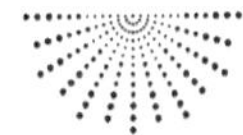

$\mathcal{R}$eg had been trying to sleep through a cacophony of bird calls in the garden outside her window, sheet pulled tightly over her head. Unfortunately, the sheet did not provide a sufficient barrier to block out their noise. All hope of sleep fled when Starlight decided it was breakfast time. He jumped down from the window where he'd been perched watching the avian activity and onto Reg's bed, yowling impatiently to tell her how hungry he was.

"Not yet, Star," Reg protested. "I'm not getting up for a couple more hours yet."

Starlight had other ideas. He pawed at her head through the sheet, not giving in.

"I didn't get enough sleep!"

He wasn't persuaded.

Reg groaned. She knew she wasn't going to be able to get any more rest once the cat decided it was time for her to get up. It was one of the joys of cat ownership that no one had bothered to tell her about. She pulled the sheet off of her face and Starlight touched his nose to hers, then rubbed the length of his cheek down hers, purring loudly. Reg pushed him away a little and scratched his ears.

"It wouldn't be so bad if I hadn't been up half the night."

Being nocturnal, Starlight already knew that Reg had been up late to hold a midnight seance for a client, which meant she had only been in bed for a few hours before the birds had started making their racket. Keyed up and overtired, the little bit of sleep that Reg had been able to get had been restless and filled with wild, unsettling dreams.

Reg yawned noisily. Starlight put his ears back, looking at her like she'd belched at a fancy dinner party.

"I'm tired," Reg reiterated.

There was no point in staying in bed any longer, so she forced herself to get up and wandered into the bathroom for her morning ablutions. Starlight didn't follow her into the bathroom as he sometimes did, wary of being flicked with water so Reg could have her privacy. He was waiting by his bowl when she made it out to the kitchen. Reg frowned, looking down at his bowl. She could swear that he'd actually eaten some of his dry kibble. Maybe he would actually eat the new brand that she'd paid an arm and a leg for at the specialty pet store. The clerk who had helped her had extolled the health benefits of the dry food, showing her the ingredients to verify that it was actually made from premium meat rather than the combination of grains and byproducts Reg had found on the label of the cheap grocery store box she had previously bought.

"Do you like that? Did you have some of it?"

Starlight just stared at her, waiting for her to hurry up and give him his morning meal.

Reg saw that her appointment book was on the island counter, which meant that Sarah had been by at some point and written someone into her calendar. Tired of surprise visits, Reg had decided to put a system in place to help her keep on top of the appointments that Sarah set up.

Sarah was not Reg's secretary, but her landlord, a senior witch whose connections in Black Sands often put her in contact with people who were looking for psychic services. She had taken it upon herself to provide Reg with the clientele she needed, as well as keep the fridge stocked and maintain everything else in the furnished cottage in her backyard in top condition.

While Reg sometimes wished for the peace and privacy she should have been able to enjoy as a paying tenant, she couldn't deny that Sarah's intrusions were an unexpected benefit and had resulted in her being able to build up her psychic services business in Black Sands much more quickly than she had anticipated.

In the past, things had always gone the opposite way. She had aged out of the foster care system without any significant skills and hadn't had any opportunities for further education. She would come up with brilliant ideas of ways to make money, but they never worked out the way she expected them to. Money just didn't come in or people caught on to her scams too quickly, and before she'd managed to raise more than a comfortable living, she was forced to move on to avoid trouble and would again be looking for a way to get rich.

She paged through the calendar to make sure she was aware of her schedule for the next few days. Starlight rubbed against her legs, encouraging her to put something more interesting into his bowl.

"Okay, okay. Let's see what we've got."

Reg opened the fridge and surveyed the contents. There was a round plastic container that was unfamiliar. She popped the lid to have a peek at the contents. Some kind of stew that Sarah had probably made too much of and was trying to pawn off on her; or else she had deliberately made enough for Reg because she was concerned about Reg's less-than-healthy eating habits—though Sarah's weren't much better.

"Let's try some of this."

Reg spooned a generous helping of the stew into Starlight's bowl and put it down on the floor. He sniffed at it for a minute, then apparently deemed it safe for feline consumption and started in on it. Reg put the container back into the fridge and looked for something better suited for her own breakfast.

* * *

Having a written calendar and Sarah acting as her scheduling secretary apparently didn't keep Reg from having unexpected guests. She had eaten her non-Sarah-approved breakfast and was just having a cup of tea and deciding how to approach her day when there was a knock at the door. If it had been Sarah, she would just have walked in, but the door didn't open.

Reg went over to look out the peephole, much more careful about letting just anyone into the house than she had been in the past. But the diminutive figure she saw through the peephole was not Corvin or some other threat. Reg opened the door, smiling.

"What can I do for you, Detective Jessup?"

Marta Jessup gave a little shrug, her Asian complexion taking on a slightly pink hue. "I hope I didn't get you up." She nodded to the tea, "but it looks like you already have the kettle on?"

"I've been up for ages." Reg stifled a yawn, wishing she were back in bed. But maybe she'd be able to sneak in an afternoon nap between consultations. "Come in and have a cup with me."

Jessup accepted her invitation and in a few minutes they were in Reg's living room, as snug in the upholstered wicker chairs as one could be. Jessup sipped at her tea, which Reg noted she had added quite a bit of sugar and milk to.

"I wonder if you would consult for me on another case," Jessup suggested.

"Sure." Reg nodded. Her consultation on the previous case, that of a missing adolescent fairy, Calliopia Papillon, had been both successful and profitable. "What can I do for you?"

"We haven't had any success in finding the missing knife."

"Hawthorne-Rose's knife?" Reg automatically ran her thumb over the healing cut in her hand. The knife was, she knew, a rare artifact. Fairy steel rarely fell into the hands of anyone outside of the kin, and especially not one that had been polluted with fairy blood. It should have been unmade before it could fall into the hands of a human like Hawthorne-Rose.

"I've talked to everyone I could in any position of authority at Corvin's club. They all maintain that when they picked up the car, there was nothing in it. No knife. They suggest that someone must have taken it out of my bag before the car was retrieved."

"Well, they would, wouldn't they?" Reg gave a shrug. If possession of such a rare and valuable object had fallen into Reg's hands, she certainly wouldn't have been eager to return it to its rightful owner. Not without significant compensation. The police couldn't prove that anyone at the club had it, so they couldn't make threats to get it back.

"I can't prove whether they have it," Jessup echoed Reg's thoughts, "or whether Corvin or someone else took it before the car was picked back up by the club."

"My money is on Corvin. It wasn't me."

"I suspect the warlock too," Jessup admitted. "Even after all the times he's assisted with investigations in the past… I'm not sure he could resist the pull of a powerful object like the knife."

"He'd be risking never being able to do any other work for you. Would he take that chance? When you've provided him with other artifacts as compensation before?"

"Could he delay immediate gratification for something he might get in the future? I don't know. He doesn't have the best record for demonstrating willpower."

There was a knot in Reg's stomach. She tried to breathe through it. Jessup didn't know of Reg's latest conflict with Corvin, but she knew that Corvin had previously stolen Reg's powers. He had returned them to her, something unheard of, in order to save Reg and himself from Hawthorne-Rose, but that didn't mean he didn't want them back again. In fact, he seemed quite determined to possess them once more.

"No," Reg agreed, "willpower is not high on Corvin's list of virtues."

"At the moment I have no way of proving that Corvin has the knife, or that his club does, or whether I'm just chasing my tail here and it's someone else altogether. So I wondered… if you could put me on the right track."

Reg nodded. "Yeah, I'd be happy to help."

She stared for a minute into her cup, at the tea leaves swirling in the bottom. It wouldn't be hard for her to locate the knife. She had located lost objects that she had no connection to in the past. The knife had drawn her blood, so she had a strong physical connection with it. She closed her eyes to focus, which didn't give her a headache like rolling her eyes back in her head. Jessup didn't need a show like less sophisticated clients. No need for over-dramatization.

She reached out with her mind, feeling for the knife. She was surprised not to get an immediate hit. She frowned, squeezing her eyes shut more tightly and drawing her brows down, focusing intently. Jessup sat quietly, waiting, and didn't distract her from the process with questions.

Reg kept her eyes closed and made a noise to call Starlight to her. She shouldn't need a psychic boost to find the knife, yet obviously she did. She heard the patter of Starlight's feet and he jumped up into her lap. The only time the cat actually came when he was called—other than for meals, which she never had to call him for—was when she needed him for a psychic reason.

Reg scratched his ears and pressed her face into the velvety fur on top of his head. Starlight was still, but it was an active, focused stillness, not like when he was sleeping or cuddling. Reg imagined the knife. She tried to conjure up a detailed picture of it in her mind. She had seen it several times. She had been injured with it. It had been joined with her.

But it was like there was a wall around the knife. She couldn't locate it. She tried to see the wall itself or the area around the wall. If it were in a box or protected by some kind of enchantment, then maybe she couldn't see the knife itself but would be able to see its location. Still, nothing came to her. Starlight dug his claws into Reg's leg. She tried to harness all of his energy and hers and to focus it on the task, but she still failed to find the knife.

Reg breathed out in a long sigh and opened her eyes. "I can't see it," she said, shaking her head. "I should be able to, I don't know why I can't."

Jessup nodded, not looking surprised. "I wasn't betting on you being able to, but I figured it was worth a try."

"I don't understand why I can't reach it. It shouldn't be that hard, when I've seen it and… err, had it in my hand… before."

Jessup's eyes flashed amusement. "Yes. Well, in my experience, these paranormal phenomena never quite work out the way you expect them to. And you can never be sure what the other person is up to… what kind of magic or other power they might have on their side."

"But if it's Corvin…" Reg wanted to say that she had a connection with him and she should have been able to use that, but she couldn't figure out how to say it in a way that wouldn't make it sound like they had a relationship.

"If it's Corvin," Jessup picked up the thread, "he's had your powers. He knows better than anyone what you're capable of and what he'd need to do to block you. It wouldn't be hard for him to guess that I'd come to you to help find it."

"I suppose." Reg still didn't think Corvin should be able to block her. They'd been so intimately connected in the past.

Starlight fluffed out his fur and looked at her contemptuously, which told her that he knew exactly who she was talking about. There was no love lost between Corvin and Starlight.

"I'm not going to see him," Reg told the cat. "We're just talking about whether he has the fairy steel."

Starlight made a little burping meow, jumped down, and walked away. Reg shook her head. "I'll never understand cats."

"It actually seems like you understand him pretty well."

"Then maybe I understand him too well."

Jessup laughed and nodded. "I'm not sure any of us wants to know what cats are thinking about us."

"Mostly, I'm just the provider of fish."

"I'm sure there's more to it than that…"

"Not a lot. If you want to know what cats think about... mostly it's about food."

"Well..." Jessup shifted, preparing to stand, "I appreciate you trying, Reg. If something comes to you later... let me know."

"Sure."

There was a hurried knock on the door that made Reg jump, and the door opened. It was, of course, Sarah. She popped into the room and looked around, her eyes wide, looking disheveled. Sarah, a grandmotherly type, always looked neat and tidy and was the master of quick changes, so Reg was surprised to see her in such a state.

"Sarah? Is something wrong?"

"My emerald!" Sarah's breathing was quick and labored. "I can't find it. I don't know where it is. My emerald!"

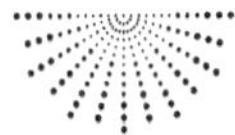

Come sit down." Reg was already halfway across the room to her, concerned about her condition. "Tell us what happened."

She reached Sarah and took her by the arm to escort her to the seating area. She didn't want Sarah to have a heart attack or faint from exertion.

"You remember my emerald necklace," Sarah said, falling heavily into the chair. "The one that I wore to the dance."

"Yes, of course. It was beautiful." Reg had never seen such a large stone. It had glowed with a life of its own and hung from a thick chain of braided gold.

"But it's gone. I don't know where it could have gone! Someone must have taken it."

"I don't think anyone could have gotten into your house without you knowing about it," Reg soothed. "You haven't been out anywhere. I'm sure it's just misplaced."

"Misplaced? You think I could misplace an item like that? I'm very careful with all of my possessions, but that one most of all. I wouldn't ever *misplace* it."

Reg held up her hands in a motion that was both a shrug and an attempt to stop Sarah's protest.

"I'm sorry. I didn't mean to insult you. I only meant…"

Sarah's eyes riveted on Jessup. "Marta, you have to help me. You can find it for me. Someone has stolen it!"

Jessup looked first at Reg, eyebrows raised, and then at Sarah. "The first thing we'll need to do is to conduct a thorough search of the house, in case it did fall back behind something or get moved somehow." She looked at her watch. "I don't know if I have the time to help out with that right now. I'll have to come back later and take a look around and take your report, if it hasn't shown up."

Sarah glared at her. "We're not talking about a trinket here," she said icily. "This is grand theft. My emerald is priceless."

There was an awkward silence, during which Reg wanted to point out that if Sarah's necklace was worth so much money, she should have been keeping it in a secure safety deposit box or safe, not just in a jewelry box or drawer in her house. She was sure that Jessup was thinking exactly the same thing, but neither of them was willing to incur Sarah's wrath by saying it.

Jessup looked at her watch again. "I really do have to go, but I'll have the department send someone over to take your report and open a file. Then I'll touch base with you again later. Okay?"

Sarah nodded, her lips pressed together in a thin pink line.

Jessup stood. "I'm sorry. I will get someone right onto it. But… the officer they send over to take your statement will likely not be a practitioner, so watch what you say. If you make them think you're a crazy old lady claiming to have lost a magical necklace, they're not going to take you seriously. Focus on the intrinsic value of the emerald itself."

"I'm not stupid."

"I would never suggest that you are. But you're used to dealing with others in the community, and the person they send over will likely not be open to the idea of… paranormal phenomena."

* * *

After Detective Jessup left, Reg did what she could to calm Sarah down, putting the kettle back on to boil and assuring her that the police department was bound to find out who it was that had stolen Sarah's emerald.

"Who are we kidding?" Sarah wailed, her normally neat blond hair askew. "The police department has no chance of finding my necklace! How are they going to figure out who it was that took it? And where it is being kept now? This is a job for a clairvoyant, not the police."

She turned her gaze to Reg, who was too drained from looking for the knife to even consider trying to locate Sarah's emerald. Reg explained the reason for Jessup's visit.

"I can't look for your emerald right now, but I'll do it later, when I have a little strength back. Right now… I just can't."

Sarah's lips pressed together again, and Reg knew she was thinking about how she was always the first one to help others, yet both Jessup and Reg had given excuses and put her off.

"I'm sorry. Really, I am. If I had known about your necklace a little earlier, I would have told Jessup that the knife would have to wait. I know this emerald means a lot to you. I'll help you all I can. I just don't have the energy right now to find anything."

"Of course," Sarah agreed, but she didn't sound at all convinced.

"I'll come over to the house and help you to look physically," Reg offered. "I can't use my powers right now but I could have a look around."

"I've already looked. It isn't in the house. Someone came into the house and stole it."

It sounded just as unlikely as it had the first time Sarah had asserted that an intruder had taken the necklace.

"Did they take anything else? Electronics? Other jewelry? Cash?"

"They took the most valuable thing in the house. Why would they need to take anything else? They knew what they were looking for. They knew exactly what they were doing."

"But you have a lot of other jewels. They weren't interested in anything else?"

Sarah studied Reg suspiciously and Reg couldn't help the flush that rose to her cheeks. She hadn't stolen anything of value from Sarah. If she had, she'd have been able to keep it from her face. She was good at lying, but she didn't have the same ability to cover her embarrassment at being suspected when she had done nothing.

Of course she had taken note of Sarah's vast array of jewelry. Of course she knew how valuable Sarah's trinkets were. Sarah hadn't exactly tried to hide them from her. But Reg hadn't taken them. If she'd taken them, she would have done it in a way that would have diverted suspicion from her, or she would have immediately left town. And no matter how valuable the emerald was, she wouldn't have been satisfied to have left everything else and taken only the one piece of jewelry.

"If it was me, would I still be here?" Reg asked.

"Maybe you thought I wouldn't believe it was you."

Reg shook her head. "If I had something like that in my pocket, I wouldn't be waiting around to see whether you suspected me or not. I'd be putting as many miles between you and me as possible."

Sarah studied her. Reg didn't know whether Sarah would believe her because Reg was being honest with her about it, or whether she wouldn't believe her because Reg was as much as admitting that she might have considered stealing such a valuable object.

"I didn't steal it," Reg said, looking her in the eye. Maybe Sarah just needed to hear it from her, straight out. "I didn't take your emerald or any of your jewelry."

"Can I trust you, though?"

Reg swallowed, looking at her. Would she have been able to resist the emerald any more than Corvin would have been able to resist the knife, if the opportunity arose? Could she have decided, in the face of such a temptation, that her life in Black Sands was more important and valuable to her than the cold, hard cash that such a prize would bring in?

"I wouldn't trust me."

Sarah nodded her agreement. "No."

CHAPTER THREE

There was a long period of silence between them.

As a child, it had always hurt Reg's feelings when someone accused her of doing something she hadn't done. It even hurt her feelings when someone accused her of something that she had done, not believing her protestations of innocence. It always seemed unfair that someone should suspect her. She had done everything she could to present herself as a good girl, and had never understood why people suspected her anyway. But the fact was, people would always suspect the foster child. The homeless person. The one who had a record. The person pretending to have paranormal powers. Guilty or innocent, people would always assume Reg's guilt.

And she would just have to accept it. There was no point in getting upset over it.

"Sarah, I know you're really upset over this... but I wonder if you can help me out with something, when it's all sorted out and you're feeling like yourself again."

She knew Sarah wouldn't be able to resist her curiosity, even if she were upset over the disappearance of her heirloom. And she was driven to help people. It was her natural instinct, even if it was something Reg herself rarely felt.

"Help you with what?"

"It's nothing. Later. When this is all taken care of and you have your necklace back."

"That could be weeks, Reg. Or never. If some sorcerer has gotten his hands on it…" Sarah shook her head, eyes glistening with tears. "It was my job to safeguard the emerald, and it's gone. If it was stolen for some reason other than its value as a rare gem… then I've failed."

"I'm sorry. Why is it so valuable? What can it do?"

"Tell me what you need my help for," Sarah said, looking Reg in the eye and clearly avoiding her question.

Reg hesitated, her own curiosity over the mysterious powers the necklace must have teasing her. "Well… it isn't really anything important. It's just that… I've always been good at finding lost things. Even before I realized that I had real psychic powers. I always had ideas, or saw where they were. I'd get in trouble because my school teachers or foster parents thought that I'd hidden things when I found them too fast."

Sarah nodded encouragingly.

"And when Jessup came over and asked me to look for the knife, I didn't think it would be any problem. I've touched that knife. I've held it and studied it. I should be able to find it anywhere. Or at least to have an idea of where to look for it."

"You didn't get anything?"

"Nothing at all."

Sarah considered the matter. She didn't jump in with an easy explanation or tell Reg that it was nothing to be concerned about.

"Your powers, at least since you came to Black Sands, have been very impressive."

Reg nodded, looking away from her. She had done a lot of things in Black Sands that she had never done before, or had never done since she was a child and had learned to hide and suppress her psychic abilities.

"Most psychics don't have the clarity of vision that you do.

They have ideas and impressions, but not actual clear visions like you have had."

"I guess, yeah."

"So which is normal for you? Was it unusual when you were having clear visions? Or is it unusual that you are not getting anything now?"

"I… don't know."

"Maybe there is something that was helping you before that isn't any longer."

"Like Starlight, you mean? Because he was trying to help me find the knife."

"As far as you know." Sarah cast her eyes about for the cat, but he wasn't in the room. "You can't always trust what you see. Especially not with cats. They can be very deceptive. Where is he now? Why isn't he out here begging me to feed him like he usually does?"

Reg frowned, looking back toward the bedrooms. "I don't know. He seems to like the new cat food, so maybe he just isn't hungry."

"Maybe he's avoiding you because he didn't choose to help you with your psychic vision."

"No. I'm sure he was helping me. It just wasn't enough. I still couldn't see the knife."

"Okay," Sarah accepted this with equanimity, "then what else could be blocking you? Maybe you don't want to find the knife."

"Of course I want to find it. Why wouldn't I want to find it?"

"Because it harmed you. Maybe you believe that if it is found, it will harm you again. You're just starting to heal now; the wound is still fresh."

Reg licked dry lips. She raised her teacup for a drink, but her tea was too cold. "Maybe. But I don't think so."

"Maybe the wound from the knife damaged your psychic abilities. Letticia didn't like the way it was just healed out of the blue when it had been so difficult to treat initially. It was suddenly better, when she hadn't even had a chance to apply the rowan berries to it yet."

"But we thought maybe that was fairy magic. From Calliopia…"

"And maybe it was. But fairy magic is unpredictable. It rarely gives you something without taking something away. Haven't you ever read the traditional fairy tales? Wishes are always granted in the worst possible way, leaving the wisher in a worse position than they were in to begin with. Maybe she healed you and took away some of your powers at the same time."

Reg's heart pounded hard. She had been trying so hard to avoid Corvin and giving him what he wanted; had she blindly given them up to Calliopia without even realizing it? She shook her head, scowling. "I don't feel the same way I did when Corvin took my powers. When I woke up after that… I felt empty and… deaf… like I couldn't hear anything anymore. Because all of the voices and feelings were gone. But that's not what I feel like now. I feel like… I'm not getting the answer to a question, but not like everything is gone."

"You might not have lost everything. You might just have lost the ability to seek. Or some other combination of powers. The folk are fickle."

CHAPTER FOUR

Sarah eventually went back to the main house, across the back yard from the guest cottage that Reg rented from her. She declined Reg's repeated offers to help her to search for the emerald necklace. She was quite sure that it had been stolen and she wasn't going to accept any theory that it had been accidentally misplaced or slipped behind a piece of furniture.

Reg watched Sarah walk back up the sidewalk to the house. When she was out of sight, Reg went to her bedroom. Starlight was sitting on the end of the bed, tall and stiff, his ears pricked up, listening.

"Where have you been?" Reg asked him. "Were you listening to the conversation the whole time?"

He just stared at her, but Reg could feel his haughty amusement. At least she still had that ability. Not that the ability to intuit a cat's emotions could be a particularly profitable skill for a psychic. Unless she started to offer pet services. Get to know your cat… understand what he is thinking… why he is acting out…

"You want to help me, don't you?"

Starlight gave a rumbling purr of assent. Reg felt a wave of warmth spread over her body and gave him a smile. She scratched his ears and his chin.

"Yeah. You're a good cat, aren't you? Maybe you just didn't want to come out while Sarah was so upset. You didn't want to stir things up more for her, since she really doesn't like cats—doesn't appreciate cats like she does some other animals."

Starlight gave a sudden twitch, focusing his gaze somewhere beyond Reg. Reg turned around to see what he was looking at a second before there was a hard rap on the door.

"Uh-oh. I don't like the sound of that. What's going on?"

Starlight jumped down from the bed and headed toward the door, so Reg followed him. He stopped in the middle of the living room and looked at the door. Reg looked through the peephole. No uniform this time, but it also wasn't anyone she recognized. A cloaked man.

"Regina Rawlins," he said through the door, his voice not raised, but still clear. He pronounced her name wrong, with a long 'i' like the Canadian city instead of her preferred Reh-JEE-nah.

"Who are you?" Reg demanded without opening the door.

"Dave Smith. I sent you a summons earlier."

"A summons?"

"I assume that you received it, though I didn't receive any response."

It took a minute for Reg to remember the summons he must have been talking about. A notification she got via a crow, informing her she would be expected to testify at Corvin's tribunal.

"Oh. That. About Corvin?"

"Would you at least open the door, please?"

Reg was even less motivated to open it knowing who he was. He was from Corvin's coven. The head of his coven. Did that mean he was like Corvin? Maybe he was even worse than Corvin. Not someone she was going to invite into her home. She preferred to keep the closed door between them.

"I don't want to."

"Miss Rawlins. I am not accustomed to having to shout through doors in order to have a conversation. Please open the door so we may talk face to face. You could have responded to my missive, and then I would not have had to come over here to speak in person."

"Okay. Go away, and I'll send you a reply. Except… I don't know where you live and I don't have a messenger crow."

He chuckled. "I did give you several other ways to reply in my letter."

Reg's cheeks warmed. "I, uh… don't read your old-style writing very well."

"Perhaps you could just open the door, then."

Reg sighed. She looked back at Starlight to see what he thought of the idea. Starlight stared back at her, not indicating that she should open the door, but not hissing or biting her ankles, either. He wasn't responding to Dave Smith the warlock the same way as he responded to Corvin Hunter.

Reg turned the handle and pulled the door open a few inches. She sniffed, but didn't smell the floral odor that Corvin exuded when he was trying to charm her. But maybe each warlock had a different smell, or different kinds of charms. She couldn't assume that they were all exactly the same. Reg opened the door a little farther to look at him.

Like most of the warlocks she had met so far, he was quite handsome. Dark-haired, clean-shaven, dark eyes. With his cloak, he looked like he had just walked out of a *Lord of the Rings* set.

"I am not here to harm you," he said, raising an eyebrow.

He didn't seem threatening. But then, neither did Corvin. That was how he attracted his prey.

"I've only known a couple of warlocks," Reg told him. "Corvin stole my gifts. Another of them gave me this." She raised her hand to show him the cut in the middle of her palm from Hawthorne-Rose's knife.

He blinked at the healing wound thoughtfully and nodded. "I repeat. I'm not here to harm you."

"I don't trust your word. Sorry, but I've been burned before."

He gave a tentative smile. "Not all warlocks are Corvin."

"Maybe not. But how do I know you're telling the truth?"

He raised his hands helplessly, knowing that nothing he said could convince her that he was trustworthy.

"Do you… have the same powers as Corvin…?"

"No. Just like with witches and mediums, everyone has different powers." Then his eyes widened and he put out his hand in a 'stop' gesture. "Oh, you mean his ability to take your powers. No, there are very few of us who have that ability. Certainly none others in our coven."

That, at least, was a relief. If he was telling the truth. She still wasn't about to invite him in. Reg folded her arms, feeling vulnerable. Another warlock, standing just inches away from her, and she had no way to protect herself.

"So what do you want?" she demanded.

"Your attendance at Corvin Hunter's upcoming tribunal was requested."

"Yeah. Do I really have to be there? Can't you deal with him without me?"

"If you seek justice, you need to tell your side of the story. We have received reports of his activities, but we cannot proceed without your testimony."

"Can I just tell you or swear an affidavit? I really don't want anything to do with his coven."

"You need to attend."

Reg sighed. She had suspected as much, even if she had hoped to get out of it. "Fine. I'll come."

"Do you need me to give you the details? If you have difficulty reading my script…"

"No. Sarah already put all of that in my calendar. Is there anything else I should know? Do I have to wear robes or observe some other kind of custom? I'm not from around here and I don't know how these things are done."

"The coven will not be sky clad. There is no expected dress for the witnesses; you can wear what you are comfortable with."

Reg blinked at him and shook her head slightly. "What?"

"Some rituals are typically observed sky clad, but not something like a tribunal. The participants will be robed."

"I don't know what sky clad means, it sounds sort of…"

Dave Smith cleared his throat and Reg thought she detected a blush. "Disrobed," he offered in a tentative voice that made it sound like a question.

"Disrobed?" Reg repeated blankly, before really comprehending what he was saying. "You mean *naked?* You guys go dancing around in your…?"

"In our birthday suits, so to speak? Sky clad really does sound better." He swallowed his embarrassment and looked at her steadily. "As I say, this proceeding is not such an occasion. The members will be robed and I would expect you would want to be as well."

Reg swore under her breath. "I didn't mean I was going to come naked. I just wanted to know if there was a ceremonial dress." She motioned to his black cloak. "You know, like that."

"Oh, right. No, you can wear what you like. I don't believe you're a witch, so you probably don't have ceremonial dress."

"No."

"Just come in your regular clothes."

Reg nodded. She couldn't help looking back at the handsome warlock, thinking about him *without* his ceremonial dress, which she was sure made her blush more than he had. What was it with the warlocks looking so ruggedly handsome. Was it a spell? A potion? Warlock face cream?

"So I can expect to see you there?" Dave Smith asked.

"Yes. I'll come." Reg scowled. "I don't really want to testify, but I want to see him get what he deserves for what he did to me."

The warlock's eyes slid away from her and he nodded. "Did you have any other questions? Anything I can do for you?"

Reg leaned against the doorframe, relaxing a bit. "You're the leader of Corvin's coven? Aren't you pretty… young for that? You look younger than he is."

"Appearances can be deceiving. I'm not."

"Oh." Reg waited for more details, but nothing was forthcoming. She assumed he meant that he was not younger than Corvin, rather than that he was not the leader of the coven. It seemed strange that someone so young could be the leader of the coven, when the leader of Sarah's coven was a mature woman in her sixties or seventies. Dave Smith looked to be thirty, tops. "Well... I guess I'll see you at the hearing, then."

He reached into his pocket and came out with a business card held between his index and middle finger, which he held out to her. "My details, in case you should wish to reach me by a method other than avian."

Reg looked at it, but wasn't sure she should take anything from him. "If you use modern technology, then what was with the bird delivery and calligraphy?"

"Err... it's traditional." Dave Smith shifted.

"Kind of showy, isn't it? When you could have just sent me an email?"

"Maybe a little," he admitted.

Reg considered, feeling out his discomfort and analyzing it. "Maybe the whole point is intimidation. You want people to feel anxious about it. Same with calling it a tribunal. You're trying to make it sound like some big, scary thing."

"This *is* something that is very important to us. The consequences could be far-reaching not just for Corvin, but for the community. It's very serious."

Reg remembered Corvin telling her about disciplinary actions that could be taken against witches and warlocks. In serious cases, they could be bound, which meant that not only were their powers taken out of the community, but that the community had to expend power in holding them. She nodded slowly. "Yeah, okay. I get it."

He wiggled the business card, encouraging her to take it. Reg considered it warily.

"Leave it in the mailbox," she said, nodding to the mailbox affixed to the outside of the cottage. She had never used it; if she got any mail, Sarah would simply leave it on the kitchen counter.

Dave Smith didn't move at first, then he nodded and deposited it into the box as requested. "You're very careful."

"I'm learning. I don't want to do something stupid. If there's some kind of spell on that card and I bring it into the house…"

"There isn't."

"So you say. I've been lied to before."

"I'm guessing a 'nice to meet you' handshake is out of the question."

"You guess correctly."

He still didn't leave. "You know you can't judge all warlocks by the actions of one or two."

"I'll have to meet a few more before I can make that decision."

She knew by the look on his face that he was going to ask her out. He'd make some lame come-on like, "Why don't you join me for dinner, and I'll show you what nice guys warlocks can be?" And she'd turn him down, and then he'd be angry at her and more likely to side with Corvin at the hearing.

He turned away abruptly. "I'm sorry to have taken up your time, Miss Rawlins. I'll see you at the tribunal."

She watched him until he was out of sight, then shut the door. She left his business card in her mailbox. She wasn't touching it until Sarah or someone else had a good look at it.

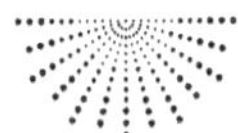

CHAPTER FIVE

*R*eg expected a visit from Sarah later in the day, telling her that she had found the necklace or giving her an update on the police investigation. But the hours passed and Reg dealt with clients and her email and advertising, and she still heard nothing from the witch.

She made herself a tuna fish sandwich, splitting the tuna with Starlight. While it wasn't a gourmet meal, she wasn't particularly interested in Sarah's stew, and it was at least healthier than ordering fast food yet again. She'd put on a few pounds since she'd arrived at Black Sands and she didn't want to get fat.

She had no evening clients, which meant that she could watch a few shows on TV and get to bed early, something she really needed following the seance the night before. She was really looking forward to the extra hours of sleep.

She would have gotten it if it hadn't been for that stupid cat.

* * *

The phone rang, and Reg looked at it blearily for a few minutes before picking it up and answering it.

"Hello?"

"It's Detective Jessup. I was wondering if I could set up a time to come by and talk to you today."

Reg grunted.

"I beg your pardon?"

"Is this about the knife? I don't know that I can do any more for you than I already have. And I kind of promised Sarah that I'd look for her emerald when I got my strength back."

"It isn't about the knife."

"Is it another job? I promised Sarah—"

"Can we set up a time, Reg?"

Reg stopped cold. Jessup's refusal to answer her question and her terse response set alarm bells ringing. Jessup wasn't stopping by for a casual visit or to ask a favor. Had someone reported Reg? Accused her of providing fraudulent services or some other perceived violation? She hadn't yet applied for a business license, which she should probably do, though she didn't like having her name on public records like that. Reg's brain went into high gear, trying to anticipate what the issue was.

"Is it something we could just discuss on the phone? We could get it over with right now..."

"How about two o'clock?" Jessup asked. "Will you be home?"

"Yes... I'll be here."

"Good. I'll see you then."

There was a double-beep indicating that Jessup had terminated the call. Reg looked at the phone in disbelief, then dropped it onto the mattress beside her. Starlight pushed his face into Reg's, purring loudly.

"Don't you try being all lovey-dovey with me," Reg growled, pushing him back away from her face. "I'm still mad at you."

He meowed, jumped off the bed, and headed out the door and toward the bathroom, looking back at her over his shoulder as if trying to prod her into following her usual wake-up-bathroom-feed-cat routine.

"Forget it. You kept me awake half the night. I'm not getting up yet. You can eat your kibble if you're hungry."

He yowled mournfully, sitting in the hallway and looking back at her.

"Cry all you like. It's your own fault."

Although she really didn't want him to start crying again. He'd been at it for hours the previous night, howling and voicing his distress, pacing back and forth across the house, peering out windows and then jumping up on the bed to talk to her again.

Reg remembered the way that Erin had described the vocal renditions of her cat, Orange Blossom. Reg hadn't believed that he could possibly have been as loud as Erin described him. Waking up the neighbors and having them call in noise complaints? She had been sure it was an exaggeration. But Starlight's cries the night before had been unnerving. More than once she had gotten out of bed and turned on the light to check him out and make sure he was not sick or hurt. He just continued to pace around the windows howling.

Shutting her door hadn't helped. She could still hear him through it. She had tried shutting him in the bathroom and shutting her door, hoping that he'd calm down when he couldn't keep pacing around the cottage, but he hadn't calmed down. She'd tried to wait him out like a parent letting a baby cry it out, but he hadn't stopped and she could hear him clawing at the door, trying to get out. She didn't want to have to sand down and refinish the door, so she let him out again, and he renewed his pacing and crying.

Apparently, once the sun was up, whatever had been bothering him had passed, and he was back to his normal self again, ready to have breakfast and start the regular routine. But Reg hadn't gotten the sleep she needed and she didn't have any morning appointments, so she was going to sleep, at least until Sarah showed up to go through her usual routine of checking Reg's cupboards and fridge, writing down any appointments she had happened to make, and whatever other mothering she was determined to do.

When Sarah got there, Reg would get up.

* * *

When noon rolled around and Sarah still hadn't put in an appearance, Reg decided she'd better stop being lazy and get ready for the day. She'd been awake for some time, playing on her phone and refusing to get out of bed just on principle. But noon was the bright line she couldn't cross. At that point she had to get up, admit to herself that for once Sarah wasn't going to come and check in on her, and it was time to get down to business herself.

Starlight was curled up on a chair in the living room sulking about Reg not getting up to feed him as he had trained her to do. When she walked into the kitchen to make some tea, she saw that his food bowl was empty, something that had never happened before. She immediately felt guilty. He'd eaten all of the dry kibble and had been left with nothing to eat. She'd always heard that cats were supposed to have food available throughout the day to graze on whenever they wanted to. The empty bowl made her feel negligent, like a mother who'd forgotten to feed her child for a day or two.

She looked over at Starlight, who was watching her through one open eye. Her emotional reaction to his empty bowl seemed overblown, and she wondered if he was feeding her emotions, making her feel worse than she would have if she didn't have a psychic connection with him. She masked her emotions and trickled some more kibble into his bowl without calling him or making a fuss over it. Just routine, like he cleaned his bowl out every day and she wasn't at all concerned. Starlight continued to watch her for a few moments. Then he closed his one eye and rolled over, turning his back to her.

Obviously, he wasn't starving.

There was no mail on her counter. Either she hadn't received anything, or Sarah hadn't felt up to bringing it around to her. She'd have to go up to the house to ask later on. Maybe offer to help Sarah look for the emerald and see if there was anything else she could do. She had thought that Sarah would have found the necklace and recovered from her upset within a few hours, but apparently that had not happened.

Since there was no mail, community flyers, or newspaper to read, Reg pulled out her phone and tapped through a news site, checking to see whether anything interesting was happening in the world. Or at least in Black Sands.

Nothing jumped out at her. No news, really, just rehashes of ongoing issues. She tapped on a morning show and watched it while she waited for the tea kettle to boil. She read the headlines for upcoming segments, again seeing nothing very interesting. Filler. Just crappy filler. She supposed she should be happy about that. No plane crashes, no horrific crimes that she might be consulted about. Just puff pieces.

The kettle started to whistle. Reg poured the hot water into her cup, only half-watching what she was doing, her other eye on the small phone screen as the hosts joked around and introduced the next segment.

It was a piece on teen poverty and homelessness, an issue that always grabbed Reg's attention. She'd seen street life first-hand. She'd pulled herself out of that, like few managed to do, and she'd found ways to make a life for herself. It never lasted for long. Something else would always come along and pull her down again, but she was determined to succeed somehow. Erin seemed to have done it. Despite having faced police scrutiny more than once, her business seemed to be thriving.

Erin seemed happy in Bald Eagle Falls, somewhere Reg would never have been able to stay more than a couple of weeks. Where Black Sands had a welcoming community of witches and mediums and other paranormal folk, Bald Eagle Falls had the Bible belt and all kinds of Christian prejudices against things that fell outside the norm.

Reg focused on the screen, trying to listen to what the reporter was saying. He was interviewing a young woman who apparently worked with one of the agencies providing services to youth. Reg squinted at the screen.

Hot water flowed over the edge of the counter, spattering her feet. Reg yelped and swore and put the kettle down. She had filled her cup to overflowing, distracted by the news show. She danced back out of the way of the pooling water, and looked back at the screen.

She knew that woman. She'd seen her somewhere before, but couldn't place her.

CHAPTER SIX

Reg had lazed in bed until noon, so the two o'clock appointment with Detective Jessup rolled around pretty quickly. She kept an eye on the front window, wanting to be aware of when Jessup approached instead of being surprised by her knock on the door. Starlight seemed to pick up on Reg's nervousness and was looking around alertly, his ears swiveling this way and that as he listened to the little sounds that Reg couldn't even hear.

"Maybe she won't come," Reg said. "Cops get called to emergencies all the time. They're always having to reschedule because something more important came up. That's the way the world works. They have to take care of whatever's a priority right at the minute. And if something else came up, she'd have to take care of it..."

Starlight studied her for a moment as if to tell her that she was babbling, so she shut up. He was right. She was just telling herself lies, trying to put off the moment of truth. She looked out the window again and saw Jessup walking down the sidewalk toward the door. She took a deep breath, steeled herself, and walked to the door. She opened it before Jessup had a chance to knock. She hoped that took the wind out of her sails a little bit. But Jessup nodded. She didn't smile in greeting or act surprised that Reg was watching for her. She walked into the house without an invitation.

"Thanks for seeing me."

"I didn't think I had much choice."

"You always have the choice of whether to talk to the police or not."

Reg shook her head. "Sure didn't feel like it."

Jessup sat down on one of the living room chairs. "Do I need to inform you of your rights?"

Reg stared. "What?"

"You are aware of your rights?"

"Am I a suspect?"

"This is just an investigation. Trying to get the facts straight. No one is being arrested."

"That doesn't answer my question."

Jessup took out her notepad and flipped it open to a fresh page. "You have the right to have an attorney present."

"Are you giving me Miranda?"

"I'm… reminding you that you have rights if you want to exercise them."

Reg sat silently for a moment, considering that. "I… I guess I'll hear what you have to say, and then I'll decide. I don't have anyone."

"If you need a recommendation, you can call the state bar. You can also have an attorney appointed to you for free."

"Yeah. I know. Go ahead and say what you're going to say. What's this all about?"

Jessup scribbled with her pen to get the ink flowing, not meeting Reg's eyes.

"You are aware of Sarah's lost necklace."

"Yes. I figured she would have found it by now. I honestly didn't think that anyone really stole it. Maybe it slipped down behind a dresser. She's got a big house. It could be a lot of places."

"I had hoped that it would turn up on its own," Jessup admitted, "but it hasn't… and we need to proceed with the investigation and act on the assumption that it may, in fact, have been stolen."

"So this is about the necklace?"

Jessup looked her in the eye. "Yes."

Reg met Jessup's gaze and didn't waver. She counted the seconds and looked away at the appropriate point. No one liked a staring contest. But the connection had to last long enough for Jessup to be sure that Reg was being open and honest with her. It took fine tuning and lots of practice to get it right.

Jessup gave a little nod. Confirmation to herself as to what she had seen.

"What do you think happened to the necklace?" she asked.

"I just said. I think she misplaced it. I don't think someone went into the house and took it from her. Who would do that? I assume she's probably had the necklace for years. Who would suddenly decide they had to have it now?"

"Maybe someone who just became aware of it."

"Me, because I'm the new girl in town?"

"You *are* the new girl in town. And you saw it for the first time when Sarah wore it to the community dance."

"And I assume she told you that I told her she should have it locked up, not just lying around the house."

"That doesn't mean you didn't help yourself to it. You knew it wasn't locked up. Maybe you felt justified taking it because she didn't follow your advice. She deserved to lose it if she wasn't going to take care of it."

"No."

"Tell me what happened, then, in your own words."

"There's nothing to tell. Like you said, she wore it to the dance. I saw her put it on. I saw her wearing it at the dance. We came home. That's all I remember about it. I didn't see her put it away, and I haven't seen it since."

"You're suggesting that she didn't put it away that night? Maybe she left it out somewhere? Maybe she was too tired after all of the night's excitement?"

"I don't know what she did with it. I'm not suggesting anything. That's the full account of what I know about the emerald necklace. I saw her with it on. At home and at the dance. I never saw it again."

"Was she wearing it when she went home?"

"I assume so." Reg closed her eyes, trying to visualize it. They had come back home in the same limousine as had picked them up before the dance. It hadn't been completely dark inside the car. But it hadn't been daylight either. Reg pictured Sarah sitting beside her. But she couldn't remember with clarity anything that had happened after her encounter with Corvin. She had been tired and confused and Sarah had helped her to the car and then home. "I can't picture it. I really don't know."

"What happened at the dance?"

Reg searched Jessup's face for some sign that she already knew what had happened. Sarah must have told her, or she'd heard about it from someone else. It was a close-knit community, and gossip traveled fast. The air waves must have been buzzing with word about what had happened to Reg going back and forth.

"It was just a dance."

"I don't think so. Something happened."

"Well, it's true that it wasn't like anything I've ever been to before. The outfits, the decorations, the food and drink. It was all amazing. Like an old English ball."

"Sounds amazing. Some of the parties out here really are phenomenal. After a while, you tend to forget how over-the-top it is compared to community center sock hops around the country."

"I don't think I could ever get used to it."

"But that still doesn't tell me what happened."

"We went, we had food and wine, networked, danced, and eventually came home."

"And what happened?"

"I just told you."

"Was it Hunter? I noticed there was… something going on between the two of you. Hunter said he'd screwed things up."

"Yeah, he did."

"What happened?"

"It's got nothing to do with Sarah's necklace."

"I'll be the judge of that. I want a full picture of what happened that night."

"It's personal."

There had been enough people who had caught at least a glimpse of what had happened that Reg was sure it wasn't something she could ever keep private, but that didn't mean she couldn't try. It was her life. She was entitled to some privacy.

"I'm not going to tell anyone else," Jessup said. "I want to know what happened and what you can remember. It's important. You were the only other person that I know of who can confirm that Sarah still had the necklace when the two of you got home."

"I told you I can't remember."

"Then tell me what you can remember. That will help to clarify it."

"Do you really have to know? Can't you just leave it?" There was a lump in Reg's throat. She wasn't going to cry in front of Jessup. She didn't cry in front of the police. Unless it was because she knew it would work in her favor—that was different.

"Just tell me," Jessup urged. "Pretend it's just you and me and you really want to tell someone about it."

Reg sighed heavily and tried to swallow the lump in her throat. She looked up at the ceiling, willing her eyes to stay dry.

"Corvin talked me into dancing with him. I made a deal with him. That I'd only dance if he promised not to glamour me."

Jessup didn't tell her that it had been stupid to try to bargain with someone like Corvin Hunter. He would never hold up his end of the deal.

"I told him that if he used any of his magic on me, then he didn't have my agreement to give him my powers. No matter what he could get me to say, I didn't give my permission."

Jessup's brow furrowed as she thought about this. She nodded slowly, a hint of a smile on her lips. "Very tricky," she approved.

"If he couldn't use his powers on you, he would never be able to persuade you to give up your gifts willingly."

"That was the plan."

"And he agreed?"

"Not at first. To start with, he got mad, said it wasn't fair, had a little temper tantrum, and went storming off."

There was no hiding Jessup's grin at that. While she sometimes hired Corvin as an expert consultant on a case, there was no love lost between the two of them, and she kept a very tight rein on him.

"After a while, he came back," Reg went on. "He had calmed down and he said he agreed with my terms. Just dancing, no magic, no trying to get my powers. He just wanted to dance with me."

Jessup nodded slowly.

"I even asked Sarah. She said she'd keep an eye on things. That I would be safe as long as I was around people. He wouldn't do anything to me while everyone was watching."

"Creatures like him don't operate in the light," Jessup agreed.

Reg pondered for a moment on Jessup's use of the word creature instead of person. Sarah had called him a beast and an animal. Reg herself thought of him as a predator. A big cat or other hunter. He did seem far closer to an animal than a human sometimes. He'd referred to it as his nature, and Reg knew that his gnawing hunger was only too real.

"So we danced... and it was wonderful. Like nothing I've ever experienced before."

"But...?"

Reg shrugged helplessly and shook her head.

"But he broke his word?" Jessup prompted.

"Yes." Reg could barely whisper it. "He said he couldn't help it. That I was just too enticing. We walked out on the porch for air, and as soon as we were away from other people..."

"How did you manage to resist him?"

"The fairies. Lord and Lady Bernier and their entourage. Lord Bernier said I was protected by the fairies."

"Because you were contaminated with Calliopia's blood."

Reg nodded. "I didn't know that at the time. Lord Bernier rescued me before Corvin could steal my powers away again. Corvin was furious. He made me… he forced me to feel his pain. His hunger. It was awful. I thought it would kill me."

"To someone who isn't accustomed to it… it probably would."

"Lord Bernier threatened to kill Corvin… so he finally took the feeling away."

"That really is awful, Reg. I'm so sorry that happened to you."

For a minute, Jessup was Reg's friend. Someone who cared about her and how she felt. But then Reg forced herself to remember that she wasn't just having tea with a friend. It was a police interrogation, no matter how well it was camouflaged.

"So… Lady Bernier gave me some kind of restorative. I don't know what was in it, but it only took a few drops… and then Sarah got there… and we went home…"

Jessup considered this. "So you were ensorcelled by Hunter, given his pain, and then administered an unknown potion or drug that might or might not have been an intoxicant."

"Yes."

"It's no wonder your memories of what happened after that are a little muddy."

Reg gave a little laugh. "Yeah, I guess so."

"You and Sarah were probably both a little off kilter after all of that."

"Yeah. I don't know how she was feeling, but I was pretty rough. And my hand was still bothering too," Reg ran her thumb over the healing wound. "You remember how bad it was."

"It *was* bad."

"We got back to the cottage," Reg remembered, "and that was when Starlight came back. And he dragged this big clump of yarrow back in with him. Like he left just to find what we needed to treat the cut."

"Sarah came here before she went home."

"Yes."

"Have you searched to make sure she didn't drop it here? Or outside?"

"I haven't. I didn't even think about that."

"And did you say you came back in a limo?"

"Yes."

"Sarah never mentioned that. We'll need to check with the limo service too. Make sure she didn't drop it in the car."

"Wouldn't they have called her if she left something in the car? Or else they would keep it and deny they ever saw it."

"If it went down the crack in one of the seats, it might not have been found. It could still be in the car."

"Okay, I guess so," Reg agreed.

"Are you going to seek it for her, like you said?"

"Yeah. If I can."

"When?"

Reg looked toward the main house. "I don't know. I thought she would have been over here before now. She usually stops in for a visit. She didn't today."

"She's in pretty rough shape. She might not have felt up to it. And..." Jessup gave a grimace, "...I might have told her not to talk to you until I'd had a chance to interview you."

CHAPTER SEVEN

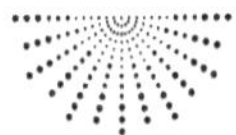

Reg clenched her teeth. Fury flamed up in her chest. She was so angry she could hardly breathe.

"Why? You really think I stole her emerald?"

"You are the newcomer here. The emerald has been in Sarah's possession for many years without incident. And you do have a history." Jessup tried to meet Reg's eyes, but Reg avoided her gaze, too angry and anxious to pull off a bluff.

"What history?"

"You've used the name Reg Rawlins before. You've left a trail."

Reg pounded her fist into her other hand, turning her anger and accusation onto herself. Why had she returned to that name? Nostalgia? Sentimentality? How stupid to go back to her childhood name just because seeing Erin had stirred up memories. Of course Jessup had run background on her. She'd probably done it before she'd talked to Reg the first time, accusing her of perpetuating a fraud by offering psychic services. She'd known then about Reg's checkered past. Maybe even about the heirlooms that had disappeared from Bald Eagle Falls, financing Reg's journey to Florida.

"I didn't steal Sarah's emerald."

"You had opportunities. At the party, in the car, back here, or in the main house."

"Don't you think I'd be out of here if I'd stolen a stone like that?"

"Yes, I do."

At least there was that. But whether Jessup believed she had taken the necklace or not, she was still investigating. She still had to look at Reg and to find either a way to eliminate Reg or evidence that she had committed the crime.

"It was someone else," Reg insisted. "Or else she just lost or misplaced it."

Jessup nodded. "We're investigating all angles."

"So are we done? Or do you need a lie detector test? Or maybe you want to search the place to make sure I don't have it in the back of a drawer somewhere."

Jessup's eyes narrowed as she studied Reg. Reg could sense her doubt and suspicion. It would have been obvious even to someone without any psychic powers. She was worried that Reg was throwing out a bluff. That she did, in fact, have the necklace secreted away in some drawer.

"I do think we should make sure Sarah didn't lose it here. It sounds like there was a good amount of confusion when the two of you got back from the party. Maybe she took it off without thinking, or maybe the clasp broke or was not done up properly."

It was a good way for Jessup to get Reg to consent to a search without accusing her of stealing it. And it would only allow her to search the more public areas Sarah would have been in. Not the bedrooms.

"Okay. We'll look together."

Jessup glanced at her sideways. Of course, she was right to be suspicious. After a glib tongue to talk people out of their money, sleight of hand was a con man's most valuable tool. If Reg did have the necklace, she could pick it up and pocket it even with Jessup working side-by-side with her. Reg was at least that good. If Jessup were going to keep up the pretense that she was just helping Reg see if Sarah had dropped the necklace and not that she was doing a police search of Reg's home, she couldn't object.

"Alright. Why don't you walk me through what happened from the time you got home. Maybe right from getting dropped at the curb. We'll retrace Sarah's steps and see if it triggers anything or we can find it along the way."

Reg acquiesced. They walked outside and around to the front of the main house. Jessup actually did walk right up to the curb, while Reg hung back at the sidewalk impatiently.

"Where along here were you dropped, do you remember?" Jessup asked, looking at the sewer grates.

Reg hadn't even thought of the possibility that the necklace could have dropped through a grate. She had recently learned about pixies living underground with tunnels that connected to the older parts of the sewer system. Was it possible that one of them could even have magicked it away from Sarah, causing it to drop down into their dirty little hands? Reg remembered the way that the necklace Sarah had given her as a ward against Corvin had simply slipped off in her hand when she decided she no longer wanted it, despite how impossible it had been to remove it earlier in the evening. Magic could certainly be used to unfasten a necklace.

"Uh… I'm pretty sure our door was aligned with the front door of the house." Reg walked over to the point at the curb, staring at the house and trying to picture it in her mind. "The driver would have expected us to go straight into the house, so he would have dropped us right here."

She looked down at the gutter and measured the distance to the nearest sewer grate. It seemed too far for the necklace to have traveled without a good deal of assistance. Jessup walked over to it anyway and shone her light down the hole. Reg tried to see without crowding Jessup. But there was nothing but the debris she would have expected. It didn't look like it had been disturbed. There were no footprints. No glint from the gold or gemstone.

"I don't see anything," Reg said.

"Nor do I. Did you go into the house before the cottage?"

"No. Straight back to the cottage."

They walked back around the house to the back yard in silence. Reg tried to remember every impression of that night. Every sight, sound, and smell.

"I guess we were about here when we saw Starlight."

"He was outside."

"Yes. He'd escaped the day before. Or two days. I don't know what time it was. I tried to go pick him up…" Reg took a few steps to demonstrate, "but he didn't want to be caught. So I stayed back from him and went into the house to get some tuna to tempt him in." Reg looked down at the pathway and the lawn. "I had taken off my shoes in the car, so I was barefoot. I stayed on the stones."

"And Sarah?"

"My back was to her. I went into the cottage first, and she was out of my sight for a few minutes while I called Starlight in… she came in, and then he did, dragging that yarrow plant."

Jessup looked down at the ground, and walked in widening circles, scanning for any sign of the jewelry. Reg didn't have any confidence that she would find it. She was sure Sarah hadn't lost it in the back yard. She walked back into the cottage, looking around with fresh eyes, trying to remember each move they had made that night. Dealing with Starlight and the yarrow plant, getting to bed.

There really wasn't anywhere Sarah could have dropped her necklace without Reg noticing it either that night or afterward. But she looked along the floor under the edges of the cupboards anyway, looked behind the sink in case Sarah had taken it off and put it down while dealing with the yarrow, checked in random drawers and the freezer. She wasn't feeling a tug toward it, as she often would if she were looking for an object. No instinct as to where it might be.

When she turned back around, she was startled to see Jessup standing there watching her, a frown on her face.

"I don't know where else to look," Reg said. "We were just here, in the kitchen, and then she went back to the house when I went to bed. I can't remember her wearing the necklace, but I would have noticed if it had been missing, don't you think? If it had fallen off or she had taken it off, one of us would have seen it, wouldn't we?"

"Maybe, maybe not. You had a pretty traumatizing night, and she would have been distracted. She might have taken it off absent-mindedly when you left the party, or when she was working in the kitchen here. She might have put it into her purse and forgotten about it. Who knows?"

"Did you ask her if she put it in her purse?"

"Yes. She said no, and she checked, but what if she used a different purse than she thought she did? She's not a young woman."

"But she wouldn't have forgotten that."

"In my experience as a detective, anyone can forget anything. Especially women going through hormonal changes like pregnancy or menopause."

"Ugh. I wouldn't want to be the one to ask Sarah that."

"I haven't. I've been trained in negotiation, but not with angry menopausal witches. Forget that. I'll use my investigative skills."

Reg laughed.

"Well…" Jessup took a cursory glance around the room. She clearly knew there was no point in conducting a search of the kitchen and living room when Reg had entered the cottage ahead of her. "Shall we see if Sarah wants you to seek the emerald?"

CHAPTER EIGHT

*R*eg's heart was thumping as they walked up to the house and knocked on the back door. She had never been so anxious about trying to locate a lost object before. Sure, there had been plenty of times when she'd been really desperate to find something, but that didn't compare to her fear that she might no longer be able to find things. She hadn't found the knife that Jessup had asked her to seek. Was that because of her history with the knife? Because someone powerful was hiding it from her? Or had she just lost the ability?

"It's going to be fine," Jessup assured her. "Once the emerald is found, I'm sure everything will go back to normal."

Reg cocked her head at Jessup, frowning. Everything would go back to normal? What exactly was she talking about?

Jessup pounded on the door for the second time. Reg had expected Sarah to open it immediately the first time, eager to greet them and get their help, but the second knock was met with silence.

Reg leaned closer to the door. She thought she could hear voices, but she couldn't make out what they were saying.

"Does she have company?" Reg asked. "There wasn't a car out front."

"Someone could have walked over." Jessup pressed her ear to the door. "I don't know. I'll try once more."

She hammered on it again. They waited, listening for any response from within. Finally, Reg detected footsteps, a few seconds before the door opened with a whoosh.

Things were definitely not normal with Sarah. She always looked very professional and put together, neat and well-tailored in her Florida granny clothes. Instead, she looked disheveled, like she hadn't been out of the house or done any laundry or self-care in weeks. It had only been a day since Reg had last seen her.

"Sarah, are you okay?" she asked with concern.

"Would you be okay? Of course I'm not."

"You look—"

"Can we come in?" Jessup interrupted, putting her hand on the door to push it open.

Sarah rubbed her eyes, bloodshot and baggy with no makeup on. She looked like she had just gotten out of bed or off a three-day bender.

"Come on," Reg said, giving the door a nudge and stepping closer to Sarah. "We want to help you. You want us to help find the emerald, don't you?"

"You're here to look for the emerald?" Sarah asked, showing a little interest.

"Yes. Why don't you take us to… the place that you usually store it," Reg suggested.

"Upstairs. I'll show you."

Jessup followed Reg into the house and they both trailed Sarah up the stairs and down a couple of hallways to a bedroom that Reg hadn't been in before.

"It was in here," Sarah said, looking around the room with cloudy eyes. "This is where it always is when I'm not wearing it."

There was little in the room other than a display case in its center. A cube of glass over a black form where the emerald necklace apparently rested when not around Sarah's neck. Reg and Jessup approached the display case with something like reverence.

Reg looked down into the empty case. She reached out and touched the glass, giving it a gentle nudge that made it click and start to rise up, bending at a hidden hinge in the back. Reg watched it move through its full range of motion before it stopped. She looked for a minute at the case, then looked at Sarah.

"There's no security? No lock or code? Anyone could open it?"

"Well, not just anyone," Sarah protested. She swept a stray hair back from her face, looking at Reg in mild confusion.

"But there was nothing to stop me."

"Of course not. But you were with me."

Reg looked around. "Is there a spell, then? A trap that catches people who come in without you?"

"No. There are wards on the house itself, but nothing specific to this room or the case in particular."

"Then anyone could access it. Anyone you let into the house."

Sarah was probably far more careful about who she let into her house than Reg had been at first. But then, Sarah was presumably a powerful witch herself, capable of protecting herself in a way that Reg wasn't.

"No. Not with Frostling."

Reg shook her head, trying to understand the word. "Is that a spell?"

"No."

Jessup looked up suddenly and Reg was about to ask her what was going on when there was a whoosh of flapping wings and a loud screech, and suddenly claws were digging into her shoulder.

Reg shrieked and flailed her hands, getting scratched and bitten for her efforts. Sarah shouted at her to stop and tried to hold Reg's hands still. Jessup talked in a quiet voice that Reg had to strain to hear under the noise she and the creature and Sarah were all making at once.

"It's okay, Reg. Calm down. You need to just relax. I'll get it off. Just take a deep breath."

Reg tried to school her reaction. She took a breath and held it, closing her eyes for a few seconds and then opening them to reset her perception of the room and what was going on. It wasn't until then that she was able to focus on the large bird, still shrieking, flapping, and digging its bony claws into Reg's shoulder.

"This is Frostling," Jessup said. "Will you help me get him off, Sarah? I don't want to startle him, but we need remove him."

Sarah stopped shouting and stilled her hands. "Yes, okay. Let me do it."

Jessup put her hand on Reg's arms to keep her calm. "Just be a minute. We'll get him off of you and out of the way. Okay?"

"Just do it. Just get it off now."

Sarah coaxed the bird, talking to it in a cutesy baby voice. "Come on, now, Frostling, come to Sarah. It's okay. Just let go."

The bird dug its claws in harder before finally relenting. Reg sighed as each foot was removed, so that she no longer had red-hot pokers digging into her shoulder. She rubbed it, wincing.

"What the heck was that? It attacked me!"

"I told you about Frostling before," Sarah said, her tone sullen. "I told you I have an African Grey parrot."

"Yes, you did. You didn't tell me it was allowed to fly around wherever it pleased and to attack people."

"You asked me how I protected the jewel."

"That didn't mean I wanted you to sic your bird on me!"

"I didn't." Sarah placed the bird on her own shoulder, stroking it and speaking to it as if Reg had attacked her pet rather than the opposite. "I just let you see what happens to people who try to interfere with the emerald."

"The bird attacks them." Reg rubbed the bruises the bird had left in her shoulder.

"He's as good as a watchdog. Better than a cat. Believe me, I haven't had anyone try to steal anything out of this room for a very long time."

"Well, yes, I can believe that," Reg agreed.

"You can't just let it attack people like that, Sarah," Jessup warned. "I know he's just doing what he's been trained to do, but you *let* Reg in here. I thought the whole point was that if you let someone in, they are safe."

Sarah said nothing. Reg wondered if maybe, just maybe, the bird had done exactly what it had been trained to do on some signal from Sarah. It didn't seem like the attack was fortuitous. Sarah's bird had attacked at just the right point in the conversation. She looked at Sarah, wondering.

"Does the bird talk?" she asked.

"Birds don't talk," Frostling answered with a croak.

Reg stared at him. She looked at Sarah.

Sarah gave a distant smile. "It's a joke."

"You trained the bird to say that birds don't talk?"

Sarah shrugged. "He's learned a lot of things. They live for a long time. And they're very intelligent."

Jessup rolled her eyes at Reg. No one said anything for a few minutes. Reg looked at the open case.

"I still don't think this is very secure."

"I agree," Jessup contributed. "We should at least dust it for prints."

They both looked at Reg, and she realized her mistake. It now had her prints on it, so she couldn't prove that she hadn't been the one to take the emerald if it had, in fact, been left in the case where it belonged. When they looked for matches to the prints on the glass, they would find hers, obliterating anything else underneath.

Reg closed her eyes. She felt the energy of the room, contemplating the absence of the jewel. That was where it was supposed to be. That was where it had been for years, maybe even decades. Its energy imprint on the room was just as tangible as the fingerprints Reg had left on the case. She could feel it around her.

"I'm going to look for it," she told Sarah and Jessup.

"Do you need anything?" Sarah asked, brightening a little for the first time that day. "Tea or something...?"

"Right now, I just want to feel the necklace," Reg said. "It left an imprint in this room and I want to see if I can find it."

Sarah and Jessup were respectfully quiet. Reg focused, widening her attention, reaching out with her consciousness, trying to track the energy signature of the necklace. It was still somewhere in the world. Reg had seen it. She could feel its energy in the room. She had found objects she had far less of a connection with.

She let her mind drift. She couldn't force it. She had to just let it come to her. Did she know the person who had it? Had it been misplaced and was somewhere in Sarah's house still? It had to be somewhere close.

"Charlatan," the parrot squawked.

Reg scowled at the bird, opening her eyes to give it a hard, cold stare. The bird just looked at her with one eye in the side of his head. He blinked and stared and blinked and stared some more.

"Why would he say something like that?" Reg demanded. "Why would you train him to say that?"

"I didn't," Sarah said. "He's entitled to his own opinions. Sometimes birds just say things."

Reg shook her head. "I can't focus with him in here. Especially with him talking."

"We'll go to another room," Sarah sighed.

She made a motion to the bird, and it flew off her shoulder and out the bedroom door. By the time Sarah made it to the door, he was gone. There was no indication where.

Jessup looked at Reg with an eyebrow lifted, which Reg took to indicate that she wanted to know whether Reg had seen anything or was having any success. Reg gave a little shake of her head.

Sarah led the way to a small sitting room. "I have some chamomile tea," she offered. "Chamomile is very calming. Maybe that would help you to perform the seek better. If you weren't so uptight about Frostling…"

"I'm not uptight about him. He just distracted me."

"He's really a very lovely bird…"

"I'm not a bird person. The same way you're not a cat person. They don't do anything for me."

"But you can talk to birds. You must have some kind of attraction toward them."

"No. I just did what I had to do that day. It was talk to the bird or cook to death. Obviously, in that kind of scenario, I was motivated to talk to the bird."

Sarah gave a little smile. "I'll get you the tea," she promised, "and then it will be easier to do the seek."

Reg didn't make any objection when Sarah bustled off to go make the tea that Reg definitely did not need in order to find the emerald. She was perfectly capable of finding whatever objects she wanted to without a cup of tea.

CHAPTER NINE

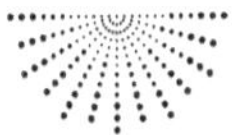

*A*re you okay?" Jessup asked. "How's your shoulder?"

Reg massaged it. "It will be fine. I don't think the dumb bird broke the skin. But it sure scared the heck out of me. You might have warned me."

"I know the parrot, but I didn't know she was using it to guard her jewelry, or I would have warned you. And warned her, too. You can't just let your pet attack people for entering a room, especially when you allow them into that room to begin with."

Reg shook her head. "Are all witches and warlocks into birds? Sarah, Corvin, Dave Smith…"

"Dave Smith?"

"He's the leader of Corvin's coven, I guess. You don't know him?"

"Davyn Smithy. I know him. When did you meet him?"

"Just… yesterday, I guess. He came by to make sure I got the order to appear at Corvin's hearing."

Jessup blinked, looking puzzled. Reg realized she might have missed giving Jessup some required details. "I guess maybe I didn't tell you that Corvin has been called up before his coven because of what he did. Because he broke his word or their rules."

Jessup chewed her lip. "That's pretty serious."

"Yeah. Well, so is what he did to me."

"I agree. It's just very rare for the coven to get involved."

"That fairy, Lord Bernier, he said he was going to see to it that Corvin had to answer for what he had done."

"Even rarer for fairies to get involved in human matters. They stepped in to protect you, I guess because Calliopia's fairy blood marked you as being protected. But to take the further step of reporting Corvin to his coven and demanding that they deal with him… that's really unusual."

Reg didn't know how to feel about that. Happy that they were dealing with Corvin? Angry that they'd had to be forced to do it by a fairy? Grateful to the fairies for not only protecting her from the immediate danger, but also for insisting that Corvin appear before the tribunal? All of the emotions were swirling around in her head, mixed up and refusing to be ordered logically.

"This will help," Sarah said, returning to the room with a tea service for all of them. "You'll calm right down, and be able to do the seek."

Reg didn't argue. Maybe she didn't need the tea to seek the emerald, but it might at least calm down the warring emotions that were making her feel shaky and vulnerable, sitting there thinking about Corvin and having to appear at his trial.

She poured herself a cup of tea, which made Sarah look a little happier. She sipped at it. It was too hot, but she needed to drink it and move forward.

"You're sure you're okay, Sarah? I'm sorry I didn't realize how important the emerald was to you… but you're obviously really upset about it being lost."

"Stolen."

"Whatever happened to it. I can see that it's really upset you. I'm sorry that it happened."

Sarah nodded and poured herself a tea as well. Reg thought that Sarah probably needed it more than she did. Jessup eyed the tea service, but didn't pour herself a cup. That gave Reg a moment of pause. Did Jessup think that Sarah had put something in the tea that she shouldn't? Or something that Jessup shouldn't be consuming on the job? It was just chamomile, wasn't it?

The smell was familiar, and although Reg didn't have the super smelling sense that Erin did, she thought herself competent enough to know that there wasn't anything else mixed in with the chamomile. She took a few more sips, waiting for it to calm her nerves.

* * *

They just sat visiting and sipping the tea for some time, but Reg noticed that Sarah's glances toward her were getting more frequent and anxious. Her heart having finally slowed to a regular speed, Reg put her cup down.

"Okay. I'm sure it will be just fine. I'm going to find the emerald. At least a clue, even if I can't tell exactly where it is. And then you'll be able to find it, and everything will go back to normal."

Sarah nodded encouragingly. Jessup didn't say anything, she just sat there observing and waiting.

Reg took a few long, deep breaths. She could do it. Her whole life, she'd been able to find things that no one else could. Some of her foster families had found this a useful trait to have. Others had refused to believe that Reg had any particular talent and assumed that it was only luck when she found something, or an admission of guilt in stealing it in the first place.

Reg visualized the necklace. She remembered how it had glowed when Sarah wore it, looking so warm and alive. And the way that Sarah herself had looked. It was important to her. More than just an item with great monetary value. It was an heirloom.

Reg closed her eyes and reached out with her mind. She needed to know where the emerald was. She needed to find it for her friend. Sarah was her friend, not just her landlord.

"Come on," she whispered.

But no matter what effort she put into it, she didn't get any feeling back about the location of the emerald necklace. Like with the knife, she simply couldn't feel it anywhere. She put her hands over her face, covering her eyes. She didn't want them to see that she couldn't find it. She didn't want to see the look in Sarah's eyes.

"Reg." Jessup's voice was soft. She got up from her chair and approached Reg, putting her hand on Reg's shoulder.

"I can't do it," Reg said, her words muffled by her hands. She felt exhausted and close to tears. "What's happening to me?"

"You're just struggling," Sarah said. "Maybe you're trying too hard."

"I should be able to feel it. I should be able to tell you something about where it is, even if I can't find it absolutely. That's the way it works!"

"Everybody has problems sometimes. It's not your fault."

"Are they gone? Have I lost my powers? This doesn't make sense!" Reg pushed the fury over her helplessness away from her violently. The door to the room slammed shut, making them all jump.

"Oh!" Sarah laughed. "I must have left the window open." Reg could hear her going over to the window, but she didn't hear the window slide shut. She lifted her face out of her hands and looked at Sarah, who was staring at the closed window. "Well, there must be a cross-breeze from somewhere else. Did I leave the back door open?"

"I closed the back door," Jessup said.

Both women looked at Reg.

"Why are you looking at me? I didn't leave anything open."

"You slammed the door," Jessup said.

"I did not."

"Just a little bit of psychic overload," Sarah said, again laughing, but sounding more anxious. "You're upset. That's all."

"That doesn't make any sense. If I've lost my powers, how could I move anything? It's hard enough to do when I'm really focused on it."

"You haven't lost your powers," Sarah assured her. "You're just having trouble with seeking right now."

"It could be psychological," Jessup suggested. "You couldn't find the knife, so you're psyching yourself out about not being able to find the necklace either. You're blocking yourself."

"I'm not. I'm perfectly calm."

Sarah shook her head, smiling. "You're just having a bad day. Everyone has a bad day now and then." Sarah looked down at herself. "I have to admit that I'm not having the best day today myself."

"Maybe not, but you haven't lost your powers."

"Neither have you." Sarah let out a deep sigh. "It's alright, Reg. I know you tried. I know you would if you could."

Jessup cast Sarah a glance. *She* wasn't quite so sure. Had Jessup told Sarah about Reg's past? That Reg was a liar and a cheat? That she had stolen and conned her way across the country? Sarah would never trust Reg if she knew everything.

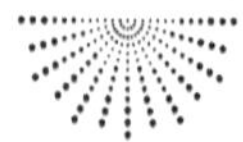

CHAPTER TEN

*R*eg returned to the cottage, tired and wrung out as she always was when she performed a task that took a lot of psychic energy. She really had done her best for Sarah, whatever Jessup might think. Reg stumbled and Jessup caught her arm. She made sure Reg was steady before letting her go again. Reg walked up to her door and leaned against it briefly.

"Something is wrong."

Jessup hovered just behind her. "What's wrong, Reg?"

"I don't know. Something."

"Because you couldn't find the necklace? No other psychic would have done any better. Some objects just can't be found that way. Maybe Sarah is right. Maybe it was stolen and whoever stole it is shielding it from any attempt to seek."

"It's not just that."

"What else?"

"There's someone…" Reg scowled, finding it hard to focus. "I can't get their face out of my mind."

She looked back at Jessup, who raised her brows. "Who?"

"If I knew that, I wouldn't have said 'someone.'"

"Where did you see this face? Was it in a vision? Maybe it's the person who is in possession of the necklace. Maybe you're seeing the possessor rather than the necklace itself."

Reg considered this. "I don't know… I don't think so. Her face was already in my mind before I tried to find the necklace. I'm not sure where I saw her." She shook her head. "It's just one of those things, like having a word on the tip of your tongue. I'll probably wake up at two in the morning and know who it is."

"Not important, then? Not related to this case?"

Reg breathed out in frustration. "No. It's nothing."

* * *

Reg was aware of people coming and going to and from Sarah's house. She didn't see them, but she heard their cars and she could feel them close to her, as if she were in Sarah's basement and could hear their footsteps and voices overhead. She remembered thinking that Sarah had been talking to someone when she and Jessup had first gone to the main house. Had there been someone else in the house that Reg and Jessup weren't aware of? Or maybe she had been talking on the phone. Or it had been the TV.

Reg felt restless, anxious for everyone to go back home so that she could have some peace. A few times she peeked through her front curtains, but she couldn't see anyone. She could just feel their presences there.

As it drew into the evening, Reg was getting hungry, but she didn't want anything in the fridge. She decided she needed to get out of the house. She'd had too much pizza and Chick fil A the last little while, so she decided to see what she could find that appealed to her at the Crystal Bowl, a hangout for the paranormal community. That was where she had originally met Sarah on her first day in Black Sands.

Bill, the barman she knew best, was on duty. He smiled at her. "Miss Rawlins. Haven't seen you around for a while."

"I've been sort of busy. But I've been around a couple of times when you were off, too."

"Well, as long as you're not starving."

"No, I get plenty to eat."

He drew her a beer and placed the glass on a napkin in front of her. Reg took a few swallows and sighed. "Oh, that feels good." She closed her eyes for a minute, feeling the warm flush spread over her. "This is a strange place, Bill."

"The restaurant?"

"Black Sands. I've never known anywhere like it."

"Don't know that there *is* anywhere like it," he agreed.

"I've never been anywhere that so many people actually... believe me."

He chuckled. "Those with powers have never been particularly well-received."

Reg nodded.

"But that's not what has you so unsettled," Bill suggested.

Reg looked at him, surprised. "No, I guess not."

"What's on your mind?"

"I'm just feeling so out of sorts. Everything seems like it's out of sync right now. People who are usually calm and happy are upset, I can't find anything, and there are just too many people coming and going!"

Bill raised an eyebrow. "It is a restaurant and bar. People are going to be coming and going all day long."

"I know that. I didn't mean here. I meant at the house."

"Your house?"

"No, not mine. Sarah's. Every time someone comes, it feels like they're walking over my grave. I get all anxious and can't wait for them to leave. And then I feel worried about why they were there in the first place. It's none of my business." She shook her head. "I know that. It's never bothered me before. But now I can't stop noticing."

"You heard about her missing emerald."

"Yes, of course. I've helped look for it."

"Maybe you don't feel safe. Like someone might steal something valuable from you."

Reg thought instantly about Corvin, then pushed him out of her mind. He wasn't going to take anything else from her. He was never going to get the chance. She thought about what Bill had said.

"I don't know. Maybe. If she valued it so much, why didn't she keep it somewhere safe? Having it right there at the house, that doesn't seem very smart. There are banks. Services that store jewels and keep them in top shape until you need to use them again. Why risk it? It doesn't make any sense to me."

"It needs to be near her to perform its function."

"What?"

"For it to benefit her. She needs to be in the same vicinity as the emerald. Having it in a bank wouldn't have helped her."

A missing piece of the puzzle was falling into place. It wasn't just valuable because it was a great big emerald, it also had magical properties.

"What exactly does it do?"

Bill looked the other way and found it necessary to retreat to the other end of the bar to polish the counter and talk with his patrons there. Reg waited for him to return to where she was so they could continue their conversation.

"So the emerald is a powerful object?" Reg asked.

He looked sideways at her. "You didn't hear it from me."

"I'm sure you're not the only one in town who knows. What exactly can it do?"

"Of course Sarah has never said directly, but…"

"You might have some idea."

"Rumors and gossip. Nothing you can put any stock in."

Reg raised her eyebrow, waiting. He seemed determined to tease her, but Reg knew how to handle a gossip-monger. She took a sip of her drink and looked away as if distracted by other thoughts. Bill couldn't stand the show of indifference.

"Word is," he leaned in closer to her, "that it provides certain health benefits."

"So it keeps her from getting sick?"

"Perhaps."

"Well, seeing as she is a witch, she probably knows about all kinds of potions and other things for her health. An apple a day…"

"This goes far beyond protecting her against colds."

"Hmm." Reg supposed that was why Sarah had bragged about being older than she looked. She was apparently in good health for a senior. She kept up her appearances, at least until recently, and while she was a little overweight, she still seemed to be strong and active. "I guess that explains why she felt like she had to keep it in the house, then. I don't know why she didn't just tell me that. And if it was me… I still would have had some kind of security system."

She realized that she probably shouldn't be gossiping with the bartender about how lax Sarah's security was when she had fantastically expensive jewelry there. That was just asking for a burglary.

"But you didn't hear that from me," Reg said quickly. "I shouldn't have said anything."

"Your secret is safe with me." Bill pantomimed locking his lips.

Reg shook her head at the contrast between Bill's appearance and the juvenile gesture.

"You want some food to wash that down?" he asked, nodding to Reg's nearly-empty glass.

"Yeah. That is actually why I came here. Whatever's fresh today."

He nodded and went to the kitchen to put in an order for her. He busied himself with other customers and cleaning up before he drifted down her way again. He looked past Reg.

"Well, speak of the devil."

Reg turned her head slightly, far enough to see Sarah just getting settled. Despite how often Sarah ate there, Reg hadn't expected to run into her. She thought that with the theft, Sarah would stay home, being miserable by herself and not wanting to deal with other people. Reg smiled at Sarah, but Sarah just stared blankly back. She sat down and got settled, not motioning for Reg to join her. Reg had been getting ready to jump off of the stool and go sit with Sarah, so the fact that Sarah didn't want Reg there threw her off balance momentarily. She perched there, body tensed, for several long seconds before finally slouching back down, a bit embarrassed and wondering whether anyone had been watching to see her spurned by her friend.

Reg turned back toward the bar, giving Sarah her back. She wasn't going to stay there gawking, looking like a hurt puppy kicked to the side. Bill was hovering nearby. He motioned to her empty glass.

"Refill?"

"Thanks, yeah."

Bill filled the glass back up, making no comment about the situation. At least he didn't try to tell her that Sarah just hadn't seen her or that things would get better and be back to normal soon.

"Your dinner will be ready in a few minutes."

"Thanks." Reg slid her phone out and started to look through her social networks, no longer wanting to talk with Bill or to engage with anyone else.

She heard the restaurant door open and, before turning to see who had just come in, Reg felt a noticeable increase in the temperature of the room. She turned her head partway to see Corvin Hunter standing in the doorway.

Reg turned and looked for Bill to tell him to cancel her order and she'd come back another night, but he had her dish in his hand, already approaching to put it in front of her. Reg rubbed the center of her forehead, which was beginning to throb, and tried to think of what to do. She'd ordered and her meal was there, so she needed to just eat it and go home. It wouldn't be fair to Bill or the restaurant owners to have to eat the cost of her meal just because Corvin Hunter had come in. They couldn't exactly ban him from eating there. Or they wouldn't want to, anyway.

Reg accepted her plate with murmured thanks and looked back over her shoulder to see where Corvin was. He had moved over to Sarah's table and was talking with her. Sarah didn't really even like Corvin, so why was she talking to him? She certainly knew that she couldn't trust him. She'd told Reg a million times.

Reg shoveled a few bites into her mouth and looked back again. Corvin was not just standing there talking to Sarah, but had sat down with her. And Sarah didn't appear to be objecting. They leaned toward each other, talking quietly, walling off the rest of the room with their bodies and paying attention only to each other. As far as they were concerned, Reg didn't even exist.

Reg didn't even know what she was eating. It was some kind of seafood, but it might as well have been fish and chips from the grocery store freezer section for all she knew. There was no reason for her to be feeling like the outcast little girl that no one wanted to play with at recess. She had plenty of things to do to entertain herself. She hadn't made arrangements to have supper with Sarah or Corvin and there was no reason they couldn't have dinner together and not invite her. She wasn't even friends with Corvin, and Sarah knew that. In fact, it would have been thoughtless of her to invite Reg over when she knew Corvin was going to be there in a few minutes.

But she still couldn't help feeling resentful of their meeting and eating there without even giving her an acknowledging smile or nod.

Reg was nearly finished shoveling her meal into her mouth and they had barely even moved, talking intently, not putting in an order as far as Reg had seen.

She put down her fork, the fish like an iron ball in her stomach. She couldn't eat another bite. She threw down enough money to cover the drinks, meal, and a generous tip for Bill, and headed for the door.

CHAPTER ELEVEN

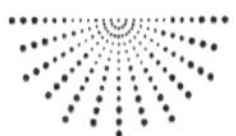

orvin's eyes caught on Reg as she moved toward them. He said something to Sarah that made her turn around and look at Reg.

"Oh, hello, Reg. Nice to see you," Sarah said, her voice and manner as bland and colorless as a bowl of oatmeal.

Reg paused, looking for something to say. She looked at Corvin, shaking her head as he started to speak.

"I didn't know you'd be here," she said flatly, "or I would have stayed at home."

"No need to cut yourself off from the world for me," Corvin's voice was as smooth and warm and enticing as it ever had been. Reg made sure to stay back, giving him a wide berth. "I've tried to call you."

"I know. I'm not interested in talking to you."

"Regina…" Unlike Dave Smith, Corvin always pronounced it correctly. Not only that, but he sounded like a lover murmuring it, intimate and sexy. "I've told you how sorry I am for what happened. It was a mistake. Everyone makes mistakes…"

"Uh, no. Not everyone makes mistakes like that. Only *you* make mistakes like that."

His face flushed and his jaw clenched. "And I've *apologized*."

He ground the word out like it was a personal affront that he should ever be expected to apologize to anyone. He thought he was special. He thought the rules didn't apply to him. As far as he was concerned, he should be able to do whatever he wanted to. And if he were forced to apologize, she should have to accept his apology.

He was a predator. That was what he was. He had appetites, like anyone else, but he thought that he should be allowed to satisfy them, no matter what the cost to anyone else. He was different, a special breed of warlock, and the world owed him.

"Is everything okay, Sarah?" Reg asked, deliberately turning away from Corvin as if he were of no concern to her.

Sarah looked at Reg vaguely. Her thoughts were probably muddled by being so close to Corvin. She was seeing Reg through a fog. "I'm fine?" Sarah made it sound like a question. As if Reg had told her that she was fine and she didn't quite believe it.

"I don't know if you are. Maybe you need to get some fresh air. Get away from the warlock's glamour."

"Corvin hasn't done anything," Sarah sighed. "What would he want with an old witch like me?" Her tone was tired and distant. Despite the fact that she had dressed and done her hair to go out, she seemed to be aging right before Reg's eyes. Her wrinkles were deeper than Reg remembered, with makeup caked between them. The bags under her eyes could not be disguised. And her dyed-blond hair was fading to gray.

Corvin raised one hand slightly so that it hovered over Sarah's. She didn't appear to take any notice of this. But Reg had seen Corvin do this before, had even been on the receiving end. This was not what he did when he was stealing powers; rather, he was boosting Sarah's physical strength. That didn't mean that he couldn't do both at once, or use the one to get the other, but he didn't lean in to kiss Sarah, as he would have to take her gifts. He just kept his hand over Sarah's, watching her face.

Reg could see that Sarah's complexion was improving, getting more pink and losing some of its dullness. Sarah put her other hand to her head.

"Yes," she said faintly, "that's better."

Corvin sat back again, pulling his hand away. Reg had to admit that he did sometimes do something nice for someone else. But there was almost always the expectation of something in return. Reg didn't know if he was expecting some kind of compensation from Sarah, but if he was, it didn't appear to be immediate.

"You'll feel better after you've had something to eat," Reg said, not looking at Corvin. "Have you ordered anything?"

Sarah looked at her glass of water, not answering. Was she slipping that quickly? Reg had always known her to be bright and engaging, on top of everything. Seeing her so vague and distant was disturbing.

"I don't understand what's going on," Reg said, whispering to Corvin in spite of her determination not to talk to him. "This is all because of the emerald?"

"She has relied on its merits for a long time."

"But at this rate..." Reg looked at Sarah again. Sarah didn't appear to be paying any attention to what Reg was saying. "At this rate of decline... she's not going to last very long."

Corvin shook his head.

"What about... other things? Couldn't she take some potion, or maybe some other emerald... even if it's not as big..."

"Letticia is putting together a restorative for her. But its effects will only be temporary, and every time she uses it, it will have less efficacy. And there is only so much strength I can give her. Her aging process must naturally catch up, and when it does... she won't survive."

"How can you say that? Even if she's older, that's not a death sentence. We can find ways to help her to stay healthy and... bright. She's always a little funny when you're around, you have an effect on her."

"Reg... you don't understand what we're talking about. I'm

not talking about her being eighty years old, or even a hundred. As her natural age catches up to her… she will die."

Reg looked at Sarah sharply.

"You can't talk that way around her. And what do you mean? She'll be more than a hundred years old? She *is* more than a hundred years old?"

"Yes. She is."

"That's impossible."

"No. Not impossible when you have a stone like that. She is much older than one hundred years old."

"No."

He shrugged. "It's an idea that takes time to get used to."

"She can't be that old."

"Not naturally. Not without something extending her life."

"Then we've got to find her another emerald."

"It isn't just the emerald itself. It's the magic that has been woven into it. Magic that takes years to develop."

"Well, there must be others around. If there is one, there are others."

"There may be others. But not that are immediately available or that anyone is willing to part with. And none so powerful as Sarah's. A lesser stone won't have the same effect."

"Then we need to get it back."

It wasn't until then that Reg really understood what was at stake. She had thought that it was valuable as far as the amount of money it was worth or the sentimental attachment Sarah had to it. But she hadn't realized that Sarah's life depended on being able to get it back. Jessup hadn't told her that and neither had Sarah.

"Then give it back," Sarah said sharply. "Why don't you just give it back to me?"

Reg stood there for a moment, stunned. She hadn't even thought that Sarah was following the conversation, but apparently she was, at least that much. But she was even more stunned by Sarah's tone of voice. Her words were sharp and angry. She stared at Reg with a malevolence Reg had never seen in her face. Behind it, Reg knew, was desperation. She needed that emerald, and she needed it soon.

"I don't have the emerald, Sarah," she said softly, as reasonably as possible. She didn't know how to talk to old people. She'd never been comfortable around them. "I didn't take it. And I don't know where it is. I've tried to find it. But… I'll keep trying."

"You took it. I know it was you."

"No. It wasn't."

Sarah's eyes went to Corvin and he gave an infinitesimal nod. Reg erupted with fury.

"What are you telling her? You're telling her that I stole her necklace? You know I had nothing to do with it! I would never steal from Sarah!"

Her words echoed around the suddenly-quiet room. Reg wanted to take them back. Not all of them. Just the ones that implied she might steal something else from someone else.

"Reg, you're making a scene."

"I'll make the biggest scene ever," Reg threatened. "You've been lying to her! Telling her that I stole the necklace!"

"I only told her what I know," Corvin said slowly, choosing his words carefully.

"You don't know anything! I didn't touch her emerald! You're the one who stole the knife, you're probably the one who stole the emerald too!"

"The knife?" Sarah echoed.

"He's the one who stole the knife from Jessup, remember?" Reg prompted her. "Remember Hawthorne-Rose's knife? He's the one who stole the knife, so he's the one who stole your emerald too."

"I did not steal the emerald," Corvin said. "You're the one who stole the emerald. You sent your cat over there, and—"

"I did *what?*" Reg demanded, her voice screeching higher.

"You used your familiar," Corvin said calmly. "You sent him over to the main house and had him steal the necklace. I saw him."

"You saw Starlight steal the emerald," Reg said. "Well, that's pretty rich. He never left the house, how was he supposed to steal the jewelry?"

Corvin shrugged. "I know what I saw."

"Which was what? Starlight stealing the necklace? If you saw that, why didn't you stop him? Why didn't you take it away from him?"

"I saw the cat crossing the yard. I saw it go into the house. Before the emerald disappeared. What reason would you have to send the cat into Sarah's house other than to take the necklace? She said she didn't invite you over. Or the cat. She didn't invite anyone over. That's the only intruder that anyone is aware of. A cat slips in, takes the necklace, and quietly leaves. The perfect plan."

"Except that it isn't true! When was the last time you saw a cat do what it was asked? You can't train a cat to steal a necklace."

"I've seen some witches with very able familiars. I wouldn't presume to dictate what a cat could or couldn't do, with or without training. We know that the beast is intelligent. That's been proven."

"That doesn't mean he went into the house and stole the neck-lace. That never happened. He's been in the house the whole week. He hasn't been outside, to Sarah's house or anywhere else."

"He was gone for a couple of days while Calliopia was missing."

"That's different. He did escape for a couple of days. Sarah was the one who let him out. Since then, we've both been really careful not to let him out. We don't want him taking off and getting hit by a car or trapped by someone."

"Or stealing jewelry."

"He didn't steal the emerald. That's the most ridiculous thing I've ever heard. Cats don't steal jewelry. Birds maybe. Crows collect shiny things, don't they?"

"I didn't see a crow going into the house. I saw the cat going in."

"It wasn't Starlight."

"Excuse me, folks," one of the waiters edged closer to Reg and Corvin. "I'm sure you don't realize how loud you are and how you're attracting everyone's attention. Maybe this is something that could be discussed outside?"

"I don't care if everybody hears it," Reg growled. "I want everyone to know that he's accusing me unjustly! He's making it all up! He wants to damage my reputation and poison Sarah against me. I did not steal anything from Sarah!"

"I can't have you yelling in here, ma'am," the waiter tried again. "Please. You'll need to carry on this conversation somewhere else. You are disturbing the clientele."

Corvin shifted as if he would stand up. "Shall we take it outside, Regina?"

"I'm not going anywhere with you!"

"People…" the waiter tried desperately.

"No!" Reg barked at him. "You stay out of this!"

At the bar, a glass broke, making everybody jump. Someone give a little shriek of surprise. Reg glanced over at Bill, but couldn't tell if he had dropped the glass.

The waiter put a hand on her arm. Reg jerked away from him.

"I told you to leave me alone!"

Another glass broke and Reg looked over at the bar quickly enough to see a third spontaneously burst into pieces. There were more shrieks from the patrons.

"Regina, calm down," Corvin soothed. "Just take a breath."

"You don't get to tell me what to do."

"You're going to break all of the glassware."

"I'm not breaking them!"

"You might not be doing it intentionally, but…"

"I'm not breaking them."

Three more glasses burst in quick succession, followed by the bottle in Bill's hand, showering liquid on the bar and floor. He looked at Reg, eyebrows raised. Reg looked at Corvin, who was sitting back with his arms folded across his chest, looking amused.

His smirk made her rage spike again, and the glass in front of him exploded, spraying all of them with water and shards of glass.

Reg swore in horror. She was more worried about Sarah than she was herself. She darted forward to protect Sarah, way too late. She swept glass and puddles of water away from Sarah.

"Don't move. Let me make sure all of this is cleaned up first..."

Corvin liberated a couple of cloth napkins from the bundles of silverware.

"Don't use your bare hand, Regina, you're going to get cut yourself. Here."

He gave her one napkin and he used the other, mopping up the water and brushing the shards of glass into a pile away from Sarah. She had some on her clothing and in her hair, and Reg worked carefully to remove them so that Sarah wouldn't cut herself. The waiter stood by with his mouth open.

"I didn't do this," Reg repeated to Corvin.

"Your powers are getting away from you. You need to rein them in. Or if there's too much for you to handle..." He gave a suggestive smile.

Reg shook her head, but tried to tamp down the rage, just in case it was her anger that was causing all the breakage. "I don't break stuff. I can move things a little, sometimes, but this... I didn't do this."

"Just like you didn't steal the emerald."

"I didn't. I'm not a thief."

Corvin met her eyes. He raised an eyebrow, challenging the statement. Reg opened her mouth to argue with him, but it was filled with cotton. She couldn't find the words to object. It wasn't because she was afraid to lie or had something against lying. She was a good liar. She just couldn't form the words.

"I have been inside your mind," Corvin reminded her. "Inside your memories and psyche. I know you, Regina. More intimately than anyone else."

He knew she was a thief. Maybe she hadn't stolen Sarah's necklace, but there had been other thefts from other women. None of them had been over one hundred years old or had been relying on the jewelry to prolong their lives, but how would Reg have known if they were?

"I didn't steal Sarah's necklace," Reg repeated.

"I think it's time for you to go," Bill suggested, appearing at Reg's elbow. His manner was apologetic. "We'll take care of the breakage, please don't worry about it, but if you could leave now…"

"It wasn't me," Reg protested again, but her protests were getting weaker. She hadn't intended to break anything, but the smashes had been extremely satisfying when her emotions were feeling so out of control.

"I'll walk you home," Corvin suggested, starting to rise.

Reg motioned for Corvin to stay seated. "I don't need an escort, especially you. Just be warned, you'd better stop telling lies about me, or I'll…" Reg couldn't think of a good threat. "You just look out."

Corvin gave her a smug smile and watched her leave.

Bill walked her to the door, which Reg thought was a bit much. There were no more broken glasses on the way. "That was quite some show," he chuckled, as they stepped outside. "I think Corvin Hunter will think twice before he starts an argument with you again."

"I… didn't mean to break anything."

"It happens. You're not the first one to break glassware, and you won't be the last. A physical fight would have broken more. I prefer the psychic sort. No one got hurt. No police. You'll feel better once you go home and cool down for a bit."

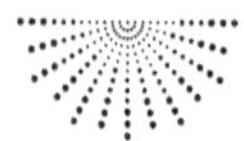

CHAPTER TWELVE

When Reg got home, she was still wound up, but there was no one to fight with except for Starlight. She confronted the cat.

"You never went over to Sarah's house, did you? The only time you got out was when you got the yarrow plant. When I was hurt. Right?"

He stared at her, not blinking. Reg gave a little laugh.

"Of course not. I know you didn't go out. It's not like you've got a cat door or can open and close the door by yourself. That's why you need humans around."

He yowled and put his ears back. He walked over to the kitchen with orders for her to put something good in his food dish and quit being such a nitwit. Reg obliged, then stood there watching him eat.

"It's a good thing you're cute and furry. Because you're causing me an awful lot of grief these days. But I know you wouldn't steal jewelry. Food, maybe, but jewelry?"

He looked up at her for a few seconds, then went back to eating. Reg shook her head. Corvin was making up stories. She had no idea why, but he was going to get her in trouble if he kept it up. People would start to believe it, even if there was no evidence or basis in fact. They would keep hearing it from different sources, and they would take it as the truth.

"I didn't steal anything and neither did you."

Starlight made no response this time. Reg pulled out her phone and dialed Jessup's number. It took a few rings before Jessup answered, and there was a lot of noise in the background, like Jessup was at a party. Or a bowling alley.

"Detective Jessup? It's Reg Rawlins."

"What can I do for you, Miss Rawlins?"

Reg should have been warned by the fact that Jessup had once again switched from 'Reg' to 'Miss Rawlins.'

"I just wanted to give you a heads-up. I know you probably wouldn't believe it anyway, but I thought you should know that Corvin Hunter is spreading rumors about me, trying to finger me for the theft of Sarah's emerald. I just thought… you should know. In case you hear it. It's not true, of course…"

"I have already heard from Mr. Hunter."

"Oh. So you've already heard his stupid story about me somehow training Starlight to go into Sarah's house and steal her emerald." Reg forced a little laugh. "What a ridiculous story. I can't believe he'd expect anyone to believe something like that."

"We have to follow up all leads," Jessup said neutrally.

"Follow up all leads. You mean that you believe it? You think that maybe I did send my cat to go steal a priceless, magical necklace?"

"We have witness statements. We need to take those seriously, no matter how ridiculous you might consider them."

"Witness statements. You know Corvin is just trying to make trouble for me."

"Why would he be trying to make trouble for you?" Jessup asked. "I thought he was already in your bad books. Why would he want to get himself any deeper into hot water?"

Reg was stymied by that. She thought about it. "Maybe he's just trying to divert attention from himself. I mean, who is a more likely suspect for having stolen a powerful magical object? If it could do all that he says it could, then it would satisfy his needs for a while, wouldn't it?"

There was silence on the other end of the phone. "What did Corvin tell you it could do?" Jessup asked eventually.

"Do you not know what it does or are you testing my knowledge?"

"How about you answer the question?"

"From what I gather from Corvin and Bill, the bartender, it keeps her from getting sick and slows, stops, or reverses the aging process."

"How does it do that?"

"I don't understand my own powers, let alone all of the other magic in the world. You didn't know this? Sarah didn't tell you?"

"She said it was a very old family heirloom and of course it had a high monetary value. That was enough to explain why she was so upset about losing it. But it does round out the picture."

"She apparently has to have it near her for it to work. That's why she's starting to… decline."

"Then wherever it is, it's not just fallen behind something in the house. If it was still in the house, she wouldn't be aging."

"Yeah. I guess." There was a knot in Reg's stomach. She had still been hoping that the necklace had just been misplaced.

"So, unless it came off and was lost in the car or at the party, it *was* stolen." Jessup's voice was hard. It didn't matter that she'd asked for Reg's help on previous cases, that she knew Reg and they had helped one another. None of that made any difference to her in the face of one eyewitness who put her—or rather, her cat—at the scene. One witness who had every reason in the world to lie.

"It must be Corvin," Reg told her. "Can you imagine how valuable something like that would be to him? If it could give Sarah a health and youth for… however long she's lived… then imagine how much power it could give to him. He might be able to go for years without having to feed on anything else."

"I don't know what the equivalency is. How much power it might translate to for Hunter."

"But you know you can't trust what he says. He has to be a suspect too."

"I really can't discuss suspects with you. But I will say that Hunter isn't the only one who suggested that it might be you."

Reg pressed her arm against her stomach. "Corvin is influencing Sarah. So if she was the other person who said I might be the thief, you can't take it seriously. I just saw the two of them at The Crystal Bowl. Corvin is feeding her all kinds of nonsense about it being me."

"I appreciate your call, Miss Rawlins. I'll be sure to keep all of that in mind."

"Detective Jessup—" Reg didn't think she was going to be able to stop Jessup before she hung up the phone, so for a moment she just waited for the beep indicating that Jessup had rung off. When she didn't hear it, she spoke again tentatively. "Detective... there must be other suspects. There were a lot of people at that party. If Sarah has been wearing that necklace for years, then everybody knows about it. It could have been lifted at the party without her noticing it. Or someone else might have broken into the house. It's obvious that Sarah's security is practically non-existent. If you think that a cat could have broken into the house and stolen the necklace, then you have to believe that it could have been a person. They are a lot more adept with doors and such than cats."

"If her burglar alarm is a bird..."

Reg felt a sudden flush of embarrassment and renewed anger. Cats and birds were natural enemies. If a cat had sneaked into the house to steal the necklace, then how would Frostling have responded? Would he have attacked, like he had Reg, or would he have flown away, frightened by the predator?

Sarah would have a better idea than anyone else, and she was apparently convinced that Starlight and Reg had stolen her emerald.

"Starlight could not have broken into the house. I'm telling you. He's been in my house since before the party. The only time he was ever out was before that, when he brought home the yarrow."

She could hear Jessup ticking off the point in her head. Starlight was a cat who was intelligent enough to figure out before any of the humans that Reg had a wound that required yarrow for magical healing. And he had gone out, found it, and brought it back. A cat that was capable of such reasoning and pre-planning was certainly capable of sneaking into the house next door and making off with a necklace.

"It wasn't Starlight," Reg insisted. "It's impossible. He hasn't left the house. Unless you think he's capable of walking through walls or apparating in remote locations."

"I'll be in touch, Miss Rawlins."

"Yeah? You want to make an appointment to come and interview the cat?" Reg regretted the sarcasm the minute the words left her mouth. Being snide and confrontational with a police detective was not the way to get her off of Reg's back.

Reg sat down at one of the stools at the kitchen island and slumped over, resting her face in her hands.

* * *

Reg sat in her favorite chair and placed the crystal ball on the table in front of her. She had only purchased it as a prop, one of those things that would help her clients to believe that she was legitimate and that what she was telling them was true. It was a solid globe of glass, with no special powers of its own, pretty but not a functional object.

Only, she had been able to see things in it. Sometimes when her thoughts were cloudy and confused, she looked into the crystal and was able to see clearly. She had seen Calliopia leaving home and being picked up by Ruan, running away with him. Callie had clearly not held her kidnapping by the pixies against Ruan. Whether he had known what they were going to do to her or not, she had forgiven him, and he had apparently deserted his realm to be with her.

Reg stared into the crystal, trying to calm and focus her thoughts. She was worried about Sarah, who would die if the emerald necklace was not found quickly. Furious at Corvin. Disappointed with Detective Jessup for not believing her. She hadn't stolen the necklace and it was unfair of Jessup not to believe her. And then there was Starlight…

Reg knew he hadn't left the house. As she had told Jessup, unless the cat were able to walk through walls or teleport himself, he had never left the cottage since he had returned with the yarrow. That was before the party, and Sarah had worn the necklace to the party.

There was a movement within the crystal. Reg unfocused her eyes instead of focusing them. She needed to see with her third eye, not her physical eyes. That imaginative, intuitive part of her brain that she had spent her whole life fighting, that only on moving to Black Sands did she realize was actually psychic ability. A gift, not the curse she had grown up believe it was. How many teachers and foster parents had told her to stop telling stories? Even when Reg had tried to tell the truth, they had still accused her of making things up. Tell a child she was a liar enough times, and that's what she would become. What was the point in telling the truth?

The figure in the ball became more clear. Reg was able to turn the shape she saw in her mind. She rotated the representation of a diminutive young woman around to study the face. She was so familiar. Blue eyes, brown wavy hair. Clothes that were neat but worn. Reg racked her brain. Where had she seen that face? Why did it keep coming back to her?

"It's the girl on TV," she whispered finally to Starlight, who she could sense hovering nearby. "I watched her on my phone the other day. She was on a news report."

But she couldn't remember any more details than those. Had

she watched the news report? Had she been interrupted? She couldn't remember anything about it.

"Come on…" Reg urged. "Come back to me. Who are you? What do you have to do with anything?"

The young woman turned and looked at her, lips parted slightly, and then she dissolved.

* * *

Reg didn't want to go to sleep until she knew who it was that had stolen Sarah's emerald. She would stay awake, do research, and figure out before the police could what exactly had happened. A little logic, a little research, and she'd have the answer. Then Sarah wouldn't have to age another day. At the rate that her age was advancing, Reg was afraid it wouldn't be too long before enough of her years caught up with her to kill her.

She wasn't sure why she felt responsible. She hadn't had anything at all to do with the disappearance of the emerald, and yet she felt like it was her fault. Maybe that was because she was being blamed for it. She wanted to prove that it hadn't been her. And she wanted to save Sarah. Sarah often irritated Reg, interfering more than she had the right to, but Reg had to admit a certain amount of affection for the old crone. It was like having a mother around. Mothers were interfering and annoying, but it was still nice to know she had someone looking out for her interests. Someone who apparently liked her and cared for her.

She couldn't just let Sarah die. She had to do everything within her power to prevent it.

A stack of books that Reg had borrowed from the public library went crashing off of her desk in the spare bedroom, making Reg jump. She hurried to see what had happened and, for a minute or two, just stared at the books where they had landed.

Maybe it was a sign.

She wasn't a reader, so she wasn't even sure why she had gone to the library in the first place. She had been curious about the history of Black Sands and the paranormal community there, and there really wasn't anything useful on the internet. But the books from the library had stayed there on her desk, untouched, for a week already. Reg didn't want to actually have to read them.

"Did you knock these down?" she asked without looking around.

There was no answering meow. And she remembered that Starlight had been in the living room with her. He had not knocked the stack of books over.

Maybe it was an omen. Maybe if she just read those books…

Reg bent over to pick one up, and flicked through it with distaste. Read all of those books? Who was she kidding? She hadn't read a single book since finishing school. She didn't even read the newspaper or the backs of cereal boxes. Having to read road signs and cold medicine instructions was bad enough.

She looked at the pictures. Early settlements in the Black Sands area. She wasn't sure where everything would be if she over-laid a map of the current city, but she was sure one of the pages in the book would show her. She looked at the black and white and sepia tinted pictures, making out small communities of witches, fairies, and other magical races she wasn't sure about. It was strange to think of how the different races and gifts had thrived long before she was born. Back through the ages, as far as the fairy tales reached back.

She turned pages slowly, not reading the words, but looking at the pictures. All of the different peoples trying to carve out safe communities for themselves. There were pictures of meetings between magical races, handshaking or signing documents that Reg supposed were the treaties she had heard of between the humans and the pixies and other similar documents. Somehow, they had managed to achieve relative peace among the disparate communities, letting them coexist side-by-side, even if they didn't generally mingle.

Reg saw the little pixies, a head or two shorter than the

humans, slender, with childish faces and bodies, their tattered clothes making them look like street urchins.

Reg sat down with a thump, letting the book land in her lap.

Street kids. That was the connection that her brain had been refusing to make. The girl whose face she had seen on TV had been talking about homeless people. Youth on the street. Runaways and throwaways. She'd been looking for her sister.

Reg closed her eyes and brought the face up again. Much more clear now that she had been able to associate some of the details. An older adolescent or young adult. She had acted like an adult in the TV interview, but when Reg had seen her in person…

"What?" she said aloud.

Starlight padded into the room and looked at her inquiringly, as if she had called him and he wanted to know what it was all about.

"When did I see her? I never saw her."

This was apparently of no interest to Starlight. He sniffed at the books on the floor, then jumped up on her desk and walked over to the window to look out. He sat on the other side of her laptop, his back to her, the tip of his tail twitching occasionally as he watched the birds and squirrels in the trees and the garden.

"She came here," Reg said, trying out the thought. It didn't matter that there was no one to talk to and Starlight wasn't really paying her any attention. She didn't need him to answer her, she just wanted to hear the words aloud. "She came here to talk to me."

Even though she didn't remember it, the words made sense and clicked into place as if she were fitting the pieces of a puzzle together.

"Okay. She came here to talk to me because she wanted help…"

Yes. That was right. Reg stared out the window for a few minutes with Starlight, letting her mind wander. She looked back down at the picture of the pixies in the book, studying their childish faces.

'I'm looking for my sister,' she heard the girl say.

She was nervous, looking around the house as if it were somewhere she wasn't supposed to be. Maybe she had been told by her parents not to pursue it. Not to talk to a psychic. Just to wait and see if her sister eventually came home on her own. Maybe they knew where she was or what had happened to her.

The reading had been uneventful. Reg didn't remember much about it. She tried to pin it down in time. It had been after the attack by Hawthorne-Rose, but before Jessup asked her to consult on Calliopia's case. The girl had initially gone to the main house, and Sarah had escorted her to the cottage to introduce her to Reg.

The girl had clearly been a pixie, though Reg hadn't realized it at the time. Since it was before Reg and Jessup had gone to the pixie realm, she'd had no idea what pixies looked like. She thought the girl had just been young and down on her luck. Knowing what she did now, the clear blue eyes, curly brown hair, diminutive height and worn clothing were obvious indicators.

The girl had been pleasant, far more polite than the other pixies Reg had met. But she had wanted something from Reg, and none of the other pixies had wanted anything to do with her.

What had the girl's name been? What was the name of the sister she was looking for?

Alice or some form of the name, Reg thought. That was the name of the sister. Something more exotic-sounding than that. The girl who had come to her had a short name. Carol?

"Not that any of this matters," she told Starlight. "It doesn't have any connection to the missing emerald. The emerald is the mystery I need to solve. Do you know where it is? Can *you* seek it?"

Starlight looked over his shoulder at her for a minute, then started to wash himself. Not helpful. He stopped and stared out the window as if something important had caught his attention. Reg leaned forward to have a look.

"What are you watching out there?"

He yowled and bumped his nose against the glass. Reg

cranked the lever to open the window an inch, and Starlight sniffed at the fresh air coming in through the screen with great interest.

Reg flipped a few more pages in the book. She needed to put it down and think of some way to investigate the theft of the necklace. Some way that Detective Jessup wouldn't have thought of.

CHAPTER THIRTEEN

*R*eg didn't know how long she had been browsing through the books, fascinated with the pictures of witches, warlocks, and others in the Black Sands of olden times when there was a sharp knock on the door. She tapped a key on her computer to wake it up and look at the time. It was late. Sarah should be in bed and Reg didn't know who else would be calling on her. She didn't like the idea of random callers late at night. Sometimes clients showed up without appointments during the day, but she didn't want anyone intruding on her after dark. She put the book down on the chair as she got up and crept up to the door.

She tried to avoid getting in the line of sight of the windows, even though the blinds should not allow anyone to peek in at her. The outside lights were hooked up to a motion detector, so she didn't have to worry about giving herself away by turning on the outside light in order to see the visitor through the peephole.

Her heart fell when she saw that it was Detective Jessup. Not there, Reg was sure, to update her on the latest developments in the case. And although Jessup had been working alone the last few times Reg had seen her, this time she had a cadre of other policemen with her. Jessup was facing the peephole stoically, and held a piece of paper out toward the peephole as if identifying herself to Reg.

Reg didn't try to talk to Jessup through the door. She knew what was going on.

She unlocked the door and opened it. "Detective Jessup."

Jessup held the paper out toward her. "Warrant to search the premises."

Reg didn't take it from her or examine the densely-written legal document. It was her worst nightmare come true. She'd spent many wakeful nights in the past worrying that someone might suspect her and get a warrant to search her property, revealing all of her secrets.

But this time, she had nothing to hide. Unless Starlight really had stolen the emerald, the search wasn't going to turn anything up in connection with crimes committed in Black Sands. And surely that was all the warrant covered.

She stepped back from the door and let Jessup and the others in.

"Please sit down on the couch," Jessup instructed, pointing. "In the middle, please."

Reg obeyed.

"I need you to stay there and not move while the search is being conducted."

Reg didn't say anything. Jessup gave a grimace, so fleeting that Reg couldn't have sworn she had really seen it, and then it was gone. She left one officer in the living room to keep guard over Reg and disappeared into the bedrooms in the back of the cottage with the others. Reg sat there, listening to the bangs of drawers, squeaks of doors, and scraping of coat hangers as the police looked through the contents of her bedroom and spare room. There were murmurs as they talked to each other, too quiet to make out. Starlight was disturbed by their movements or sent on his way and wandered out into the kitchen to look at his bowl, and then walked up to Reg and sat looking at her.

"Well," Reg asked him, "are they finding anything interesting?"

Starlight began to wash, starting with the tip of his tail. The policeman guarding or supervising Reg stared at her, but looked away when he caught her eyes on him. At least he was trying to be respectful.

Starlight chewed and licked at his fur as if he were filthy from a roll in the dirt, rather than just having jumped down from the dust-free desk. It was, Reg sensed, a snub of the policemen, showing them just how distasteful Starlight found it that they had invaded his living space.

"I know," she told him. "Me too."

She was going to have a shower when they left. In fact, she was going to want to clean the whole place once they were out of there, wiping away all of their fingerprints, vacuuming up all of their footprints.

Jessup walked out of the spare room and approached Reg, one of the library books in her hand. Reg looked at it, raising her eyebrows in query. A library book was certainly nothing for the police to be concerned about. It wasn't even overdue. Jessup sat down in the chair across from Reg, putting the heavy history book down on the coffee table between them, oriented toward Reg.

"I thought this was interesting," she said in a neutral voice.

Reg shrugged, looking at the book. Maybe Jessup liked history books. Jessup fanned the corners of the pages with her thumb, stopping and sliding her thumb in where one of the pages had been dog-eared. Reg looked at the page spreads, looking for what had interested Jessup. Scanning over the pictures, she stopped at one and cocked her head.

There was a black and white photo of a woman who looked like Sarah. She was wearing a large hat, standing proudly outside a tent, smiling at the camera. She was slimmer than the Sarah Reg knew, with fewer wrinkles, but looked remarkably similar.

"Wow. That must be Sarah's grandmother," Reg said, "there sure is a family resemblance."

Jessup just stared at her. Reg looked down at the page to see if there was something else she was supposed to have noticed. When she couldn't find anything else of note, Jessup put her finger under the picture, pointing to the caption. Reg squinted at the words.

Sarah Bishop stands outside the new cookhouse.

Reg's jaw dropped. She looked at the black and white photo more carefully, and searched out the four-digit number underneath.

"That's more than a hundred years ago."

Jessup glanced over at the policeman standing guard, and gave a tiny nod meant only for Reg's eyes. She looked at the picture again.

"Her grandmother had the same name," Reg tried, looking for a logical explanation.

"No. That's Sarah."

"It can't be. She might have looked like that five years ago. Not... no. That doesn't make any sense."

"You knew this," Jessup said, tapping the photo with her finger again. "You had these books out on your desk. You've been researching Black Sands history. You found this and you marked the page. You knew that Sarah was... long lived. You did some more research to find out why. And you learned about the emerald necklace."

"No." Reg shook her head vehemently. "I never saw that picture until you showed me just now. And if I had seen it, I never would have thought it was really Sarah. Just someone who looked like her. Someone from her family."

"The lies are starting to pile up, Reg," Jessup said quietly. "Why don't you stop while you can? You knew about Sarah and you found out the reason for her longevity. You thought that the necklace would do the same for you. You probably didn't realize that taking it would have such a negative effect on Sarah. You thought she would live out her life at the usual pace. But now you've seen what's happening to her. If you didn't understand before now, I'm telling you. She'll be dead within the week if you don't give the necklace back."

"I don't have it! I never had it. It doesn't have anything to do with me. If I had it, yeah, I'd give it back. I don't want to kill anyone. But I don't have it. So I can't give it back."

Jessup looked back toward the bedroom, where Reg could still hear the police conducting their search. They were being very thorough.

"If it's in this house, we're going to find it."

"It isn't. I didn't take it and I couldn't find it when I tried. If it was right here in my house, don't you think I would have been able to find it?"

"Of course."

"You think it was all an act. That I was never trying to find Sarah's necklace at all."

"You know the truth."

"I know the truth," Reg agreed. "Someone else stole the necklace. Why aren't you talking to Corvin? You know he's the one who stole the knife. Why wouldn't he steal the emerald too? He needs power. That necklace would give it to him."

"I know there's no love lost between you and Corvin. What he did to you was reprehensible. He's certainly on the list of suspects in the theft of the emerald, but I don't have any eyewitnesses putting him at the house."

"What if I told you I'd seen him there?"

Jessup shook her head. "You would have told me before now."

"You think you know it all, don't you? You've got it all figured out."

"I wish I did have it figured out, so that I could get the necklace and give it back to Sarah. But I need your cooperation for that."

"It isn't me you need. You need Corvin or whoever really stole it!"

There was a crash from the back of the house, making all of them jump.

"What the heck are they doing back there?" Reg demanded. "If they damage my property…"

"I'll go see what happened."

Jessup went to the bedroom and talked to the officers there, voices raised much louder than before.

"It all just came crashing down off of the shelf!" an aggrieved male voice protested. "Neither of us was anywhere near it!"

Jessup's voice was quieter, a low, reasoned tone that Reg wasn't able to make out.

"We didn't stack anything. It just came down by itself!"

There was some more back and forth and eventually Jessup returned to the living room, holding both hands palm-up. "I don't know what happened, but there doesn't seem to be any damage to anything. If there is, you can file a report with the department for compensation."

"It's not like I have a ton of stuff crammed into the closets. I've barely got more than fit in my suitcase."

"I know. I really don't think there's anything to worry about. It was loud, that's all. It startled us. But it wasn't anything to be concerned about."

"I wish that would stop happening."

Jessup looked questioning. "You wish what would stop happening?"

"That… things would stop… happening."

"Like?"

"Like stuff falling from the closet shelf. And doors slamming. And glasses breaking. It's really getting on my nerves."

Jessup opened her mouth.

"And don't say that I'm causing it, because I'm not!"

There was another, quieter crash and a curse from one of the policemen.

"Uh, no… of course not," Jessup said. She raised her voice to call out to the other officers. "Everything okay back there, guys?"

A grumble that Reg couldn't quite make out in response.

"It was the books," Jessup said, when she saw that Reg hadn't heard the answer. "He must have knocked them off the desk."

Reg didn't bother to tell her that they had also fallen off of the desk earlier when there had been nobody in the room to knock them over, even the cat.

"There aren't… earthquakes here, are there?"

Jessup shrugged. "No, not a lot. Maybe the floors are sloped."

It was as good an explanation as any, and didn't require Reg to admit that there were an awful lot of strange things happening around her lately. Strange things had always happened around Reg; that was nothing new. It didn't mean she was causing all of them. Black Sands was a hotbed of unusual people who could do unusual things. Reg wasn't the only one.

* * *

Reg turned and looked toward the main house.

"What is it?" Jessup asked.

"They just got home." Reg shook her head, frowning. "Where have they been all night? With Sarah being so tired and sick, they should have been home from dinner a long time ago. What else have they been doing?"

"Sarah and…?"

"Corvin. I told you, she was out with Corvin tonight."

"No… I don't think you did."

"I saw them at The Crystal Bowl." Reg stared at Jessup fiercely. "I told you that. That's why I called you. They were there together at The Crystal Bowl for supper. And Sarah was looking bad then. Why would they just be getting home now?"

"I don't know. It isn't any of my business."

"It is if he's filling her head up with lies so that she tells you she knows that I'm the one who stole her emerald necklace *when I'm not!*"

They both waited for the echo of Reg's shout to fade away, waiting for something else to happen, but this time nothing fell down or broke. Starlight stopped his grooming routine to glare at Reg.

"Oh, you don't like Corvin either, so don't look at me that way," Reg told him. "He says you're the one who stole the necklace. That's why the police are here, you know. To see if you really did."

Starlight looked at her for a moment before jumping up onto the couch to join her. Reg caught the policeman Jessup had set to guard her staring at her. He probably thought she was completely bonkers, raving and talking to her cat that way. Reg scratched Starlight's ears and chin, trying to use his calm aura to settle the anger and anxiety that had her chest and stomach on fire. He purred and rubbed against her and the knot loosened a little.

"I don't know what Corvin and Sarah were doing tonight," Jessup said. "Maybe he took her somewhere they could replenish her strength. I'll try stopping by to see if they offer anything. But how do you know...?"

"What?"

"That they just got back."

Reg opened her mouth to shoot back an impatient answer, then stopped herself. She couldn't see a car pull in front of the house. There was no change in the lights on inside the house. There were no raised voices to indicate their presence. But she had felt them come back in just as surely as if she'd seen or heard them.

"I, uh..." she glanced at the other policeman and kept her voice low. He didn't appear to be aware of the supernatural happenings around him. "I just... felt them."

"Were you trying to see them coming back?"

"No. It's just like... living in the basement and hearing them walking overhead. I wasn't trying to see or hear them... it's just obvious."

"Is it always like that?"

Reg shook her head. "Just lately. All of the comings and goings today have been driving me crazy. I can't concentrate with every-thing going on over there."

Jessup looked toward the house, which looked perfectly peaceful in the dark, with just a few lights on.

"You make it sound like there's been a party going on."

"It feels kind of like that. When a neighbor is keeping you awake when you're trying to go to sleep. But it's more like… heavy construction. Listening to bulldozers grinding and crashing and making their stupid back-up warning beeps." Reg shuddered. "That's what it feels like."

"Sounds like you're really sensitive right now. Psychically, I mean."

Reg ran her fingers through her braids. "Except that I can't *find* anything."

Starlight looked at Reg and shook his head, his ears making a flapping sound. Reg studied him, trying to read his thoughts. Lots of warmth and calming influence. He was trying to soothe her raw emotions.

"What if Starlight *did* steal the emerald," Jessup suggested, "and you didn't know anything about it? Corvin insists that you sent him into the house to get it, but what if he just did it on his own, like when he got out and brought the yarrow back?"

"I told you, he couldn't have left the house."

"You don't know where he is all the time. Maybe he went out and came in sometimes when Sarah came over here, dropping off the mail or something, and she didn't notice? You wouldn't know, if she was the one who let him in."

"She would have noticed. And she never said she saw him. Only Corvin did."

Jessup didn't answer. Reg thought about what she had said.

"Why would Starlight steal the necklace? That's not the kind of thing cats do. You think he actually planned to go over to the house, steal Sarah's necklace, and bring it back here?"

"Your cat is unique. I wouldn't expect a cat to know anything about medicine, botany, or the treatment of magical injuries either, but he clearly left here to look for yarrow to treat your wound. That tells me he does have... more human-like intelligence than I would expect from a cat. Maybe he is possessed or a reincarnate."

"Why are you so sure he stole the necklace?"

"Because I have two independent witnesses who put him there. And so far, he's the only being who we know was in Sarah's house during the right time period, other than Sarah herself."

"It's ridiculous."

"He could have done it without you knowing."

"He didn't."

"He could be the one blocking you from finding it. Because he doesn't want you to find it right here in your own house."

Reg looked at Starlight. He looked back at her, his imperious eyes giving nothing away. He continued to push quieting feelings at Reg, but there was something in his manner, an awareness that told her he perfectly understood what they were talking about.

"He didn't steal the necklace," Reg repeated.

Jessup shrugged. "I'm doing the best I can." She rose to her feet and indicated the book still lying open on the coffee table. "You've been studying Black Sands history. You knew about Sarah's longevity. Maybe she told you it was due to the emerald, or maybe that little tidbit is buried in here somewhere too. You can't profess ignorance, and doing so only makes me more suspicious."

"I didn't read any of those books. I was just flipping through the pictures in one of them today, and I don't think it was even that one."

"The page is marked."

"The page is dog-eared. Maybe it got folded by accident. Maybe the person who borrowed it last did it intentionally. Or someone who borrowed it years ago. How old is it? Go ahead and check for my fingerprints on that page. You're not going to find them."

Jessup looked down at the book, obviously considering it.

Eventually, she shrugged. "That picture doesn't prove anything one way or the other, so neither will your fingerprints."

* * *

It was a long time before the police finished their search and left Reg's house empty-handed, having found no sign of the emerald necklace. Of course, Reg had known that they wouldn't find it, but it was still a relief to have them leave. There was always the danger that the police would plant something that they could arrest her with, or the bizarre billion-to-one chance that Starlight had, in fact, stolen it and hid it somewhere in the house.

The cottage was finally quiet and so was the main house, Corvin having left and Sarah deep in sleep. Reg wandered through the rooms of the cottage, straightening items that the police had left askew or slightly out of place, knowing that she wouldn't feel like it was hers again until she'd had a chance to dust and clean everything, ridding it of the psychic imprints the police had left behind. But it was too late and she was too tired to do it before bed. She showered, scrubbing her skin until it stung, pulled on her softest jammies, and climbed into bed.

Starlight sat at the bedroom window watching outside for a long time. At some point in the night, Reg felt him jump onto the bed and curl up against her.

CHAPTER FOURTEEN

Get out! Get out! Get out of here!"

Heart pounding, Reg jumped out of bed, sure she was under attack. It took a few seconds to realize that the yells were coming from outside. She looked out the window and saw Sarah, wild-eyed, wielding a broom threateningly.

The intruder was not a trespasser, but a cat Reg had never seen before, skinny and black. It tried several times to get past Sarah, but was cornered, and every time he ran forward, Sarah thumped the broom down, and it was all the cat could do to avoid being flattened. Sarah was decimating her flowers, but hadn't made contact with the cat while Reg had been watching. She was yelling at the cat to leave, but then not letting him go.

"Sarah!"

Sarah looked toward the window, not able to see which one Reg was calling through.

"Just let the cat go," Reg said, "he can't get past you."

"He's chasing my birds!" Sarah's voice was outraged.

"Are you trying to kill him?"

Sarah lowered the broom slightly. "No."

"That's what it looks like. How can he get out of the yard if you won't let him?"

Sarah took a step back and watched the cat, her eyes flashing. "He'll just come back again when he thinks no one is watching."

"I don't think he'll come back here again."

The cat streaked past Sarah, ears pressed down against its head, its body low to the ground to make itself a smaller target. In seconds, it was gone. Sarah looked around the garden and the damage she had done with the broom.

"Oh… look…"

"It will be okay. It's just a few flowers. Everything else will spring back up again within a few days."

Sarah rubbed her eyes. "I won't be around long enough to see them."

"Don't say that." There was a pain in Reg's chest. "Come inside and let's have a cup of tea."

Sarah stood there for a few minutes, looking lost and forlorn.

"Come into the cottage," Reg urged again, afraid Sarah had already forgotten the invitation. "It will be okay. Let's have tea."

Sarah looked vaguely in her direction, then started to walk around to the front of the cottage. Reg darted through to meet her at the front door, calling to her once more to make sure she didn't forget Reg's invitation and simply go back into the main house.

"Come in for tea, Sarah."

Sarah walked in the door and looked around. Her face was haggard. She had no makeup on and the wrinkles were turning into deep crags. Her eyes were sunken deep in the sockets, looking small and dark.

"Have a seat," Reg motioned to the furniture in the living room. "I'm just putting the kettle on. It won't be long."

Reg herself was still in her pajamas, sticky from sleep, her heart pounding wildly after being awakened so abruptly. At least with her hair done up in cornrows, her hair wasn't messy on rising.

"I hate cats in my garden," Sarah said vehemently. "You shouldn't let them in there!"

"Me? It was nothing to do with me. I've never seen that cat before."

"He's not yours?"

Reg shook her head and swallowed. "No. Some black cat I've never seen before. It wasn't Starlight. He's still inside."

Reg cast a quick look around. Starlight was nowhere to be seen. She hadn't noticed when she had woken up whether he was still on the bed or not. He must have been. It was unusual for him not to make his way immediately to the kitchen to beg for food, but maybe he thought it best to avoid the crazy woman with the broom, or was confused by Reg not following her usual morning routine, heading for the bathroom before the kitchen.

She put the kettle on. "I'll be right back," she told Sarah. "I'll be back before that starts to whistle."

Sarah stared out the living room window. Reg used the bathroom quickly, worried Sarah would wander off or start chasing down other people's pets before Reg could get back.

She peeked into the bedroom and was relieved to see Starlight sitting on the bed watching her.

"You should go keep Sarah company. Make sure she doesn't leave before we've had tea."

Starlight made no indication he would do so. If Reg were a cat, she probably wouldn't either. As a human, she was much better equipped to handle an old woman armed with a broom.

She used the bathroom and gave her teeth a quick scrub to banish morning breath, and returned to the kitchen. The kettle was not yet boiling, and Sarah was still sitting where Reg had left her.

"How are you feeling this morning?" Reg asked.

"Bone tired." Sarah's voice quavered. "You can't even imagine how tired and sore this old body is."

She had seemed able enough a few minutes earlier, banishing the strange cat from the yard. But sitting down she seemed tireder and more shrunken, as if she were rapidly shrinking in upon herself.

"We'll find the emerald," Reg encouraged. "Hang in there."

Sarah didn't answer. But at least she didn't accuse Reg again of having stolen it.

* * *

The tea stretched out far longer than Reg would have wished, but she was reluctant to tell Sarah it was time to leave or to let her go somewhere unsupervised.

She was trying to figure out what to do when there was a knock on the door. Reg got up, trying to see through the blinds who it was before going to the door. She opened the door and was faced with a tall, pouchy-faced woman with a flowered pink scarf wrapped around her hair, turban-style. Reg knew she had seen the face before, but couldn't place her.

"Do you know where Sarah is?" the woman inquired. "I expected her to be home, but she's not answering the door. I fear…"

"Yes, she's here." Reg opened the door wider to allow the woman to step in and see Sarah in the seating area.

The woman saw Sarah and looked relieved. "Oh, good. I was looking for you, Sarah!" She nearly shouted, as if Sarah were hard of hearing.

"Of course I'm here," Sarah said.

"That's good. I was afraid something had happened to you."

"Nothing happened," Sarah said querulously, "I'm capable of taking care of myself, you know."

"Yes, dear," the woman agreed, taking Sarah's hand to shake and patting it with her other hand. "Of course you are perfectly capable. Are you ready to go?"

Sarah looked at Reg. "I don't want to go out anywhere. I'm much too tired. Maybe another day."

"Well…" Reg looked at the new woman, not sure what to say. "Maybe Sarah's not feeling up to it today."

"We'll go back to the house, then," the woman said, giving Sarah a little tug on the hand she was still holding. "Come on."

"I don't want to go."

"Just to your house, so you can rest," the woman soothed, and Reg was suddenly overcome with the desire to climb into her bed and rest her own weary bones. She was still in her pajamas, and she looked toward her bedroom with longing.

Then Reg remembered who the woman was. Marian. Another psychic, one of Reg's competitors. Reg didn't know her specialty or all of her skills, but Marian seemed to have a remarkable ability to influence the desires of people nearby. She had previously attempted to nudge Reg toward getting intoxicated at the community dance.

Marian's power over Sarah seemed to be effective, as the old witch was attempting to get to her feet. Marian leaned over to put her hand under Sarah's elbow to try to get some leverage. She managed to hoist Sarah up to her feet, then supported her around the waist as they walked, even though Sarah had been able to get around under her own power just an hour earlier.

"We'll get out of your way, then," Marian told Reg. "You look like you could use a rest too."

A surge of weariness went through Reg. She glared at Marian. "Don't do that!"

Marian raised her brows. "Don't... what...?"

"Don't try to push feelings onto me."

"I'm sure I don't know what you're talking about." Marian moved more quickly toward the door.

"Isn't there some kind of rule against making people feel emotions or desires that aren't their own?"

"I've never heard of such a thing. How could there be? How could such a thing ever be tracked or determined?"

"If you do it to me again, we're going to find out."

Marian's eyes met Reg's for a moment, cunning and challenging, and then she looked away. "You have a nice day now, dear. You don't find *that* offensive, do you? Or a smile, intended to brighten your day? People influence others' moods all the time, in all different ways."

"Like I said, you'd better not try it with me again."

Marian stopped. "You are the newcomer to Black Sands. If you don't like the way things are here, maybe you should just leave. I'm sure that wherever you came from is far more sophisticated and enjoyable for you than Florida."

The vitriol hung around her like a black cloud. She hated Reg. There could be no doubt of the fact. Why, Reg wasn't sure. Certainly there could be two psychics in town without professional jealousies breaking out. There was plenty of work to go around, and Marian and Reg weren't the only ones in town with psychic powers. Reg had no idea why Marian disliked her so much.

Reg chewed on her lip, waiting for Marian to go, not engaging with her any further. No point in pushing her luck. Reg didn't need yet another person running to the police and pointing an accusing finger at her because she was jealous of Reg's success.

Or maybe Marian was the unnamed second witness who claimed to have seen Starlight in Sarah's house.

* * *

Despite the feeling of heaviness Reg was left with after Marian's departure, she forced herself to shower and dress and eat something, and before too long, she was feeling more like her normal self again.

She hadn't been to Letticia's house before, but she felt like it was important to go see her and see if there were anything she could do for Sarah. Letticia should already know how the witch from her coven was faring, but maybe she didn't know how quickly she was going downhill, or she could tell Reg some way to help Sarah or to get her finding skills back.

The address was in the old-fashioned black address book Sarah had left in the kitchen drawer for the use of whoever rented the cottage from her. It was much more useful for tracking down particular practitioners than an internet search, as many of the old-school witches didn't adopt modern technologies. Some of them didn't even have landlines and could only be contacted by mail, in person, or through some messenger service. In the magical community, it wasn't unusual to send a message through a real bird rather than Twitter.

Reg input the address into her GPS and let it guide her to the outskirts of town, where she soon found herself in a dark forested area that could have come straight out of Hansel and Gretel. The GPS lost its signal in the canopy of the trees, and Reg stared at the sketched lines on the screen, trying to match them up to the rough roads cut through the dark green forest. The other option was to turn around and follow her electronic breadcrumb trail home. But she wasn't ready to give up without at least giving it a try.

Letticia's house was somewhere off the edge of the map. Reg decided to just keep following the road she was on until she couldn't go any farther. If she didn't find the coven leader, she would go home.

The road got smaller and rougher until it was barely a track through the trees. When it finally came to an end, Reg was within sight of a little cottage.

It wasn't the gingerbread house of Hansel and Gretel. It was more like the thatched houses of Three Little Pigs, but it looked like it had been there for a very long time and had at least stood up to the weather.

Anxiety crawled in Reg's stomach. She was completely out of her element. She was a street-savvy, city-bred girl, used to looking after herself in the urban jungle, but being out in the Everglades was something different altogether. She was all alone, approaching a house that might or might not belong to a powerful witch. She was by herself and had no experience in how to protect herself from harmful magic. The little house in the woods might just as easily belong to an evil huntsman or recluse serial killer.

The door opened, and at least one question was answered. Letticia stood in her doorway, her face pinched and disapproving.

"Are you just going to sit in that contraption all day or are you going to come in?"

Reg cleared her throat and forced herself to climb out of the car to face the witch. "Sorry. I wasn't sure if this was the right place and was just trying to decide how to find out…"

"The way people have found out for hundreds of years. By walking up to the door and knocking."

Reg nodded, feeling the red flush creep across her face. "Yes, of course, you're right. I just… I was a little nervous." Reg stopped for a moment before crossing the threshold into Letticia's house. "I don't even know what to say."

"Come in."

Reg steeled herself and entered.

The house was small, but neat and well-appointed. In the kitchen area, there was a black cast-iron stove that Letticia must have used to make her meals and potions and to warm the house when the temperature dropped too low outside. And it was not, Reg didn't think, large enough for her to crawl inside.

"How is she this morning?" Letticia asked.

Reg was startled. "Sarah, you mean?"

"Is it not about Sarah that you came?"

"Well, yes… of course… I just didn't think…"

"Why else would you come here? Sarah is your friend and your landlord, and she's dying."

There was a lump in Reg's throat. "Don't say that. Don't say she's dying."

"Everybody must die sooner or later. Sarah has had a long and productive life, and it would appear that it is time for it to come to an end. While none of us want to see her go, she has to follow her destiny."

"So… you don't have any suggestions? There's nothing I can do to help her? There's no potion you can make for her?"

"I have many helpful rejuvenation charms, creams, and tonics, but none of them will stop death from coming for Sarah."

Reg sat down on an upholstered chair Letticia waved her

toward, her knees giving way. Even with what Corvin and Jessup had told her, it hadn't really hit her that without her emerald, Sarah wasn't just going to die. She was already dying.

"She woke me up this morning chasing a cat out of the yard," she told Letticia, wiping a tear from the corner of her eyes. "She was yelling and scaring the crap out of some poor stray that had wandered into her garden. Trying to beat it to death with a broom!"

Letticia smiled understandingly.

"But then after I got her to stop trying to kill the poor thing… she just seemed to fade away. She looks worse every day. Her mind seems to be wandering. I just… I feel so bad watching her decline."

"Death is rarely seen as a kind deliverer. Old age is not for the faint of heart. But maybe it is time for Sarah to stop running from it."

More tears squeezed out of Reg's eyes and her nose started to run. "I was just getting to know her. She has been so kind to me since I came to Black Sands. She just took me under her wing without knowing anything about me, treating me like her own family. I never had a grandma. But that's what she's been like to me. Like a grandma or a mother… and a friend."

"The best thing you can do now is to be with her. Spend some time, before she fades further."

"There's no way to stop it?"

"Only by finding the emerald, and I fear that it becomes less and less likely that anyone will find it in time. Even now, it may be too late for it to have any kind of effect."

"Somebody took it. Somebody must have come into her house and taken it away."

"Perhaps," Letticia agreed.

"How else could it had disappeared? It's not in her house. It's not in my house. And no matter what anyone says, it was not stolen by my cat!"

Letticia didn't agree or disagree.

"Letticia…" Reg sat on the edge of the chair, leaning forward toward the witch. "Is it okay to call you that…?"

"It is my name," Letticia said dryly.

"I know… but it seems disrespectful to call you by your first name. Is there an honorific…"

Letticia gave a smile that seemed to smooth the hard ridges of her face for just an instant.

"Letticia is fine, Regina. No special title is needed. Witches don't have a hierarchy. I am no more important than Sarah or than you. We are all children of the earth."

"Okay. Letticia. How could anyone have gotten into the house to steal the emerald? I thought that she was silly not to have it in a bank, and to be relying on her parrot to attack anyone who tried to steal it from her. But… didn't she have wards and protections to keep anyone from breaking into her house? I mean, she put wards up at the cottage to keep Corvin from coming in uninvited. Surely she must have even better protections on her own house and on something as important and valuable as the emerald. If it is what keeps her alive, wouldn't she have done everything she could to protect it from thieves?"

"Yes. She does have wards and spells in place to protect herself and her home. And the emerald."

"Then how could anyone steal it?"

Letticia sighed, shaking her head. "As you said, it would have to be someone she had invited in."

"Someone she trusted and thought was a friend."

Letticia gave a solemn nod. Reg leaned back in her chair and closed her eyes, her heart aching, causing her actual physical pain.

"May I get you something?" Letticia asked softly, and she got up and went into the kitchen area without waiting for an answer. Reg didn't know what to say. There was nothing Letticia could say that would heal a broken heart.

"How could anyone do that to her? How could someone she loved betray her like that? Taking away what was left of her life?"

Letticia put tea into cups and switched on an electric kettle.

"Maybe it was someone who felt it was her time to go. She has been resisting it for some time. Some of us have noticed certain declines in her mental faculties even before the disappearance of the gem."

Reg shook her head. "No. She was so kind and she was always on top of everything. She didn't just take care of herself, she was always mothering me too." Reg sniffled. "She *was* on top of everything."

"No. Not everything. In time, she would have had to let go of the emerald. I wish that she had done it of her own accord."

Letticia poured the tea and took a cup to Reg. Reg sniffed the tea, not sure what herbs she could smell. A hint of licorice, maybe. Erin would have been able to identify it immediately. A never-fail party trick. Reg sipped it and a warm feeling spread across her chest, easing the knot of tension slightly.

"No one took it just so that she would get old and die," Reg insisted, sure of this fact. "Someone took it because it is powerful. They wanted to harness the power for themselves, one way or another."

Letticia just looked at Reg.

"It wasn't me," Reg snapped.

"I did not say that it was. Do not put words in my mouth."

"Sorry. The police searched my house last night. Corvin is saying that it was me. Someone else too, I think maybe Marian the psychic. It feels like everyone thinks I took it. Even Sarah. Because that's what Corvin told her."

"The warlock is a force to be reckoned with. But he can only influence her while he is directly with her. The same is true of Marian. Her skills are strong when she is present, but over a distance... she isn't like you. She cannot reach out to someone or something that is not in the same room."

"So if neither one of them is there with Sarah, she won't believe that I took it?" Reg tried to swallow the lump in her throat. What did it matter whether an old lady believed her or not? Reg hadn't taken it. That was all that mattered.

"They can only directly influence her when they are with her."

"Okay. That's something, at least. And there isn't anything I can do for Sarah? Other than to find the emerald?"

Letticia shook her head. "No. And I believe you've already tried to seek it."

"Why didn't it work? I can find things that don't matter. I can find things that I've never seen or touched before. Why can't I find something that's so powerful and important?"

"I think you already know the answer to that."

Reg's head whirled. "What's that supposed to mean?"

"I mean that in all likelihood, if you look deep down in yourself, you'll understand why you are not able to find it."

"I've already done that. I've done everything I could to see it."

"Except look at yourself."

"I don't have it."

"You have that power inside you. You know you do. And you are the best one to know why you can't access that power."

"It must be because of Calliopia," Reg said. "Nothing has been the same since she brought me back from the shadow realm. I've been so mixed up and things have been happening around me, but I can't *find*. I can't find anything."

"Fairy magic is unpredictable. And a fairy who has just come into her own is both powerful and unpredictable. It takes a few decades for them to settle in and get used to their powers. Like a horse or a teenager filling out after shooting up."

"So she could have had an unexpected effect on me. She might have… enhanced some powers and taken others away."

"Taking powers away would be very unusual. Other than witches and warlocks like Corvin Hunter, there are not many things that can take a practitioner's powers away. It's more likely suppressed than removed."

"What's the difference?" Reg snapped.

Letticia opened her mouth to explain, and Reg waved the explanation away. "I know the difference between being suppressed and removed. I'm just saying that for practical purposes, it's the same. Either way, I can't find the emerald."

Letticia nodded. She looked down at her wrist. "I'm afraid I have an engagement I must get to. I've been asked to observe a…" She trailed off, looking at Reg.

"What?"

"You need to be there too. Weren't you informed of Corvin's appearance before his coven?"

CHAPTER FIFTEEN

*R*eg's heart thudded. "Is that today?"

Letticia raised her brows.

Reg wasn't really surprised she had forgotten the date of the hearing. She hadn't looked at her calendar in a couple of days, and she didn't want to think about the hearing and had pushed it as far as she could from her mind. She was surprised that it had arrived so quickly. Didn't both sides need time to prepare their cases? No one had questioned Reg ahead of time as to what she was going to say. She didn't feel at all prepared to testify.

"Uh… yeah. That's today, isn't it? It's just that with everything going on, I kind of forgot."

"Do you know your way there?"

"I… I'm not sure where it is."

"Do you want to follow me? I would suggest going together, but you won't want to come all the way back here to get your car after."

"Yeah, that sounds good. What do you drive?"

"Not a broomstick or a horse-drawn carriage," Letticia said dryly.

Reg's face warmed. "I never suggested that."

"You wouldn't be the first. I have a car. Stay close, and I'll get you there."

"Okay. Thanks."

Reg took another long sip of her tea but didn't finish it. She returned the cup to the kitchen and went back out to her car. She waited for Letticia to appear with her station wagon or whatever kind of boat she drove.

A low riding, sleek white convertible pulled around the cottage. Letticia looked back at Reg, large dark glasses on and a scarf wrapped around her head to prevent her hair from getting windblown. Reg thought she detected a hint of a smile on Letticia's sharp face.

Letticia pulled around Reg, out the road that Reg had used coming in. Reg turned her car around as quickly as she could and followed Letticia out. They bumped over the roads, much faster than Reg had traveled them on the way in, bouncing around and bruising her tailbone. She didn't really have good shocks. She shuddered to think what the roads were doing to Letticia's expensive little convertible.

But Letticia pretty much lived off the grid and couldn't have had many more expenses than the taxes on the land she lived on, so maybe she could afford to replace her car or her car's suspension every year or two. They zoomed back toward Black Sands. Reg was happy to hit the familiar roads again. She'd half-expected to get lost in the forest and never return.

* * *

The tribunal was held in a hotel meeting room. Reg had expected some dark dungeon or a gathering in a clearing in the woods. And she was happy to be meeting during the daylight hours rather than at midnight. Maybe the warlocks were not quite as uncivilized as she had expected.

Letticia bustled Reg up to the front where the members of the tribunal were gathering and speaking with each other.

"Regina, I'd like you to meet Davyn Smithy, my counterpart in the coven of the Black Sands warlocks."

Regina nodded to Dave Smith. "We've met. So do you have one name for warlocks and another for non-magical folk?"

Dave looked a little awkward. He nodded. "Dave Smith is nice and normal and anonymous for day-to-day use. Davyn is my real name."

"Uh-huh." Reg knew the benefits of being able to stay anonymous and fly under the radar when your business or personal life were unconventional. "Got it."

Davyn offered Reg his hand to shake and she didn't take it. Davyn looked at her, then over at Letticia, giving a wide shrug. Letticia raised one severe, querying eyebrow. "Do you really expect her to show you any social courtesies after her experience with Corvin?" Her mouth drew down at the corners into a deep scowl. Davyn swallowed and dropped his hand back to his side.

"You may be seated over there, Miss Rawlins," he pointed to a chair prominently isolated at the front of the room.

Reg looked at it and shook her head. "No. I don't think so."

"I beg your pardon?"

"I'm not on display here. I'll sit in the audience until it's my time to speak."

He opened his mouth and seemed to be at a loss as to how to react to her defiance. There was a snicker from another warlock who had not been introduced to Reg, which she thought was rather rude.

"This is a formal hearing, Miss Rawlins. There are protocols to be followed."

"I'm sure there are. And I'm sure that trying to humiliate witnesses or victims isn't one of them."

"Of course not—"

"Then I'll be sitting where I choose." She looked at Letticia. "Where are you going to be sitting?"

Letticia gestured to a couple of rows of chairs angled in the front corner of the room. "Over there, with the tribunal."

Reg didn't want to be sitting with the tribunal, either. So she walked over to one of the audience chairs, near the front and on the aisle, so that she could easily get up when she was called upon. She sat down and made herself as comfortable as she could under the glares and laughter of the other warlocks who had witnessed the whole process.

She sat back, folded her arms across her chest, and watched the warlocks prepare for their meeting. Davyn Smithy looked her way a few times, but each time he found her glaring back at him, he looked quickly away.

Her anxiety grew as the chairs behind her filled. She hadn't expected so many spectators. Why would any of them care what Corvin had done or how she had been victimized? They didn't even know Reg.

She hadn't seen Corvin come in, but looked up and saw him watching her. He ventured a little smile when he saw her, and crooked a finger for her to join him. Did he really think she wanted anything to do with him? That she would let any of the others in the room see her consorting with him? He looked around him to see what the others were doing, then approached her chair. He again gave a warm reassuring smile.

"Regina. I wondered if I could get a private word with you."

"Are you kidding?"

"Just for a moment, I won't take a lot of your time…"

"No."

"I just want a moment the two of us could be alone for a minute."

"After everything, why would I do that?"

"Because I think that you and I could work something out that was mutually beneficial…"

"What is this, a plea bargain?" Reg couldn't even believe he was approaching her. Surely doing so was against some rule? And trying to get her alone as the minute of his trial approached…? It didn't make any sense.

Corvin shook his head. "I'm not going to do anything to you. Look at all these witnesses…" he gestured to the gathering crowd.

"If you want something, you can tell me right here, because this is where I'm staying. I'm not going somewhere else with you and I don't care about privacy. My whole life is about to be put on display here."

Corvin considered for a moment, then slid into the chair in front of her, casually turned around to talk to her face-to-face.

"I know that you can't be much happier about this whole thing than I am," he acknowledged. "Neither of us wanted it to come to this. I made a mistake, and I've apologized, and I think we both just want to go on with our own lives, not to have to deal with this whole… circus act."

Reg's anger, already at a low bubble just being in the same room as Corvin, flared up.

"You think I just want to forget about this? I don't want to forget about it. I don't want you to forget about it."

"And I'm not going to. I've learned from it. I didn't realize that I was so weak. I'll make sure… it won't ever happen again."

All the same, he couldn't seem to talk to her without laying on the charm. It came off of him like shimmering heat waves over the sidewalk.

Reg stared away from Corvin, not wanting to seem friendly toward him and not wanting to take the chance of being pulled in by him yet again.

"Whatever you've got cooked up, the answer is no," she said firmly. "I'm not letting you off the hook. You deserve whatever discipline they decide on."

"Of course, I know. I agree. Whatever they judge is just… I'll accept."

"You'd better go get ready, then, they'll be ready to start in a few minutes."

"You still haven't heard me out."

"I've heard enough." No matter how sorry he said he was, Reg saw no sign of repentance. No indication that he was going to change or try to act differently in the future.

"Reg." He said her name more firmly and Reg felt a shift, as if he'd put handcuffs on her or whispered a command. She stared at him, waiting for him to finish so she could move again. "I really think we can help each other out. What you say here has an effect on my future. My freedom and ability to practice. Just like you don't want to have your freedom restricted by getting thrown in jail."

Reg couldn't believe he would be so bold. "I don't see what one has to do with the other."

"Oh, don't you? I could be of service to you, in taking care how I tell my story about you and Starlight and the missing necklace. And you can be of service to me by taking care how you tell them about my… mistake."

"You want me to trade my testimony, and you'll keep me out of jail if I do."

He smiled, nodding. "You see? It really is simple. I know that you don't want to go to jail for stealing Sarah's jewel."

"I wouldn't even be on the suspect list if you hadn't made up that nonsense about me training Starlight to go into the house and help me to steal jewelry away from Sarah. How ridiculous! Does anybody really believe it?"

"The more witnesses there are, the more difficult it becomes for you to avoid what will certainly come."

"You put Marian up to witnessing against me. And who knows how many other people you've tried to tempt into helping you. But they won't, because it's all made up."

Corvin's jaw clenched. He stared at her, anger clear in the heat of his gaze. He had thought he could talk and cajole her into shading her testimony to not portray him in such a bad light, sure she would do it in order to get out of the way of the police and their spotlight.

"Nobody is going to put me in jail for stealing that necklace," she told Corvin with more certainty than she felt. "I'm not serving a day, because I didn't steal it, and you know it."

He got to his feet, saying nothing. Reg had done it this time. He could no longer even pretend to be saying and doing nice things for her. He was done with the charm.

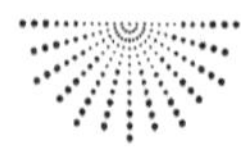

he session is called to order," Davyn Smithy declared. "Please take your seats and refrain from speaking unless you are called upon."

Women settled into the seats next to Reg's, casting surreptitious glances in her direction. Even though she was sitting in the audience, people clearly knew what her role there was.

Reg clenched her teeth and pressed her lips together hard, trying to look calm and collected. She needed everyone to think that she was there of her own choice and was calm and clear-headed. They didn't need to know that she had forgotten about the trial and would probably have missed it if Letticia hadn't needed to be there too.

Reg was not the one on trial. Corvin was on trial, because of what he had done to her. It was her chance to turn the tables on him and make him pay for what he had done.

Davyn outlined the various charges in a monotone. He looked out over the room and stopped for a minute, waiting for the audience to quiet again.

"Corvin Hunter, what have you to say about these charges?"

Corvin was sitting in one of the lone chairs at the front of the room. He got to his feet, rubbing his chin thoughtfully. Just how far could he throw those charms? Reg had usually been right next to him when he had turned his glamour on her, but she had been able to sense when he entered a room. Was he warming up the charm now, seeing if he could influence all of them? Such an endeavor would surely fail. There were some people that seemed to be immune to his charms. One day, maybe Reg would be one of them.

"I challenge the validity of the charges," Corvin said in a warm, resonant voice. "I challenge the fairness of laws made requiring me to resist my own nature."

Reg looked at Davyn for his reaction to this position. He gave no indication whether he approved or disapproved. He picked up a quill, dipped it in an ink pot, and wrote long words and sentences. Reg watched, fascinated. She'd never actually seen someone write that way, even though she knew it used to be done all the time. The advances in writing instruments, computers, and other methods of communication had killed off those old, traditional methods. Or at least, that was what Reg had assumed up until that moment. Apparently there were still some pockets of people practicing the old ways.

Davyn laid his pen down. "Do you wish to address the appropriateness of the laws at the beginning or end of the hearing?"

"I'll wait until the end," Corvin said. "I think most of you have heard these arguments before, so it is best if I just refresh you at the end."

Reg clenched her fists. She, too, had heard his argument of how it was unjust to ban someone from doing what came naturally to him. She had been swayed before by his hunger, by his intense need. She had since had a chance to reconsider that position. There had to be laws to protect the innocent. Those with baser instincts and desires could not be allowed full rein to do whatever they wanted, harming others. The laws were needed to protect those who were vulnerable.

"I believe we will get right into it, then." Davyn got to his feet, stretching a little. "I call Miss Regina Rawlins to present her testimony."

Reg stood up. Davyn gestured to the chair he had indicated she should sit in earlier.

"If you would," he encouraged.

She did as she was asked. Her mouth was as dry as cotton, but she was sweating buckets. She had no idea what she was going to say and how she was going to convince them that Corvin needed to be punished. She deserved recompense.

"Miss Rawlins, could you describe for us what happened on the date in question?" Davyn Smithy picked up his papers and read off the date of the party.

Reg nodded and swallowed. She explained how they had gotten there to the party and what they had done once they got there. Davyn nodded his understanding. His face was clear of any emotional response.

"Now before we go forward, Miss Rawlins, let us review the facts. You were aware of Mr. Hunter's powers."

"Yes."

"How did you become aware of these powers? They are... something of a taboo to talk about in the community."

"I don't get that," Reg said, shaking her head. "It would have been much better if people had explained everything to me, instead of just saying to stay away from him."

"We will get to that before too long. If you could answer my questions in the order they are asked."

"Okay... what was the question?"

"How did you become aware of Mr. Hunter's powers prior to the date of the party?"

"Oh. Well... because I was tricked into relinquishing my powers to him before."

There was a burst of noise from the audience. Clearly, they had not been expecting that tidbit. Reg kept in mind the one thing that everyone agreed upon about men like Corvin who sucked the gifts out of unsuspecting victims.

Once they took someone's powers, they never gave them back.

"You had relinquished your powers to him before," Davyn said, as if stunned.

"Yes. I know… that doesn't make any sense to you, but it's true. He took my powers away completely, so I was…" Reg shook her head and tried to describe the horrible feeling of waking up to silence. No voices in her head. No feelings. No chatter. It had all just stopped. "I was so… empty. And quiet. I didn't know what he had done at first. I didn't know what to do. But then later, Corvin helped me… I was being tortured by this man… this Hawthorne Rose. He wanted something… I no longer had."

"One of your powers?"

"Memories. But I could only remember them or pass them on if I had my powers, and I didn't anymore. It was all just a blank."

"And this torture prompted Corvin to give you back your psychic gifts."

"Yes."

There was another murmur through the crowd. It wasn't good for Reg's position. The fact that Corvin had given her her gifts back meant that she owed him. That's what he had told her.

"I didn't ask for them back," Reg clarified. "He did it spontaneously, because he wanted to stop Hawthorne-Rose."

Davyn stroked his beard, thinking it through. "We'll leave it at that… for now. But we may need to revisit this point. So… you were aware that Corvin could take your powers because he had done it before."

"Yes."

"So after that… you avoided being near him."

Reg nodded. "Yeah."

"For how long?"

"What?"

"How long did you avoid being around Mr. Hunter? Once you had your gifts returned to you, you stayed away from him for… how long?"

"I don't know. I avoided him the best I could, but sometimes I'd run into him… or we would need to work on a case together."

"How is that?"

"What?"

"What kind of cases? You are not a police officer, are you?"

"No. I was just consulting… and the police needed Corvin's input too. So… we were both there at the same time."

"That sounds awkward. You didn't ask the detective on the case for you to appear separately, so you didn't have to run into each other?"

"No. I didn't think it would do any good and we were kind of in a hurry. Lives hung in the balance."

"I see. So you avoided Mr. Hunter…. unless there was some sort of business that the two of you needed to discuss."

Reg shrugged. "We did talk," she agreed.

"You did more than talk."

"The night of the party, you mean?"

"You did more than talk to Mr. Hunter the night of the party."

"Not to start with."

"You danced. Surely that wasn't 'business.'"

"Well… no. But we *were* just talking."

"Were you? I would suggest that there was a lot more going on than just talking."

Reg wiped her forehead. She desperately wanted a drink of water but no one offered her one.

"It was Corvin's idea to dance. He kept begging me."

"So you gave in."

"No… I told him that I would only dance with him under certain conditions."

"Conditions."

Reg caught a glimpse of Corvin as he watched her testify. She could have sworn that he was laughing. Anger lightninged through her chest and she tried to control it.

"Explain what these conditions were," Davyn requested.

"I told him that he couldn't use his magic on me. That if he used magic, then I didn't consent to him doing anything, to taking my powers. If he used magic to make me say yes, then I still didn't consent."

"An interesting thought. And how did this go over with Mr. Hunter?"

"He didn't like it. He stormed off. But after a while, he came back, and he said he'd agree to my terms. He said he wouldn't use his magic on me. That he just wanted to dance with me."

"I see." Davyn picked up his pen and wrote down several lines of information. Everyone waited, watching him intently, shifting restlessly in their seats.

"So did you feel confident that you would have no further trouble from Mr. Hunter?"

"Uh… no. Not at all. I asked Sarah what she thought. She said that everything should be fine if we were just dancing and we stayed where there were other people. She said that he wouldn't do anything if there were other people around."

"So to summarize, you knew that he could take your powers because he had before. You laid strictures on him as to the use of his magic, and you believed that if you stayed around other people, you would be safe from him."

"Yes."

"Then what happened?"

"We danced. It was hot. I wanted some fresh air."

"Ah. So you left him and went outside…?"

"No." Reg felt the first warning bells, warning her things were not going to go in her direction.

"Clarify then. You went outside…?"

"We walked outside together. To get some fresh air. We wanted to be somewhere we could talk, and the balcony was open."

"So there were a number of other people on the balcony with you."

"No. It was just us." Reg swallowed. "I could still see the

crowds through the door. I thought… that people were still close enough that nothing could happen."

"I see. So you went out alone with him on the balcony, after being warned about being alone with him, when you had doubts about whether he could control himself, and when you had previously had your powers stolen by him."

"It wasn't like that."

"What was it like?"

"It… I don't know. But it wasn't like that."

"It sounds to me like you made the decision to join with him of your own free will and choice. No magical influences."

"No."

"You abandoned any pretense of protecting yourself against him. You decided that you were going to give him your gifts back," Davyn said more aggressively.

"I did not! I would never do that. He was magicking me—"

"So you say. But I don't see anyone here who is going to testify otherwise."

"I could smell the roses," Reg insisted. "He was definitely using his glamour to make me do what he wanted."

"Yes. So you say."

"As do I," a new voice announced.

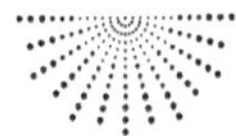

CHAPTER SEVENTEEN

*E*veryone turned to see where the voice had come from. A tall, pale man stood at the back of the room with several attendants. Seeing that he had the council's attention, he walked regally to the front of the room.

"Lord Bernier," Davyn greeted in surprise. He bowed his head deferentially. He picked up his pen to make note of the fairy's appearance. "What is your interest in this case?"

"I was there. When the child was attacked, I was the one who stepped in to stop the warlock from feeding."

"What did you find? What did you see and hear?"

"I saw the child in his arms. She was clearly ensorcelled. She didn't know what was going on."

"When you say 'the child,' you mean Regina Rawlins?" Davyn motioned toward Reg.

"Yes."

"And the warlock was Corvin Hunter?" Davyn indicated Corvin, who twirled in his chair as if he were enjoying being on display.

"Yes."

"What did you see that made you think she was ensorcelled?"

"I could smell his scent. Very strong. She was limp. Her eyes were closed. When I interrupted them, it took her a considerable length of time to wake up enough to be aware of what was going on and the danger she had been in."

"But you didn't hear their conversation. You don't know whether she yielded to him before your arrival."

"There is no way for me to tell you what happened before I was there," Lord Bernier said logically. "But if she had yielded to him without magic, then there would have been no need for his charms and glamour."

Davyn gave a small shrug. Reg looked around, wondering if there was anyone who was going to question her from the other side. She had thought that he was supposed to be unbiased, one of the judges in the tribunal, but it seemed clear Davyn was on Corvin's side. There didn't seem to be anyone on Reg's side, making accusations against Corvin, to prove that Reg had been an innocent party and that Corvin had again forced her against her will.

"He did, however, apologize," Lord Bernier said, looking over at Corvin. "He tried to deny that he had used his magic, and when that failed, he apologized and said he had not meant to do it and had broken his word. I assume your kind do not apologize for what they have not done."

"I see. That does shade things," Davyn admitted, making another notation on his page.

"That is not all the creature did," Lord Bernier stated, waiting for Davyn to pick up the questioning again.

"The creature?"

Lord Bernier made a motion toward Corvin. "The fallen one."

"Corvin Hunter. What else did Mr. Hunter do?"

"When he realized that he was not going to get the opportunity to feed, he put his hunger into her."

"How did he do that?"

"Like this."

Davyn suddenly went rigid in his seat and grasped the table in front of him with both hands. He opened his mouth but seemed unable to get any words out. There was a rushing tide of sound as everyone in the room started to talk, wanting to know what was going on and unsure of how to react. Bernier made a small motion with his hand, apparently releasing Davyn from whatever spell had bound him.

Davyn breathed heavily for a few minutes. He helped himself to a bottle of water. "You know that it is against our laws to force your thoughts and feelings on someone else."

Lord Bernier shrugged. "You asked how it is done. I showed you. Is that not what you asked?"

"No. You could have just answered the question. No more demonstrations of any kind."

"Corvin Hunter put his pain into the child," Lord Bernier reiterated. "This is against the laws of both of our peoples."

"Yes, it is. Did he say why he did it?"

Reg was outraged. Davyn was clearly on Corvin's side, now trying to find an excuse for why Corvin had done what he did.

"He said if she felt his pain, she would give him what he want-ed," Lord Bernier answered.

"So eventually, you… managed to break the spell?"

"Yes. I threatened to kill him."

There were a couple of laughs from the audience. Reg held her head. It had been a terrible thing to live through once. Having to relive it as she testified and heard it described was bringing the slowly bubbling anger to the surface, and Reg wasn't going to be able to hold it down much long.

"Is there anyone else who can testify as to what happened that night?" Davyn asked.

"My wife was there. Several of our consorts. They would all tell you exactly the same thing."

"No doubt," Davyn said dryly. "But that's it? There was no one else there? No one who could testify as to what happened before that? When Mr. Hunter and Miss Rawlins left the dance? What was said and occurred between them?"

Lord Bernier shook his head. "They were alone when I came upon them. She is protected, so we stopped to provide assistance."

"She's protected?" Davyn repeated.

"She is protected by our kind."

"Fairies?"

"It is so. She carries the blood of Calliopia, daughter of the house of Papillon."

There was a low murmur from the audience. Davyn wrote down a line or two and nodded. "Thank you, Lord Bernier. We appreciate you making the trip to assist this council, and the efforts that you made to ensure Miss Rawlins' safety."

Lord Bernier gave a regal nod, then he and his escorts swept back out of the room.

Reg wanted to scream. Davyn was so clearly trying to bias the tribunal against her and to show Corvin leniency. What was the point in her having attended at all? He finished writing another line and looked back at Reg, his eyes hard and challenging. But he kept a soft, reasonable voice as he spoke to her, making it sound as if he cared for her and what had happened to her.

"You had doubts as to whether Mr. Hunter would keep his word and not glamour you."

"Yes."

"Why is that? Did you doubt his honor?"

"I doubted his ability to resist his hunger and do what he said he would."

"Really." Davyn tapped his finger thoughtfully on the table. "How much did you know about this hunger?"

"I'd... felt it before. Not like when he put it on me that night. I'd just... got a glimpse of it before."

"At the time he'd stolen your powers."

"No. Uh... it was after that. He allowed me into his mind and I felt his hunger then."

"He allowed you into his mind?" Davyn said doubtfully, and looked over at Corvin. "That's a very personal thing."

"She's new to all of this," Corvin said, with a beneficent smile,

"I'm sure she didn't realize at the time that it was a violation. I defended myself against her once I realized what was happening and pushed her out, but… she did, as she says, get a taste of my need."

Davyn looked back at Reg. "And having felt the magnitude of this hunger, you did not believe that he would be able to resist using his powers on you."

"Yeah. Exactly."

"Believing he wouldn't be able to resist, you walked with him out onto the balcony, where there was not anyone to protect you."

Reg saw the trap he'd laid for her. A hot flush rolled over her face. "Why are you blaming me?" she demanded. "I'm the victim here! I told him I did not yield my powers to him even if he managed to make me say yes with his magic. I told him no over and over again, and he still glamoured me!"

"Miss Rawlins, this issue of *consent* seems to be one that you hold some very strong opinions about."

"Of course I do."

"This idea that you can preempt your own consent is not something that has been tested in our community before. We do have rules, as you know, that a warlock of Mr. Hunter's persuasion cannot take your powers without your permission."

"That's what you say. But I haven't really given my permission if I didn't know what I was agreeing to or my judgment has been clouded by his magic."

"That might be seen to be… reaching."

Reg shook her head in disbelief. "That first time, when he stole my powers, I had no idea what I was consenting to. I thought…" Reg knew that her face was turning a brilliant shade of red, but there was no reason she should be embarrassed. She had been taken advantage of and she wanted to help to prevent others from being taken advantage of in the future. Corvin was the one who should have been ashamed of his behavior, not Reg. "I thought I was just consenting to… physical intimacy. I didn't have a clue he could take my powers."

"But that is how it is done. Through physical contact. You give up your gifts in exchange for physical pleasure. Which, I might point out, you ended up getting for free."

"I didn't know, though. I didn't know what he could do."

Davyn waved this aside. "That is beside the point. We are not here to discuss what happened on *that* occasion. There was no complaint filed and you admit that you did give consent. Not only that, but you got back your powers. One might even suggest that you still owe him the fulfillment of that contract."

Reg could see Corvin smirking. He had, in fact, tried advancing that argument before. "What is wrong with you people?" she demanded. "I don't owe him anything! You might have some fun pretending you're living in the twelfth century with your quill pen and bird messages and living without electricity, but this is the twenty-first century!"

"And what does that have to do with this case?"

"This whole issue of consent! I told Corvin and I'm telling you, if you have to magic someone to get consent, it's not consent! No more than it would be if you roofied them!"

There was silence in the room. A few seconds ticked by. "Roofied…?" Davyn repeated uncertainly.

"Oh, good grief, this is exactly what I'm talking about. Twenty-first century. Get with it. You should know what's going on in the world around you! Drugged. If you drug someone to get them to do what you want, they can't give consent. It doesn't matter what they say. If they're too drunk or stoned to know what's going on, you back off."

This seemed to be a totally new idea for Davyn. He sat there, thinking about it, tapping his finger on the table. The warlocks in the seats behind him whispered to each other. Letticia was sitting with the tips of her fingers pressed together, staring at Davyn. She seemed to sense Reg's gaze and shifted to look at her. She gave a slight nod. At least there was one person on Reg's side.

"This isn't something I'm just making up," Reg told Davyn.

"It's been upheld by the courts. Someone who is under the influence can't give consent, and I say that includes magical influence."

"That has not been tested in our community."

"Then the idea that he has to get consent is all just a sham. You don't require him to get consent. He can use his magic to do whatever he wants. There are no limits."

Davyn scowled. "There most certainly are. Cases like this are rare and difficult to try. Setting aside the issue of whether he could use magic to get consent, it would seem that you had full knowledge of what he was, what he could do, and how to protect yourself, but you chose not to."

Reg tried to formulate an answer, but couldn't think of what to say. He clearly expected the tribunal to vote Corvin's way. She had been roped into appearing and telling her story, only to be told that she was the cause of her own troubles.

* * *

"If I could speak now?" Corvin suggested. "It sounds like we're getting down to the nuts and bolts of it now..."

"Are there any other witnesses?" Davyn asked, looking around.

"Sarah Bishop was going to testify," Letticia said. "However, she has fallen ill and was not able to attend."

Corvin smirked. Reg felt a chill. Surely he wouldn't have stolen Sarah's necklace just to keep her from testifying at his tribunal? After all, what could Sarah say that hadn't already been discussed? She was a second witness to the conversation Reg and Corvin had before going out on the dance floor, but she wouldn't have had anything to add.

Davyn nodded. "Alright. Mr. Hunter, then. You have the right to defend your actions."

Reg got up from her chair and returned to her seat with the audience. It was obvious by the way that everyone looked at her that she was expected to stay in the assigned seat, but she had no desire to remain on display to everyone as Corvin told his side of the story and vilified her. Corvin watched her sit down and waited for a moment, letting the tension build, before he spoke.

"I have apologized to Ms. Rawlins repeatedly for any action she saw as inappropriate on my behalf," he said smoothly. Which was true, but he made it sound like he didn't think he'd done anything wrong, and that hadn't been his tone when he'd begged for her forgiveness. "I deeply regret any distress I might have unintentionally caused her."

Reg made a noise of disbelief. It carried through the quiet room, as she had fully intended it to.

"I know what it is to have your powers stripped from you." Corvin's voice was quiet so that everyone in the room had to strain to hear it. Reg didn't believe he had any idea what it was like. "That doesn't excuse any wrongdoing on my part, of course, but I would like to share my experience."

He stood up and walked across the room, shaking out his arms and legs like he'd been folded into the chair for too long. He frowned and paced, struggling with where to begin.

"As most of you know, this... condition that I suffer from is one that is inherited, usually passed from father to son. My father also suffered from it. You might think that made it easier for me, because I had someone else who could understand what I was going through. But my father was not a compassionate man."

Corvin linked his hands behind his back as he paced, looking like a university professor mid-lecture.

"My father did not ask for permission before draining my powers."

There were gasps and whispers through the crowds. Reg studied their wide, surprised eyes. This was clearly not the usual order of things.

"On more than one occasion, coming home angry and hungered after a fruitless day trying to provide for himself and his family, he would set upon me. It was terrifying. Having my own father assault me and take what was not rightfully his..." Corvin wiped his mouth with the back of his hand.

Reg remembered the vision she'd had of him, the hunger eating away at him, writhing on the floor and crying to his mother to provide for him. And instead, his mother had allowed his father to abuse him and take away what powers he had.

"Most people can only ever have their powers taken once," Corvin said, his voice rough. "Once, and they are gone, and they learn to live without them. But for someone like me, with the ability to build up my powers again… it meant I was repeatedly drained by him. It didn't happen just once, but over and over again. Just as I refilled my powers, he would again take them away."

Reg could imagine his desperation. The starving boy who had the food snatched from his hands over and over again. She had felt his pain for only a few minutes, and it had been devastating. She had been physically ill and exhausted. Corvin must have been incredibly strong to be able to survive the constant hunger and repeated assaults from his father.

"There are few people here who know what it is that I suffer," Corvin said, looking around. "And yet, you think yourself entitled to judge me."

"No need for grandstanding," Davyn said, bringing him back down to earth. "There are not enough of your kind around to demand a jury of your peers. You're better off appealing to our better natures than trying to make us feel guilty. We are not likely to feel bad that your kind are dying out, after a story like that."

"Those of you who know me know that I have done the best I could to fill my needs without causing undue harm or distress. I regret my haste with regard to Miss Rawlins. But for this council to judge me by the standards of those who do are not afflicted with this condition…"

"These standards have been in place for many years. You deem them to be too harsh and Miss Rawlins thinks they are too lenient, which perhaps tells us that we have hit a fair balance. We cannot make the rules so strict that they prohibit you from feeding at all, and yet we wish to protect the members of our community." Davyn turned his head to look at the colleagues who sat behind him. From what Reg could see, he mostly got encouraging nods.

How could they think that they had struck a fair balance when that meant that unsuspecting women were being attacked? Reg shook her head in disgust.

"Before the members discuss appropriate disciplinary measures, I would like one more opportunity to plead my case," Corvin said.

There were impatient sighs and movements from the gallery behind Davyn. Davyn himself leaned his chin on his hand as if too fatigued to remain upright without the support.

"I trust this will be short."

"In hearing from Miss Rawlins today, the council may be under the impression that she is an innocent victim who suffered a harm at my hands. I can assure you that nothing could be further from the truth."

Reg straightened with a squawk. "What?"

Davyn gave her a glare. Reg opened her mouth to argue with Corvin, but the woman to her left gave her a nudge. "If you want to argue, you have to let him have his say first," she whispered. "Don't start a shouting match or they'll have you ejected."

Reg closed her mouth with a great effort. She sat there with her arms folded, giving Corvin the worst glare she could, imagining burning him up with her eyes.

Corvin turned away from her, facing Davyn directly, his shoulder and back toward Reg.

"Regina is not the one who brought the complaint against me," Corvin said in a low, confidential tone. "She and I know each other and have worked together both before and after this incident. While we both regret it, I don't think that she would ever have brought charges if left to herself. In fact, these complaints were not brought by any human, but by fairies."

There were mutterings among the spectators and council members. Fairies and humans associated loosely with each other, but left to their own devices, usually dealt with their own kind and were suspicious of each other. There were treaties and understandings between the various races, but even so, they all tended to be a little xenophobic.

"Lord Bernier has already spoken today," Davyn pointed out. "He was present and therefore entitled to bring these charges to bear."

Corvin nodded. "Just as you say. But without Lord Bernier's… *participation*… in the process, I don't believe there would have been any hearing. Regina and I would have been able to work things out between us, just as we have before."

There was no comment from anyone else about this statement. Corvin nodded and went on.

"As you noted, Regina was not an innocent who was a stranger to my condition. She had full knowledge of what I was. Perhaps she is one of those people who likes to flirt with danger."

Reg opened her mouth to object, the but woman next to her pinched her arm. "Don't say anything. He's baiting you."

It was a struggle for Reg to remain quiet, but she did.

"Or maybe she enjoyed the power struggle," Corvin went on, "her attempt to dictate her own terms and see who came out on top… If you were to look into her background, you would find that Reg has a long history of con jobs and brushes with the law. She is being investigated in connection with the thefts of two valuable objects. She is not the innocent victim she would like to paint herself as. And it's not the first time she's made false allegations—"

CHAPTER EIGHTEEN

Reg felt like something snapped in her head. She saw nothing but red. Corvin's dapper cloak burst into flames. For a moment, everyone in the room froze, including Corvin. Then he was suddenly moving, tearing the cloak away from himself and throwing it to the carpet, which luckily seemed to be flame resistant and did not catch fire or start melting. Corvin turned to look at Reg, his face angry and at the same time frightened.

While she was staring at him, his nose started bleeding. Corvin raised his hand to touch the blood and looked at it in disbelief. He pinched it and tried to give instructions to the various witches and warlocks who started to swarm around him, giving advice and trying to physically assist him. Davyn stood up and raised his arms, trying to get everyone's attention.

"Ladies and gentlemen, everything is alright. Just a little technical difficulty. If everyone could please take your seats unless you are called upon to assist. We don't want to end up with injuries due to panic and crowding. Please take your seats."

A few large security men moved into the room. Reg wasn't sure whether they were hotel staff or whether magical tribunals often broke into violence so they had their own security on site.

They started to push and redirect the spectators to clear the area at the front of the room again.

"You see?" Corvin demanded, pinching his nose. He gave a little laugh. "You really think she is a victim here? She has remarkable psychic abilities. She's perfectly capable of taking care of herself. She doesn't need any tribunal."

"It could have been anyone in the room," one of the warlocks in the tribunal soothed. "You wouldn't want to unjustly accuse anyone of—"

"Look at her!" Corvin insisted. "Ask her! She's—" Corvin's jacket burst into flames and he howled and pulled at it, unable to get it off as quickly as the cloak. The man helped him to pull it off, trying to pat out the flames while doing so. Corvin glared at Reg across the room. His face was bloody and he wasn't able to keep pinching his nose while he tried to wrestle his way out of the burning jacket. The flames just flared higher when they tried to pat them out. By the time Corvin got the jacket off, an alarm was ringing.

"It's fine. I'm fine!" Corvin insisted, trying to push the helpful hands away from him. He tried to advance toward Reg, but the others could see his goal and were not about to let him go after her.

"If you keep it up, pretty soon I'm not going to have any clothes left!" Corvin growled at Reg. "There are much easier ways to get me to strip."

Reg marched toward him, determined to punch him in the nose and give it a real reason to bleed. Several people grabbed at her as she moved past them, until one pair of hands managed to get a good hold on her and closed tightly around her arms, forcing her to stop and be still.

"Miss, that's not a good idea," the owner of the hands whispered in her ear. "Try to calm down before this gets out of hand."

"I'll show you out of hand!"

"No, you won't."

Reg whipped her head around to look at the unfamiliar

warlock. His hair started to smolder, a twist of black smoke ascending into the air. He didn't let go of her, but the smoke disappeared as if the fire that had started had been snuffed out.

"You are a dangerous woman to cross, aren't you?" he chuckled. He was one of the big men who had moved into the room when things had started to get exciting. Magical security, not hotel security, if he wasn't fazed by his hair spontaneously igniting.

"Let me go."

"I don't think so. Somebody needs to keep an eye on you."

"It isn't me. I'm not causing all of this."

"I'd say it's definitely coming from your direction."

"How could you know that?"

"How about we all just take a deep breath here? Nobody needs to get hurt. Just relax."

"I told you, I'm not doing it. I can't light fires. I have a hard enough time lighting matches!"

"And you weren't wishing just now that Mr. Hunter would burst into flames?"

Reg frowned. Strange that he should ask that. "That's not one of my talents," she reiterated. "I wouldn't know how to light a fire with my mind even if I wanted to."

"You'd be surprised what you can do, especially when under stress."

"It's not me. There must be someone else here doing it."

"Perhaps."

It was some time before things settled down again. Reg stood by, waiting to see what was going to happen next. Corvin eyed her as he sat back down in his appointed seat. The excited crowd quieted.

"Did you have more that you wanted to say, or were you done?" Davyn asked Corvin.

"I guess… I was done. I wanted to point out that Miss Rawlins wasn't a defenseless victim here, and I guess she's proven my point."

Davyn considered this and nodded. He didn't write it down

on his record. "The council has a lot to consider. I think it would be best at this point for us to adjourn the public hearing, and discuss it privately. I do not expect to be coming to a decision today on guilt or innocence or on appropriate disciplinary measures."

The noise from the crowd was a long sigh, and then a moment of silence while everyone considered this and then prepared to leave. Davyn wrote one more note on his scroll and then stood up, going over to the rest of the council to talk to them.

* * *

Reg looked at the security guard who was still standing with her, though he was no longer holding on to her.

"So that's it?" she asked. "We're done?"

"We're done," he agreed. "They will take some time now to discuss all of the points that have been brought up in the hearing before coming to a decision."

"How much time?"

"Anywhere from a few hours to..." the guard trailed off. He shrugged. "I don't think there's any outside time limit. It's not like courts or regulatory agencies that have to come to a decision in a defined length of time. It will probably be a few days... or weeks."

"But it could be longer."

"Could be."

"What about the right to a speedy trial?"

"Well, you're not on trial, so I'm not sure you could demand one. And that's the regular court system... which this is not."

"And in the meantime, Corvin's allowed to walk around doing whatever he wants?"

"He hasn't been convicted of anything. And the warlocks won't be eager to bind him if he is found to be guilty of the charges, either. They don't like to do that."

Reg sighed. "Yeah... I remember him saying something about that."

The guard looked at her. "That must have been an interesting conversation. How did it come up?"

"Not about this…" Reg made a gesture to indicate the hearing. "It was a case we were working on."

"Ah. I see." The guard glanced around. "Are you, uh, by yourself? Maybe I could walk you to your car…?"

"No, I'm fine."

"You don't want any of these people harassing you because of something that was said today. Why don't I just see you safely to your car. I'd feel better about it."

Reg was about to say no again when she caught something in the guard's expression. He wasn't offering out of a sense of duty or because he thought she might be in danger. There was a particular glint in his eyes and looseness in his manner that telegraphed that he was interested in her. And after the experiences she'd had with men lately, Reg could really do with one who was squarely on her side.

"Well… I don't think you need to. But if you want to."

He grinned broadly. "I do."

Reg laughed. "Okay, then. It's out this way."

As they headed toward the exit, Letticia made a motion to get Reg's attention. "Everything okay?"

Reg nodded and gave Letticia a wink to clue her in. "Just getting an escort to my car," she said, "for safety reasons."

Letticia stared at her for a moment, and then she nodded, her expression blank, giving nothing away.

* * *

On her return home, Reg remembered that Corvin's trial was not the most important thing in her life and there were other things to be concerned about. Like Sarah, and whether she would even survive until they found the emerald. *If* they found the emerald.

She was pondering the whole mess on the way home, not even turning on the radio because she wanted her mind clear to puzzle through all of the pieces. The answer had to be right in front of her face. She knew Sarah. She knew where the emerald had been kept. She knew the suspects other than herself. The motive for the theft was obvious. It was valuable, and someone wanted it either for its monetary or magical value. They either wanted lots of cash or health and long life.

She couldn't stop thinking that it was Corvin himself. He was the one who had thrown the blame in her direction. He was the one who had a need for powerful magical objects to feed his hunger. Would it cure him of his hunger, if it were a genetic disease like he had suggested? Or would it just give him the power he needed to survive from one day to the next to sate his hunger?

Corvin and Sarah were friends. Reg had never understood their exact relationship, being so far apart in age. And Sarah had warned Reg that Corvin was bad news and she shouldn't have him around. But she had also admitted to being attracted to him and had been eating with him at The Crystal Bowl. Could Corvin really be that cold-blooded? Pursuing his own appetites and watching the old crone die? Did he think, as Letticia had said, that Sarah's time had come and it was time for her to give up the emerald and let nature take its course?

Letticia herself could have taken the necklace. Sarah would have let her into the house upon request. Letticia was Sarah's coven leader. Sarah would probably have shown her the necklace or let her hold it if asked. Then all Letticia had to do was throw some kind of confusion spell on Sarah and walk away with the priceless treasure. If she felt that it was time for Sarah to accept the inevitable, maybe she had decided to hurry things along. Or maybe she wanted the rare jewel for herself.

Reg wasn't paying much attention as she crossed the back yard to the cottage, and gave a little shriek when a black shape broke out of one of the bushes and streaked across the pathway in front of her in its hurry to get away. Reg stopped where she was, holding her hand over her heart and waiting for it to stop racing.

"It's just a cat," she said softly. She followed it with her eyes. A black cat. Bad luck. Was it the same one that Sarah had been trying to whomp in the garden? "Kitty, kitty?" she called softly.

The cat, in the process of jumping over the fence, turned and looked at her.

"Kitty, kitty, kitty?" Reg called. "You want to come in and get some food?"

It balanced there, looking at her, but the instant Reg took a step forward, it was gone. Over the fence and out of sight. Reg shrugged. She walked up to the cottage and let herself in.

Starlight was on the back of the couch looking out the window. When Reg entered, he jumped down and started meowing.

He and the cat outside were about the same size. Both were black. The cat outside didn't have the same tuxedo markings and star that Starlight did, and it was skinnier, but she had only had a fleeting glimpse. There could have been other similarities. Reg frowned, thinking about that as she got Starlight something to eat.

"Were you looking out the window at the other cat?" she asked him. "Did you see him?"

Starlight stopped meowing and looked at Reg expectantly.

"Hmm. Maybe you did." Reg tried to reach out to him mentally. She could often feel what he was feeling, but he wasn't close enough to human for her to actually understand his thought processes. "What did you think of him?"

She didn't need any words to explain the warm feelings that came from Starlight. He obviously wanted to meet the new cat. That was why he'd been wandering around at night howling at the windows and watching outside intently. He wasn't sick and he wasn't trying to drive Reg crazy. He wanted to make friends—or maybe more—with the newcomer.

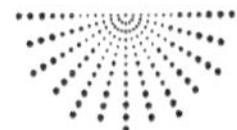

CHAPTER NINETEEN

Reg fed Starlight and left him to eat while she walked across to the main house. She watched the door carefully as she opened and closed it, not wanting Starlight to escape or to let the new cat sneak inside. She knocked on Sarah's door and tried to open it, but found it locked. She waited a bit, then rang the doorbell, beginning to worry that Sarah might have taken a turn for the worse. And there wasn't much further to go.

The door opened. It was Marian. Her lips tightened when she saw Reg. "So it's you. What do you want?"

"You're the psychic; guess." Reg pushed past her, entering the house. "How is Sarah?"

"She's sleeping. It's probably best if you just let her rest."

"I need to talk to her."

Reg hadn't actually been in Sarah's bedroom before. It was a big house, and there were lots of bedrooms full of clothes and other goodies. She struck off toward the stairs, feeling for Sarah, and went directly to her bedroom. She peeked in and saw that Sarah was sleeping, as Marian had said. Reg walked in and sat on the chair beside the bed. Still warm from Marian sitting there keeping an eye on her friend. Reg didn't like Marian, but softened a little, realizing how devoted she'd been in staying by Sarah's side in her time of need, while Reg seemed pulled in every other direction.

"Sarah." She put her hand on Sarah's. She seemed to have lost weight, her limbs shrinking, the skin loose and fragile. "Sarah, can you wake up?"

It took a few more prompts before Sarah started to move and to blink blearily. She looked at Reg for a few minutes and then smiled weakly, a little drool collecting in the crease that ran down from her mouth.

"Reg."

"Hi, Sarah. How are you feeling?" It was a struggle to sound cheerful, but Reg didn't want to sound like she was visiting a friend at her deathbed.

"I've had better days." Sarah attempted to smooth her nightgown and look presentable. "I suppose it won't be much longer now."

Reg tried to ignore the suggestion that Sarah was going to die. Not if she could help it. Not if Reg could find the emerald in time.

"Sarah, did you actually see Starlight come into the house? Or did Corvin just tell you that he did?"

Sarah stared at her and Reg was afraid she didn't understand what Reg was saying. She opened her mouth to prompt Sarah further. Sarah gave a little shake of her head.

"Starlight wouldn't come into the house."

"No," Reg smiled, relieved. "He wouldn't, would he? Do you think Corvin really saw something? Do you think maybe he saw a different black cat?"

"The one in the garden?"

Reg let out a puff of breath. "Yes. The one you saw in the garden. Do you think that's the cat Corvin saw?"

"A cat didn't steal my necklace."

"I saw it too." Marian was standing in the doorway, listening in.

"*What* did you see, though?" Reg demanded. "Did you see a cat in the house? A cat with the necklace? Or a cat in the yard? Corvin says it was Starlight, but Starlight hasn't been out of the house, so maybe he saw the other stray that's been hanging around."

"I saw the cat in the yard. Corvin saw it going into the house."

"How? It couldn't get in through a locked door."

Marian considered for a moment, then shrugged. "Through a window? A hole in the screen door?"

"How did he *say* it got in?"

"I don't know. He didn't specify."

"I think he's making it up. Maybe he saw it in the yard like you did and it gave him the idea, but I don't believe he ever saw it go into the house."

"Frostling wouldn't have let a cat steal the emerald," Sarah said, her voice quiet and whispery.

"Cats are predators. Wouldn't he have been afraid?"

She chuckled. "Haven't you ever seen a mama bird go after a cat? A parrot is a big bird. No cat would stick around if he was attacking."

"What about another bird?" Reg asked, thinking about Davyn using birds to send his missives. "What if someone sent a raven or something to steal it? Or maybe one saw it through the window. They like shiny things, right?"

"Corvin?" Sarah asked.

"Him. Or another warlock. Or someone else. Is it a possibility?"

Sarah's shoulder lifted in a little shrug. "I don't know. I don't know how Frostling would have responded to another bird. Do you really think Corvin took it?"

Reg sighed at the wistfulness in Sarah's voice. "I think he's the most likely suspect."

"I thought that was you," Marian said.

Reg gave her a warning look. She wondered how Marian

would like it if *her* hair ignited. She suppressed a smile at the image and tried to block Marian from reading her.

"Corvin needs magical artifacts more than anyone," Reg pointed out. "Something as powerful as the emerald… it would be a huge temptation for him, wouldn't it?"

"But he couldn't come into the house. I have wards against those who enter with the intent of doing harm."

"He came in with you yesterday."

Sarah looked at Reg, her eyes clouded with confusion. "I didn't see Corvin yesterday."

"Yes, you did. You had dinner with him over at The Crystal Bowl. He and I had an… argument. You weren't home until late, hours after that."

"I didn't go out yesterday. I was just home, resting."

Reg glanced over at Marian, looking for her opinion of Sarah's confusion. Marian gave a shrug. Sarah was an old woman. Ancient, if Reg were to believe what she'd been told. Memory slips were normal. But it didn't help Reg to solve what had happened.

"So if Corvin came in with Sarah yesterday," she spoke to Marian, "then either his intentions were good, or Sarah invited him in, right?"

"I'm a psychic, not a witch. I don't know all of the ins and outs of spells and charms."

"Sarah." Sarah was starting to drift and Reg touched her arm to rouse her again. "Did you invite Corvin in? Have you invited anyone in lately?"

"No. No one."

"How could someone get in if you didn't invite them? Is there another way around the wards?"

Sarah brushed a fringe of gray hair away from her face. "Wards are not the strongest spells. They have to be very specific, and it is best to have several of them. You can talk someone into releasing their ward, or inviting you in. Or if they have something that belongs to you…"

Reg thought about that. Her mind flashed to the business card that Davyn had given to her, which she had insisted he put in her mailbox rather than touching it or bringing it into her house. She never had taken it out.

"If you have something that belongs to them... like what? Anything? What if I left something here on purpose and came back for it later? Could I get through the wards?"

"I don't have wards against you," Sarah said. "Not unless you wish me harm."

"I don't!" Reg said immediately. Her eyes got suddenly hot and stung. "I don't want anything to happen to you. I want you to get better. I want you to be well again. But what if Corvin—or someone—gave you something, and then came back for it later? Would that allow him past your wards?"

"Yes, probably."

Sarah covered a yawn. Her eyes were drooping. Reg could feel waves of exhaustion emanating from Marian. She scowled. "Stop that!"

Marian's eyes widened. "What?"

"I'm trying to talk to her. Stop trying to make her more tired."

"I wasn't..." Marian trailed off. "You can feel that?"

"I can feel everything you do. So stop trying to influence me or to influence Sarah around me."

"But I wasn't... She needs her sleep. It's better for her if she just rests. The more energy she expends, the faster she's going to fade."

Reg looked down at Sarah, her eyes closed peacefully. "Okay. I don't want to run her down. I was just hoping she could help some more. Anything she can tell us about who might have been here or who might have been able to get past her wards... I'd really like to be able to find the emerald before it's too late."

"It might already be."

"I know. But... I can't accept that. I'm going to find that necklace. I'm going to find it, and it's going to be in time to help her."

"Do you really think you're getting any closer? Whoever took it must be long gone by now. Why would anyone take it and then stick around?"

"Someone like Corvin? He has such a huge ego… he'd be sure no one could ever find him out."

Marian gave a shrug that conceded the point. Reg was sure that she wasn't the only one who found Corvin to be a huge pain in the neck, with an ego as big as a hot air balloon.

Devastatingly handsome with the magnetism to match, but a huge pain in the neck.

* * *

"I want to take another look in the room the emerald was displayed in before I go," Reg said.

Marian raised an eyebrow. "I'll come with you."

"I don't need an escort."

"Well, if I'm with you, no one can accuse you of having taken anything."

"The emerald is already gone. It's a bit late for that."

"True, but Sarah has other items of value. If any of them were to go missing, you wouldn't want to be a suspect. Especially since two valuable articles have already disappeared."

Reg breathed deeply. Two artifacts. Not just the emerald, but the knife too. Which made her all the more sure it was Corvin. A blade imbued with powerful fairy blood was just the sort of thing he would want. It was not the kind of thing that a treasure-hunter after valuable jewelry and gems would have been attracted to. It was a fine blade, sharp and well-wrought from fairy steel, but it wasn't the type of thing that would have caught the eyes of someone who was looking to make a bit of quick cash. That's the kind of thing that would only be appreciated by someone who knew its story. And if that person were also able to imbibe in the powers it held…

"Let's go, then."

She led the way to the room Sarah had previously shown to Reg and Detective Jessup. It looked just as it had. Reg looked around carefully before stepping in. She caught sight of Frostling, snoozing on his perch, and kept a close eye on him. She didn't want to get attacked again.

"This is where it was," Reg said unnecessarily, pointing to the glass-encased display.

She and Marian walked over to it reverentially. Reg had opened the case when Sarah had shown it to her previously, but it was closed again. Reg touched the glass, engaging the spring-loaded opening mechanism, and watched it open just as it had the first time. She and Marian just stood there for a moment. Reg glanced over at Frostling, watching for any sign he was ready to attack. But he seemed to be asleep. Maybe the loss of the emerald was making him age as well, or his health was tied to Sarah's.

Reg examined the display case closely. The molded form that normally held the necklace in an attractive configuration. The lock. The edges. She looked at the glass from several angles, looking for fingerprints or tool marks. But surely the police had already dusted it for prints and anything else that was out of place. Reg's eye caught on the edge of something with a soft shine, and she ran her fingertip along one of the tracks that the display case settled into to dislodge it.

"What's that?" Marian asked.

"A ribbon." Reg held up the long curl of black ribbon that had been camouflaged by the black velvet and black tracks of the display case. She examined it. "This must be the ribbon that the emerald was strung on."

Marian nodded. "It's about the right length. But would she just have tied it on? That doesn't seem secure."

Reg looked at the ends of the ribbon. There were no creases where it had previously been knotted. "It doesn't look like it. Maybe she puts a fresh ribbon on each time, and this was a fresh one for next time. Or maybe it was for something else." She glanced over at the slumbering bird. "Maybe it's the bird's. It had just fallen into the crack, here."

Marian peered at it. "Can I touch it?"

Reg wanted to say no just out of spite. Marian was her rival and had not been very gracious toward her. But it wasn't Reg's ribbon and she had been able to touch it. Maybe Marian could get a vibe from it that Reg wasn't in tune with.

She held it toward Marian, the ribbon lying on her hand. Marian reached out to take it, and their hands touched, sending a sharp jolt through both of them.

* * *

Both women immediately jolted back.

"What was that?" Reg demanded.

Marian eyed Reg suspiciously. "When I was young, there were these little trick toys called joy buzzers. You hid it in your hand when you were going to shake hands with someone, and then gave them a jolt. Just like that."

Reg was still holding her hand out in front of her. She splayed her fingers, making it obvious that she wasn't holding anything hidden from Marian.

"I don't know what it was," Marian said. "Some kind of psychic connection? Or aversion?"

"Yeah." Reg's fingers were tingling, but there was no damage. She dangled the end of the ribbon for Marian. "Do you want to take it?"

Marian reached out carefully. She touched the ribbon. With both of them holding it, it was like a living thing, warm and substantial.

"Very odd," Marian said. She closed her eyes, focusing her psychic powers. Reg took a deep breath and did the same. If it was the ribbon from the emerald, then would touching it allow her to find the emerald? If she and Marian worked together…?

Neither of them spoke or moved for some minutes. The

ribbon was weighing heavily in Reg's hand. She inched her hand toward Marian's, feeling for a shift in the current between them. She reached a point when the air between their fingertips seemed to be buzzing, and pushing any closer was uncomfortable.

"It's like when I tripped a pixie spell," Reg told Marian. "I was in the shadow world and whenever I tried to touch anyone who was part of the real world, it was like this. And to come back, I had to hold hands with someone in the real world, even though it hurt."

Marian stared at Reg, scowling.

"What?" Reg asked.

"Are you making all of that up?"

"Of course not. Ask Detective Jessup or Corvin. They were there. Corvin was invisible too. And Jessup was the one who had to bring him back."

"Who brought you back?"

"Calliopia. A fairy."

Marian still looked angry and disbelieving. "This... polarity between us... you're not doing that intentionally?"

"No."

"Let me hold it."

Reg dropped her end of the ribbon into Marian's hand. Marian examined it and ran the satiny fabric through her fingers.

"A pixie spell."

"Yes," Reg agreed. "That was what made me invisible. There is this whole thing between the fairies and the pixies..."

"I'm aware of the animosity between them. But I'm not sure how you got mixed up in it."

Reg took a breath to explain, but Marian raised her hand to stop Reg. "I'm not actually asking. I'm just thinking about what I know of pixies." She looked down at the ribbon.

"What about them?"

"They tend to be dressed in rags. Not because they don't value fine clothing, but because they wear them forever... until everything is worn and patched and falling apart. Something like this…" She wound the ribbon around her fingers. "This would actually be very valuable to them."

"A ribbon?"

Marian nodded.

Reg didn't argue it. She didn't know enough about the other magical races in Black Sands to advance any opinion or theories. "The pixies that I've seen have been pretty dirty and worn," she agreed. Ruan and his family. The pixies that they'd fought underground. They all had the same blue eyes, messy brown curls, and tattered clothing.

"The thing is," Marian said slowly. "Pixies are fond of swapping."

"Swapping what?"

"Swapping one item of value for another. They don't have the same concept of ownership as we do, but they do believe in a sort of a rudimentary payment system, where if you take an object from someone, you pay for it with another object of value."

"Bartering."

"No… not exactly. When you barter, both parties have to agree on the value of the item or service, and have to agree on how one is going to pay the other. But a pixie's swap is different. They will take an object and replace it with one that they deem to be valuable, without agreement with the owner."

Reg had no idea where Marian was going with the lesson on pixie currency. She motioned to the ribbon and opened her mouth to make a flippant comment, and then she stopped, her words frozen in the air. She gasped like she'd taken a punch in the gut.

"You don't mean… that a pixie might swap, say, a fine ribbon for an old emerald."

Marian nodded. "Look at it. It isn't worn at all. It's never been tied. Pixies never have anything brand new. It would be very valuable."

"But surely they would know how much more expensive the emerald was."

"Emeralds come out of the earth. Pixies like to lay claim to anything that comes out of the earth. They probably have unheard of treasures in their vaults. Sarah's little trinket… they'd see it as something that was already theirs and should be returned to them."

Reg swore. Had Marian cracked the case?

"Can you see it?" she asked. "If you try to find the emerald, can you see it now?"

Marian looked at Reg like she was crazy. "I can't do that."

"Well, not before, but now that we have a better idea of where it is, and you have the ribbon in your hand, can you focus on the pixie caves and see where the emerald is?"

Marian shook her head. "I've never been able to do a seek, Regina. I don't mean I just haven't been able to find the necklace. I mean I've never been able to do one at all."

"Not at all," Reg echoed. "Really? Never? Not even when you were a little girl?"

"It took me a lot of time to develop my abilities. When I was little… it would never have even occurred to me to try to find something using just the powers of my mind."

"Oh." Even though Reg had been told by several of the residents of Black Sands that her psychic powers were quite powerful, she hadn't really believed that they were better developed than those of any other practicing psychic. But Marian was confirming it. She had never even been able to find an object. "I… didn't know that. I just assumed that everybody else was like me. I didn't mean…"

Marian shook her head. "Don't try to apologize, it just makes it that much worse. You take it." She tossed the ribbon to Reg. "Can you get anything?"

Reg was glad to get the ribbon back into her own hands. She felt so much better being able to hold it. If only she could use it to find the emerald. She concentrated, trying to remember the way Sarah's emerald had looked the night of the dance. So warm and bright and alive. It had not been threaded on a black ribbon. It had been on a gold chain. One that looked as if it had been braided like rope.

"Where is it?" she murmured aloud. She wasn't grandstanding, but needed to talk it through. She needed to hear her own voice somewhere other than in her own head. "The emerald is in the pixie realm. Show me where. Let me see the cave."

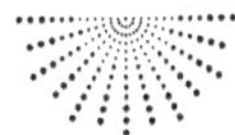

CHAPTER TWENTY

All she could see was… nothing. Not blackness, but blankness. No cave. No avaricious pixie. No vault. No necklace. Reg was so angry she wanted to throw something across the room, but all she had in her hand was the insubstantial ribbon. She wanted to hit the wall. She wanted to hit the person who had stolen the necklace. She closed her hand around the ribbon, squeezing it tightly. If it were a living thing, she was going to crush the life out of it.

There was a squawk of alarm from Frostling on his perch. He flapped his wings suddenly, and Reg immediately cringed, throwing up her arms to protect her face, sure he was coming after her again.

Marian laughed. "It's alright," she assured Reg. "It's just a bird. It's not going to do anything to hurt you."

"Last time it attacked me," Reg snapped back. But it didn't appear the bird was going to leave his perch this time. He eyed Reg, standing tall on his perch and flapping his wings wildly and emitting a loud squawk. "Darn bird! Why don't you just shut up!"

There was a poof of feathers from Frostling, and for a moment Reg panicked, worried she had blown up Sarah's bird.

Frostling gave another squawk, proving that she hadn't killed him. Reg laughed weakly.

Marian was staring at her. "What did you do?"

"I don't know. Things like that have been happening lately. I just... I can't control them."

"I think we'd better get out of here, before he gets really mad. I don't want him to wake Sarah back up again."

"The way she looked... I don't think anything is going to wake her up. Do you... how long do you think she has?"

Marian shook her head. "Not much longer. I'm just trying to keep her quiet and peaceful... make her last few days or hours good ones."

"What am I going to do if she dies?" Reg shook her head, feeling overwhelmed. Sarah had been Reg's pillar since the day she had moved into the community. Sarah had given her a place to live, had helped her get her business established, even checked in to make sure that she had enough to eat, took care of herself, and got to know others in the community. Without her, there was going to be a big hole in Reg's life. She didn't know if a hole like that could ever be filled. For the first time, she'd felt like she had a grandmother who cared about her. She'd felt like she belonged in the community. She hadn't had feelings like that for a long time... or ever.

"I don't know what any of us are going to do," Marian said. "She's been there for all of us... for so many years."

"How old is she, really?"

"I don't know. Older than—"

"I know. Older than I think. That's the answer I get whenever I ask her. Or someone else."

"I've learned that it's true. Sometimes it's best just to accept the answer you're given."

They walked down the halls, and then down the stairs, neither directing the other, just moving together with one mind.

Reg stopped in the kitchen, looking at the back door. "How

would a pixie get into the house? Aren't they affected by the wards?"

"Oh, yes. I'm sure Sarah would not have allowed an exception for pixies. They can provide helpful services, but they are too unpredictable to count on. It's best not to let them into your house in the first place."

"Then how?"

"The only way is if Sarah invited one into the house."

"But she wouldn't do that. And if she did, she'd know that it was the pixie who stole her necklace. There wouldn't be any question of it."

"I don't know all of the rules. But if the pixie had left something here, they might be able to come back for it later, when Sarah was not aware there was anyone in the house."

"That must be it, then! She thought that she was safe, because she didn't know the pixie had left anything behind. But the pixie had, and then when Sarah was sleeping or out or just doing something else… the pixie could come back and steal the emerald."

Marian nodded thoughtfully. "I just… can't think of why she would have invited a pixie into the house to begin with."

"Maybe she didn't know it was a pixie. Oh—" Reg grasped for the thought. She knew there was something she should remember. Something she had been thinking about before. "Pixies… what is it… I know there was something about Sarah and pixies and… I can't think of what it was."

Reg looked at her watch, then looked back toward her own house, trying to find the lost thought. What if Sarah hadn't known that the visitor was a pixie?

"Yes! That's it! I had a young woman come to talk to me. Something about her long-lost sister. And I didn't realize it at the time because I didn't know anything about pixies, but when I was thinking about it later, I thought she must have been a pixie."

"Once you've met a few of them, it's pretty obvious."

"Well, she wasn't… not really obvious, I mean. She didn't have those same brown, worn clothes. I mean, she didn't look like she was rich, but she didn't look like the ones I saw underground. Maybe some of them leave…" Reg thought about Ruan picking Calliopia up and running off with her. Where had he taken her? Not back to the burrows, surely. She had already spent too much time down there and was too eager to leave. She would not have consented to go back there so quickly. She'd been happy to see Ruan and to go with him. Reg had assumed at the time that they had both left their communities. They would run away to somewhere nobody knew them, or their history, or what they really were, and try to make their way in the normal human world. Or maybe there was another community like Black Sands where magical folk were accepted and would not be considered suspicious or dangerous.

"What are you thinking?" Marian asked.

"There must be some pixies and fairies who break away from their communities. Join the non-magical world, or travel to other places. They wouldn't necessarily look the same as the pixies in the community here. If they were trying to blend in with non-practitioners, they would learn that they needed to get new clothes, and how to get them from the Salvation Army or some outreach program. They wouldn't have to dress like pixies for the rest of their lives."

"No. I suppose not," Marian admitted. "But if this pixie was living in Black Sands, then she must be part of their community here."

"I don't think she is. I saw her on TV the other day. That's what made me remember her. She was talking about homeless kids. Runaways and other kids on the street, and what kind of programs they need or are available. She was talking about her sister, who I guess was a runaway."

"Runaway pixies," Marian mused. "Who knew. I always thought… I don't know. I thought they were different from humans that way. That they always stayed with their communities and took care of each other."

"I don't think so. Ruan and Calliopia, they didn't stay."

"What did this pixie want? The one who came to see you?"

"She wanted me to find her sister. To reach out to her and find out if she were still alive and if I could give her any direction as to where she might have gone."

"And did you?"

Reg thought back to the session. It had been before Jessup had brought her into Calliopia's kidnapping. So much had happened in the intervening time that her memories of the young woman were, at best, hazy. They'd had a session. Reg had told her some things… vague suggestions… she had assured the woman that her sister was, in fact, still alive, and if she kept looking, she would find her. "I couldn't tell her much. But I did my best. She didn't seem too disappointed. As far as I know, she didn't lay any kind of curse on me," Reg said, with a lame laugh.

Marian didn't crack a smile. "But that was your house, not Sarah's?"

"Uh… yes. But both houses are Sarah's property, and if she set wards on the whole property, then wouldn't her being invited into mine allow her to get back into Sarah's? Do you think?"

"Someone with better knowledge of wards than me would need to answer that question. But I would think that a direct invitation into her domicile would be needed… I don't think inviting her into just any other property would do it."

Then, in a flood, it came back to Reg. When the young woman had first called to set up the appointment, Reg had told her about being in the house in the back, and that the woman needed to come in through the back yard. But despite Reg's instructions, the woman—the pixie—had gone to the main house. Sarah had kindly escorted her to Reg's house.

"She… came here first. Sarah brought her to the cottage. I completely forgot that."

"And if she came to the front door…" Marian bit her lip, considering, and turned her head to look toward the front of the house.

"Then did Sarah just invite her in and walk her through the house to the back...?"

Marian nodded. "Oh, dear."

"I can't believe it. I can't believe neither of us remembered that."

"A lot of things happen in our lives," Marian said philosophically. "It's easy to forget something so… uneventful."

"I didn't even remember. Sarah invited her in. Why would she do that?" Reg pounded her forehead with her fist, overcome. "Why didn't she just tell the pixie to go on around the house to the back?"

"I'm sure she didn't even think anything of it. A young woman asking for you wouldn't have seemed like anyone dangerous."

"It's just like the witch with the poison apple…"

Marian looked at her.

"Snow White?" Reg prompted.

"How is a runaway pixie like a witch with a poison apple?"

"Because she looked harmless…"

"Oh. I see."

But Reg didn't think she saw at all.

* * *

Reg returned to her own house, head whirling with the new discoveries, while Marian remained with Sarah to see that she continued to rest peacefully and had all of her needs taken care of if she woke up.

Starlight was sitting on the kitchen counter, staring at the door, waiting for Reg to return. Reg felt like a teenager arriving home late at night to find her parent still waiting up.

"What is it?" she demanded.

Starlight stared at her. Reg felt compelled to tell him the details. Rather than being embarrassed about talking to her cat like he was a human or that she was essentially talking to herself, Reg started to fill him in on the latest developments. She walked up to him and picked him up from the counter. He purred as she walked to the couch and sat down with him, explaining about the ribbon and the pixie. His eyes were alive with interest.

The anger and tension bled away. She didn't feel so frustrated with herself for not having known the significance of the pixie and with Sarah for having let the young woman into her house.

"So now we know who she invited into the house," Reg said. "She thought it was just to walk the pixie through the house and that there was no harm in it. She didn't realize that the pixie left something behind and went back for it later."

Starlight rubbed against Reg's hand. Reg scratched his ears. "So what do I do next? I guess… I go find the pixie."

Starlight put his ears back in a kitty scowl.

"I know. But she's not in the burrows. She's left there and is looking for her sister. So it isn't dangerous for me to go find her and talk to her. She's just one pixie, and she came to me for help before. I'll just say that I'm following up. Maybe that I've had a vision of her sister, and give her some more nonsense about how she wishes she could be reunited with her family again, but circumstances are preventing it right now. You know, general stuff that she'll just drink up."

Starlight didn't seem to think that was any better. Reg gave Starlight long strokes down his back, making him purr even louder. She laughed at the way his rump lifted every time she got past the middle of his back.

"Hopefully, they keep archives of their shows on their website," Reg said, pulling out her phone. Which station had it been on? She tried to picture the hosts and searched through morning shows, looking for something that would trigger her memory. She tried a few different search terms, looking for the segment on teen homelessness, and eventually found faces that looked familiar.

"Bingo! There you are."

She clicked on the link, and the video of the interview started up. Reg waited impatiently for the pixie's face to appear, nudging the progress meter at the bottom of the video forward every few seconds. Then the woman showed up.

"My sister didn't have an easy life. We weren't raised together, but I remember when she was born, how proud I was to have a sister. Recently… well, some bad stuff happened to her and she ran away. I've been looking for her, trying to get in touch with her. I want to help her out. I don't have a lot, but I'm happy to share what I have. I… really miss her. Alicorn… I really miss you. Please let me find you. If anyone knows where she might be, please contact the show."

The feed changed from the woman's pleading face to a fuzzy picture of a little girl and a baby, the little girl holding the baby's face proudly up to her own. Two curly-haired little girls, cute as buttons.

Alicorn? What kind of name was that? Was that the girl's real name, or a cute nickname, one of those affectionate baby names that parents gave their children?

But focusing on the lost sister wasn't going to help Reg to find the pixie who had visited her. She ran the video back and copied down the name from the screen when she was first introduced.

Karol Blackmoor. That was the woman's name. That was who she had to find.

Google was the usual starting point for tracking someone down. But Reg didn't go there immediately. Instead, she closed her eyes and focused on the name and brought the woman's face into her mind. Karol Blackmoor. Karol was looking for her sister. She was a pixie, but she didn't live in their ancestral home. She was living somewhere else, maybe on her own and maybe with friends. Maybe she lived in a shelter or on the street while she searched for her sister; her clothes hadn't exactly been clean and pressed. Where would Reg find Karol?

Finding Karol didn't work. It didn't produce any more results than finding the knife or the emerald had. Why could she suddenly not find the things she was looking for? It had always been one of her strongest gifts.

"Thief!"

The memory of one of Reg's foster mothers erupted into her thoughts. Fat, red-faced, shaking a wooden spoon in Reg's direction.

"I won't have a little thief living in my house! 'I just found it.' You really think anyone is going to believe you? You little ungrateful tramp!" The woman grabbed her, dragging her closer, her fingers digging like bird-claws into Reg's tender shoulder.

Reg resisted, trying to pull away, but her foster mother was not to be deterred.

"I was just helping," Reg protested, unable to understand why the woman would be angry when Reg had just helped her to find her missing watch. She asked for help. She had been so upset over the loss of the watch, it gave Reg a pain in her heart. She followed the pull of that pain and it led her right to the watch, which she presented to her guardian with delight. That was when things had turned bad.

"You think you can lie and steal and get away with it? That may have happened at other homes, but believe me, I'm not putting up with that kind of behavior here!"

Still hanging on to Reg with one hand, she started to whale into her with the wooden spoon in the other. Reg fought back, kicking, hitting, trying to tear away. She wasn't going to stay still and submissive for a punishment when she hadn't done anything wrong. She had been a good and helpful girl, and she was unfairly beaten for it. Her mother threw her to the floor and got in a couple of kicks before Reg managed to scramble to her feet and run, leaving the woman screaming and brandishing the wooden spoon threateningly behind.

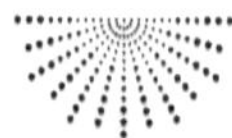

CHAPTER TWENTY-ONE

*R*eg managed to tear herself away from the memory, but it left her shaking, her heart thumping in panic, desperation, and fury over the unfair treatment. How could her foster mother scream at her and beat her for doing what she was asked? "Help me find my watch," she had begged, and then punished Reg for doing so.

Starlight's front paws were on Reg's chest, and he bumped the top of his head against Reg's chin and jaw urgently as he purred away. Reg pushed him down, wrapped her arms around him, and cuddled him close.

"It's okay. I'm okay. It's nothing. That happened a long time ago." She'd buried it deep down, pushing away the pain and betrayal. Sure, it was unfair. Life was unfair.

She hadn't been able to understand at the time why her foster mother had been so angry with her, but as an adult, looking back on it, it made logical sense. Things disappear in a foster home. Kids with nothing are tempted by pretty things. Sometimes not even pretty things, hoarding food or twist ties or used toothbrushes. The way Reg had found the watch, wedged back behind the books on a shelf in the out-of-bounds study, it was obvious that it had not just been dropped or misplaced. Reg had gone directly to it when asked for help. Since no one but the thief could have known where it was secreted away, she was obviously the one who had stolen it in the first place.

Reg never did find out which one of the children had really stolen it. One of them had watched her being beaten for what he had done and not spoken up. At least one of them watching had known that she wasn't the culprit.

Reg had learned over the years to obfuscate. To look around for an object even when she knew where it was. Put on the show of doing a thorough search. Look in places where she knew it wasn't. Continue the search after all other searchers had given up, and then turn it up by luck, happening to stumble across it by mere chance. That was the way to find a missing object. She had honed the act over the years, but in spite of her dramatic ability, people had still suspected her. People like Reg would always be suspects, no matter how innocent they really were.

Letticia's words came back to Reg's mind.

If you look deep down in yourself, you'll understand why you are not able to find it.

She had told Reg that the flaw was in herself, not in some outside force. She didn't suggest that whoever held the emerald had put a blocking spell on it. She didn't say that it was too far away, or buried underground, or any of the other things people had suggested to her. She had simply told Reg that she knew she had the power, and that if she couldn't do what she knew she could do, it was because she was blocking herself. Something deep down inside of her was preventing her from finding the emerald and the other things she had sought. Reg herself was the problem.

"Okay. If I'm blocking myself, then I can unblock myself."

Reg breathed long and slow. She focused her thoughts. She settled Starlight in her lap, intending to use his psychic powers to amplify her own. She put away her phone and looked into the crystal ball, where she had before seen Calliopia running away from home and joining up with Ruan. Reg was calm. She was focused. She was in that meditative, alpha-wave trance that would allow her to access her psychic gifts most easily.

"Karol Blackmoor. I will find Karol Blackmoor."

Her mind didn't stay in a calm, meditative trance. As soon as she voiced the desire, her brain exploded with data. Words and images and sound burst into her mind, not in sequence, but all at once, like a computer error log. Too much data to process. Reg pulled back, trying to harness it all, and then it was gone. Just like that, everything disappeared, and she was left looking at an empty room.

"What the heck was that?" Reg demanded, furious with her brain for the change of tactics. Had her foray into the shadow realm or her rescue from it left her with permanent brain damage? Had Calliopia healed her or had she caused further harm in that flash of brilliant white light when Reg was restored?

A fairy who had just come into her own was dangerous. Powerful, without full understanding or control of the powers that she held. It could take a few decades for her to settle down. And Calliopia was different. Reg didn't have a lot of experience with fairies, but Calliopia struck her as having retained some of her former pixie nature. She was sly and secretive. She didn't have the regal, stately bearing that her parents and Lord Bernier had achieved. She had run away from her family. Maybe the first time she had been kidnapped, but her desire to return home turned out to be little more than wanting to escape from the dungeon she had been held in. As soon as she had been free, she had run away.

Maybe she had damaged Reg's abilities because she didn't want Reg to be able to track her down once she escaped again. So she shackled Reg's abilities, leaving her too disabled to find Calliopia again.

The ironic thing was, Reg hadn't even tried. She had seen Calliopia's escape in her crystal ball merely by chance, never intending to, and she had not attempted to follow or find her again. Her parents didn't ask for help. As far as Reg knew, aside from the Papillon household, she was the only one who was even aware that Calliopia had left again.

Too frustrated to continue with the fruitless attempt to find Karol using her psychic abilities, Reg got up and marched to her office to see what she could find on the internet.

As she walked through the kitchen, a glass burst in the sink. Reg winced and went on without stopping to clean it up.

* * *

Searching for Karol's name had not turned anything up, but then, Reg hadn't really expected it to. A pixie, even one who had left the realm, was not likely to have left much of an electronic trail. But the interview footage had provided plenty of clues when Reg examined it more closely. Organizations that Karol was working with were mentioned. The video footage of the streets where she searched for her sister revealed the names of other businesses and made it easy to track down the area it had been filmed in, whether that was where Karol was living or not. Once she got there and started asking questions, she was bound to pick up Karol's trail.

Reg painstakingly copied and pasted the various organizations and addresses into her phone and headed out. She needed to get moving if she were going to track Karol Blackmoor down and try to recover Sarah's emerald. Time was running short.

When she got to the dusty street Karol had been filmed on, it was even more dismal-looking in the sunlight than it had been in the night-time footage. She got out of her car and, taking a deep breath, tried to reach out to Karol Blackmoor. Not to find her, but to touch her mind, to try to communicate with her. If she were nearby, it would be easier. The farther away she was, the harder it would be.

There was an immediate connection. Reg smiled in satisfaction. Karol Blackmoor was very close. She looked around, fully expecting to find her on the street, looking back at Reg. Reg couldn't see her immediately, but that didn't mean she wasn't there. Reg could feel her. She walked slowly down the street, watching in doorway and alley entrances. She'd lived on the street. Not much; no more than she could help, but she had experience in staying out of sight of searchers. She didn't try to communicate anything to Karol and didn't try to enter her mind. She just kept in touch with it, like a game of warmer/colder. If she started to get farther away from Karol, she'd be able to tell.

She was strongly tempted to speak aloud to Karol, to call softly to her that she was coming. She had to bite her tongue and keep from saying anything. She didn't know how the girl was going to react when Reg confronted her. Reg wanted to keep the upper hand.

Her eyes swept the gutter and the alleyways, places that a pixie, used to living in damp underground tunnels, would be comfortable. Their children and sentries played in the streets above the underground city. Karol would be quick to observe any behavior that was out of the ordinary or of concern.

And then they were staring into each other's eyes. Karol flinched and jerked back, ready to run. But then her muscles relaxed.

"I know you," she said softly.

"You came to me. Asking for help to find your sister."

Karol looked around, as if waiting for someone else to appear. "Is she here? Did you bring her?"

Reg blinked at her. "No. I don't know for sure where she is. But I saw you on TV. I wanted to make sure that everything was okay."

Reg shifted, making sure she was close enough to grab the pixie in a flash. At some point in their conversation, Karol was going to realize that she was in trouble, and she was going to try to run. Reg had seen pixies disappear, but they seemed to need a running start, and Reg knew if she held on to Karol, she could not become invisible. Reg needed to succeed. For Sarah.

"Oh." Karol's tentative smile dimmed. "I thought you had called her."

Called her. Reg knew by the way that Karol emphasized the word that, like find or seek, call was a psychic or magical action. Not call out or call on the phone, but *call* her. Reg shook her head slightly.

"I'm sorry… things have happened. I haven't had much of a chance to think of your sister. I've been worried about my friend." She met Karol's eyes. "You remember the woman who showed you to my house. Sarah."

Karol tried to move, but she wasn't fast enough. Reg had been ready. She held Karol tightly by the wrist, ignoring the girl's writhing and wailing. She held on for all she was worth. It wasn't nearly as bad as when she had been brought back from the shadow world, at least not for her—Karol's cries certainly sounded agonized.

"No!" Karol protested. "No, you can't. I need it. Don't. Let me go!"

"Don't let you go? Don't worry, I won't." Reg gave a grim laugh. "You have some explaining to do. I need that emerald. I need it right now, before my friend dies."

"She's lived a long life," Karol objected. "Much longer than humankind are meant to live. Her time was up many years ago."

"That's not up to you to decide. You can't just arbitrarily decide that someone is too old to live. And you can't walk into someone's house and steal their possessions. That's what you did."

"No." Karol again tried to pull away from Reg. "I was invited. I did not breach the woman's home."

"You were allowed to walk through her house to get to mine. That's not the same as being invited. Even if it was, that doesn't give you the right to steal."

"Stealing is what humans do when they take stones out of the ground," Karol countered. "They do not belong to humans. They belong to the piskies."

"Just because you live underground, that doesn't give you the right to everything in the earth."

Karol looked at her with a stubborn expression. That was exactly what she did believe.

"The emerald was Sarah's and she is dying without it. I want it back now."

"It is not here," Karol said quickly. Far too quickly. Reg immediately knew she was lying. She pulled back the pixie's shirt to see if she were wearing the necklace, but her dirt-smudged neck was bare. Keeping a tight hold on Karol's arm, Reg patted her pockets, feeling for the stone. Karol kept twisting her body away, keeping her left side away from Reg, telling Reg as obviously as if she'd held up a neon sign where she was hiding it.

Reg jerked Karol closer to her, their faces and bodies right against each other, then grabbed Karol's left coat pocket. She didn't care if she tore the jacket, she needed the emerald far more than Karol needed a coat in the Florida heat.

"Give it to me."

"You are the thief! You! It is not yours!"

"It's Sarah's. But she's not getting out of bed again without it. I'm going to take it back to her."

Karol flailed wildly as Reg clawed at her pockets. Then Reg's hand finally closed around something that was hard and heavy and clinked when she moved it.

CHAPTER TWENTY-TWO

Karol shrieked as Reg pulled the emerald necklace out.

Reg gritted her teeth, maintaining a tight grip on the pixie. Detective Jessup had told her that pixies had superhuman strength, and Reg believed it. It was like trying to hold on to a gorilla. But she was determined and focused every ounce of her physical and psychic strength on holding on to the pixie.

"What's going on? Let go of her!" Crowds were starting to gather around the two women. People seemed to think that Reg was beating up on Karol because of the way the pixie was wailing and writhing to escape.

"Call the police!" Reg growled at a man who tried to step in and separate the two of them. "She's a thief!" Reg brandished the necklace. "I'm not letting her go until I'm sure she's not going to get away!"

"It's mine!" Karol screamed. "I didn't steal it, it's mine! It doesn't belong to your kind!"

"My kind?" the tall black man repeated. "What are you talking about?"

"She's crazy," Reg said. "She doesn't even mean you. Just get the police. Tell them to call Detective Jessup. This is her case."

"You should let go of her. She's not going anywhere with all of these people around. They'll make sure she can't run."

"No way," Reg said, teeth gritted. "She is not disappearing on me."

The black man's look clearly communicated that he thought she was the crazy one, but he pulled out his phone and went about trying to get the police there and to get them to call Jessup in.

Reg felt like she was going to have to hold on to the flopping fish forever, but eventually, Karol stopped trying to escape her, crying and whining and trying to cajole Reg into letting her go with promises that she wouldn't run away or disappear. She just wanted to move her arm. Reg's grip was hurting her.

Reg just glared at her, keeping her eyes on Karol and her grip tight. She wasn't about to lose the necklace or the culprit.

A police car finally pulled up, siren blaring, and a couple of uniformed officers stepped out, growling instructions and trying to get things under control. They pushed back the crowd and shouted at Reg and Karol.

"Step away from each other. Break it up. I want both of you to put your hands over your head. Come on, get them up."

Reg wasn't moving. She wasn't going to let go of Karol and she wasn't going to put her hands up.

"She's a thief," she told the male officer, the one closest to her. "If I let her go, she's going to disappear. You secure her first and make sure she's not going to get away, and then we can talk."

"You don't want me to have to get rough, now, do you? Just let her go. Trust me, we can take care of this."

"You have no idea. I'm not letting go until you've got her in handcuffs." Reg wasn't sure that handcuffs would be enough to hold a pixie. What if she just disappeared in a poof of dust? But it was the only thing she could think of. Hopefully, Jessup would be there soon and would be able to tell them how to properly secure the pixie so that she wouldn't be able to get away. Karol needed to be sent to jail and forced to live behind bars for a long time. Whatever magical power was required to hold her there.

"She's hurting me," Karol whined. "I'll stay here if you can just make her let me go. This is all just a misunderstanding. She just attacked me out of the blue. I have no idea what her problem is."

"She stole my friend's emerald," Reg said, holding up the necklace. "This is what she's trying to get away with."

The woman cop gave a low whistle. "Isn't that pretty," she admired. "Where did you get it? I'd really love to put on some bling like that."

"It's a family heirloom. It's not just sparkly, it's a real gemstone and real gold. Check your briefings, it was reported stolen. You must have some kind of record or information sheet you can access."

"That's not real," the woman said, laughing.

"It is!" Reg insisted. "And we need to get it back to its owner right away. She's dying, and it's... it would really comfort her to know that we found it and could return it to her family. Please, you need to get Detective Jessup here. She knows all about it. She'll confirm everything and she'll know what to do to make sure that this... woman doesn't escape. She's really good at escaping custody. You don't want to be the one to blame when she disappears into thin air."

"Let's put them both in cuffs," the male officer suggested. "That way we don't have to know which one actually owns the emerald, if either one of them. We'll prevent them both from taking off and Detective Jessup can fill us in on the situation when she can get here."

"It needs to get back to the owner right away," Reg insisted. "She's dying. She needs to know that it's safe."

"That will wait until the scene is secured and everybody has been called." The big, burly cop grabbed Karol's free hand and twisted it behind her back in one swift movement. He patted her down one-handedly, focused mainly on her pockets and legs. Then he put his hand on her other arm, which Reg was still holding on to stubbornly. "I need you to let go now, ma'am."

"You have to hold on to her tight. She's super strong and she's tricky. If you don't hold on to her, she's going to get away…"

He slapped the first bracelet over the arm Reg was holding, and then brought her other hand closer.

"She's not going to get away."

He was just about to slap the second cuff into place when Karol gave a sudden twist and a ferocious growl, ripping her arm away from him.

Reg had maintained a tight grip on the other arm, knowing that Karol was going to do whatever she could to get away. The cop felt his quarry slip away, but Reg jerked Karol back, pulling her to the pavement in a heap. The cop looked at Reg in surprise, his mouth open in an 'O'.

"She's—I just—"

"I told you."

He was more careful the second time, bringing her hands together into a prayer position behind her back before trying to chain them both together again.

"Okay, she's secured. Now let her go," he told Reg.

Reg took a deep breath. "If she disappears the moment I release her…"

"She's not going to disappear into thin air. I have the cuffs on her."

Reg hoped she was right. She needed someone to say some kind of prayer or incantation to keep Karol there. Something more than Reg's wishful thinking.

She let go. Karol remained where she was, slumped on the concrete, crying softly.

"Now it's your turn," the woman cop said briskly. "Hands up. Lace them behind your head."

Reg obeyed. The officer took the necklace away from her. "The police will hold this for now. It will be returned to the rightful owner in due course."

"Due course better be today, because she's—"

"She's dying. We heard that part."

Reg was tired and sore. Her whole body ached from trying to deal with Karol. Even holding them up to the back of her head made her arms shake with fatigue.

"Why did you do this?" Karol cried as the two of them were marched over to the police car to sit on the curb while the cops took their statements and called their dispatcher for the various pieces of information they needed.

"You stole it," Reg growled. "Sarah is dying because you stole it from her. You had no right to go into her house and take one of her possessions."

"I needed it," Karol insisted. "You led me to it. I knew when I walked into that house and felt it that that was why I had gone to you. Not so that you could look into your crystal ball. I needed the stone."

"Needed it for what? You already have a long life, right? You're barely started in life."

"No, I needed for Alicorn. You would find her, because you are connected. The emerald would return her to the pixies. It would turn back her time so that she could be one of us, not one of them."

"What? What are you talking about?"

"Reg Rawlins." Reg heard Jessup's voice, heavy with frustration and fatigue. "What have you done now?"

* * *

"I found it," Reg said with relief. "Get it from your cop friends. The woman. She has the necklace."

Jessup had been studying Karol with narrow, suspicious eyes, and the mention of the necklace made her snap her attention back to Reg.

"What?"

"This is the pixie who had it. The one that Sarah invited into her house. She left the ribbon and took the emerald. I don't understand why she took it, but she thinks since it came from under the ground, that it belongs to the—to her people, you know?" Reg eyed the other cops, making sure they were out of hearing range.

"What are you talking about?"

"This afternoon, when I went over to Sarah's house, then Marian and I—" Reg realized that she was going too fast and Jessup wasn't understanding because she hadn't been filled in on all of the details in the proper order. Of course she was confused. She hadn't been a part of any of those conversations. "We looked at the display case again, where the necklace had been displayed, and I saw a ribbon that had been missed by the investigators. Marian explained to me how the pixies swap when they see something they want. And we figured that it must have been a pixie and that she had gotten into the house because Sarah had walked her through the day that she came to see me to find her sister."

"Still not following it all. You think that the police missed a clue? This ribbon?"

"Yes. It was down in one of the tracks of the display case and must just have been overlooked—"

"Or someone planted it there after the police search."

"But they didn't. I found the pixie and she had the emerald."

"And now we have someone to blame. Very convenient. You have produced the jewel, and have cleared yourself of all wrongdoing. You're the hero now. Right?"

Reg felt that same sick, sinking feeling that she had as a child when she was accused of having stolen something that she had found. But the rage that surged up in Reg was something new. As a child, there had been anger, frustration, and rebellion at the injustice of false accusations, but not the overwhelming fury that Reg had felt lately.

Reg literally saw red. Everything in the world around her suddenly hazed over in red and she thought she was going to black out. She thought she was going to have an aneurysm. The pressure in her head and the volcanic rage with nowhere to go overwhelmed her and for a few seconds, she was outside her body, looking down at everything that was going on around her. She saw the police and the onlookers and Karol, looking small and vulnerable sitting on the curb. She saw herself, flushing red, the eyes rolling back in her head,

"Reg—" Jessup reached toward her.

The windows in the police car shattered and burglar alarms started blaring up and down the street. Jessup pulled back, changing her mind about touching Reg. Maybe she'd heard news of what had happened at the hearing and didn't want to risk immolation.

"Reg, cool it," she breathed. "Calm down. You're going to find yourself locked up in a psych facility if you're not careful."

Reg was back in her body, all of her muscles going rigid. She let out a howl of pure rage, and then she cut it off. She did not want to end up in hospital or some other locked down facility. So she forced the anger down and tried to control it.

They had the necklace and they had Karol, and that was all that mattered.

They could sort everything out. They would find that what Reg had said was true, Sarah would recover, and everything would go back to normal again.

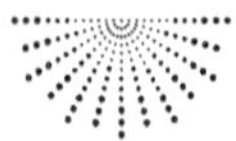

CHAPTER TWENTY-THREE

It seemed like it took forever for Jessup to get things sorted out with the other officers and Karol Blackmoor, but eventually, she and Reg were in Jessup's car, headed back toward Sarah's house with the emerald. Jessup had refused to let Reg take her own car home.

"You can come with me, or you can go to jail, it's your choice. We've got to get this thing sorted out. I don't think you're in any shape to be driving."

"I'm fine. Just tired out."

She was more than tired out. She was exhausted and her whole body hurt. Holding on to a pixie wasn't an easy job. But she knew it wasn't just her physical condition that Jessup was worried about. Reg needed to get a handle on her emotions before she ended up causing some real damage. A couple of broken glasses was one thing. A damaged police car was quite another. Maybe they couldn't reasonably say that she had broken the windows and charge her for their replacement, but Jessup wasn't likely to be asking her to consult on any cases if she couldn't keep her psychic abilities under control.

"It's been a tough week for everyone," Jessup said. "You've had a lot to worry about. How did things go at Hunter's hearing?"

Reg looked over at her, wondering whether she had already heard anything. "Not so well," she admitted. "You know… they really are chauvinists, stuck hundreds of years in the past."

"You're telling me," Jessup sighed.

Reg imagined she probably dealt with a lot of those attitudes as a police detective. People who thought that women didn't belong in the workforce, let alone the police department or its higher ranks.

"Their opinion seems to be that I brought it all on myself, because I should have known what Corvin was going to do."

"Sorry to hear that. I think they're probably just afraid."

"Afraid of what?"

"Hunter is a powerful warlock. They don't want to have to discipline him. If they can put the responsibility on you rather than him, maybe they don't have to do anything more than censure him."

"He glamoured me even after he promised he wouldn't! If the fairies hadn't been there and decided to defend me…"

"You're better off pushing the breach of covenant than assault. Like you say… they're pretty dark ages as far as their treatment of women goes."

"Too late to do anything else now. All of the testimony has been presented. It's just a matter of what they decide to do about it."

Jessup nodded. "I'm sorry it happened to you. I don't know what it is about you and Hunter… he's kind of obsessed with you. Normally, it's just about opportunities… feeding wherever and whenever he can. But with you, it seems like he's not willing to be reasonable or wait for some other opportunity to come along."

"Maybe it's because he's already held my powers. He won't give up until he has them back again."

Jessup pursed her lips. "Yeah, could be that. Or maybe he just has a crush on you."

"Oh, please," Reg's stomach twisted at the thought of Corvin Hunter actually liking her. As much as she hated him for what he had done to her, that didn't change the fact that he was handsome and had the means of making himself very alluring when he turned on the charm. Her heart started to beat faster whenever she thought about him, despite what had happened in the past. "Did you know that his father was abusive?" she asked Jessup. "He used to hurt Corvin and to drain his powers?"

"Really. No, he's never shared that. No reason to, I guess. The old man's not around anymore."

"Did you know him?"

"Hunter's father?" Jessup gave a laugh. "I'm not old enough to have known him."

"He died young?"

"No. But he was gone long before I was around. I'm not that old."

Reg frowned. "Well, how old is Corvin? I didn't think you were that far apart in age."

"Decades." Jessup glanced aside at Reg. "That's one of the things about a community like this. You can't judge people's age by the way they look. People like Sarah and Corvin who don't look anywhere close to their actual chronological ages. Fairies and pixies and any other long-lived races. People here have memories that go back much farther than yours and mine. They have grudges and feuds that might go back hundreds of years."

That made Reg think. She had assumed that Corvin was a young man, still in his thirties. 'Decades older' than Jessup put him into his sixties or even older.

Jessup answered a call on her cellphone, listening to the wireless earpiece and scowling. She did not sound at all pleased with what she was hearing. Reg hoped that it wasn't some kind of report on her, saying that because of her past, Jessup had to bring her into the police station no matter what Jessup thought had happened on the street. As far as Reg knew, there weren't any active warrants out under the name Reg Rawlins, but if they had connected up one of her other identities, things could get sticky.

Jessup gave a few terse acknowledgments, then hung up the call. She looked at Reg.

"The pixie."

"What happened?"

"She escaped. They're looking for her, but you know they're not going to find her if she's disappeared into the shadow realm."

"I warned them!"

"They're not used to dealing with pixies. Eventually, they'll learn weird stuff can happen around here and they'll be better about following instructions. But in the meantime… they don't believe that releasing a detainee from handcuffs is going to allow her to vanish into thin air."

"But you've got the emerald, right?"

Reg knew this to be true, but she had to hear it. She had to know that they were going to get the emerald back to Sarah.

"I didn't turn it in," Jessup said. "That may be against policy, but I'm not going to put policy above my friend's life."

"Now you know that she's the one who stole it, not me."

"How?"

"Because she ran away. Why would she run away if she wasn't guilty?"

"Because she's a pixie. No other reason needed."

"But isn't she required under the treaty between humans and pixies to be governed by our laws? Doesn't she have to stay in custody and let justice take its course?"

"That's not the way these things usually turn out."

"So she gets away with stealing a precious heirloom and almost killing someone in the process."

"She wouldn't be charged with anything in relation to Sarah's death. Our justice system doesn't accept magic as a means of murder or wrongful death."

"Maybe it should!"

"Really? You want the Spanish Inquisition all over again? Magical crimes have to be dealt with within the community of the perpetrator, not the human justice system. Covens, councils, kingdoms… they all have to deal with their own. Magical laws can't be part of the same system as civil and criminal."

"Then she should be charged under those laws."

"Under pixie law, humans don't have ownership over precious gemstones. Putting Sarah in the wrong for having it in the first place. Taking it away from her—especially if she swapped something of value for it—can't be a crime under pixie law."

"This is crazy."

Jessup sighed. "That it is!"

They pulled up in front of Sarah's house. Reg saw Jessup look carefully up and down the street. She didn't get out of the car immediately, just sat there looking.

"What is it?"

"Unlike certain people, I don't like to run pell-mell into the unknown. I'm just looking at all of the angles. What about your abilities? Can you feel any other presences? Any traps?"

Reg looked around. "Like what? It's just Sarah's house, and it's protected by wards. No one can get in who intends to do her harm."

"They might still intend to do us harm. And if they left other things here, they might be able to come back for them."

"Oh. I guess." Reg was exhausted, but she turned her thoughts outward, feeling for any unexpected presences. There were people in the other houses, but no one else in Sarah's. And magical traps? Reg didn't know for sure how to tell. But Jessup was right, they didn't want to end up caught in some trap again.

"I don't sense anything. But let's move slowly. I'll try to scan each room before we enter it…"

"It is just Sarah's house," Jessup said with a little laugh. "I'm sure I'm being overcautious."

"Better too cautious than not cautious enough."

They got out of the car. Reg looked at the storm drains, wondering whether there were pixies close by. Did they plan to swarm out of the sewers and steal the emerald back? But she couldn't sense anyone there.

"Okay. Let's go."

Jessup headed toward the front door, but Reg shook her head. "Can we go in through the back? I'm just more comfortable that way."

"Yes, if you think that's important."

"I don't… I just feel more comfortable with it."

"Back it is."

They walked around to the back yard. Reg looked around slowly. Nothing seemed out of place.

She heard a yowl from the house, and when she looked toward the sound, she saw a black cat scamper away, across the garden and up over the fence.

"Starlight?" Jessup asked.

"He's inside. It's that other cat. The one that's been hanging around."

"You think that's what Hunter saw?"

"Yeah. Except he says he saw it going into the house, and I don't think he did. I think he just saw the cat in the yard and it inspired his story."

"If he was lying to me, he's going to have some explaining to do."

"You know he was lying to you. Because you know I wasn't the one who stole the emerald."

Jessup looked at her. "I hope you didn't. That's not the same thing."

Reg went to the back door and knocked without a word. It was a few minutes before Marian got to the door. She looked grave.

"It's too late," she whispered. "Just let her go peacefully."

"It's not too late. We've got the emerald!"

Marian's eyes widened. "You found it?" She stepped back from the door to allow them in. "I still don't think… it may not be of any use to her at this point."

"We have to try."

They went into the kitchen. Reg looked around. Marian caught the look and frowned.

"Why don't you make her some tea?" Reg suggested. "She's going to need something."

Marian looked like she was going to argue, then shrugged her shoulders. She stayed in the kitchen and let Reg and Jessup continue on their own. Reg was glad to be rid of her. She wanted to see Sarah alone, not with another psychic there, feeding them emotions and trying to manipulate them. Reg was emotional enough without outside influences.

They paused in each doorway. Reg thought Jessup was probably right. It was Sarah's house. There were wards all along the way. Unless there was something else that belonged to the pixies there.

What about the ribbon? Was it still in the house? Could they claim that it was lost or taken when she had left it in exchange for the necklace? Reclaim it now that the necklace had been taken back? Reg stopped in the hallway and Jessup bumped into her.

"What is it? What did you feel?"

"Nothing… it's just…" Reg turned around and retraced her steps to the kitchen. "Marian… where is the ribbon? Is it in the bedroom? Or do you have it?"

Marian frowned. She pushed her hands into her pockets and felt around. "Yes… there. But why do you need it?"

"Throw it outside."

"What?"

Reg wanted to snatch it from her and do it herself, but she didn't want to chance getting a shock.

"Just do it. Get it out of the house right now."

Marian moved slowly. Reg watched with anxiety, thinking that the pixies were going to suddenly swarm the kitchen any minute, taking both the ribbon and the necklace. But then Marian was outside, and she walked back behind the fence where the garbage bins were. She returned to the house, no sign of pixies with her. But they could be invisible. They could be watching out there, unseen. Reg couldn't sense them, but she didn't know if she'd be able to. She had sensed Karol, but she didn't know if she would sense other pixies, or be able to sense them while they were invisible. The three women looked at each other, and then Reg nodded.

"Okay. Let's go see Sarah," she told Jessup. They walked back to Sarah's bedroom, a little more confident this time.

* * *

The drapes were drawn and Sarah's room was only dimly lit by a lamp. Reg felt like an intruder creeping into the quiet, dark room. Sarah lay in the bed, her body seeming so insubstantial under the sheets that Reg could barely believe it was her. Not that she had been a fat woman, but she hadn't been the frail woman who now lay under the sheets, unmoving.

"Sarah?" Reg's voice broke as she moved toward her. *Was* it too late? She'd been warned that even if she found the emerald, Sarah might be too far gone for it to do any good. After her age had caught up with her, it couldn't prevent her death.

Reg put her hand on Sarah's. So thin, dotted with age spots that hadn't been there before. Skin that was wrinkled and almost translucent.

"Sarah, wake up. We have something to show you."

She studied Sarah, looking for the rise and fall of her chest. If Sarah were already gone, just as they returned with her emerald…

Sarah snorted and opened her eyes. She gazed up at her ceiling and did not appear to see Reg standing next to her or Jessup farther away.

"Sarah…?"

Reg reached toward Jessup for the necklace. Jessup took it from her pocket and removed it from the plastic evidence bag. Reg sensed that Sarah would have to touch it directly. Being close to it wouldn't be enough at that late stage. Reg wasn't sure what to do next. She held it close to Sarah's eyes. "It's your necklace, Sarah. Your emerald. We found it and brought it back to you."

Sarah stared, seemingly blind and deaf. Reg picked up Sarah's hand and pressed her fingers to the emerald. The emerald glowed and pulsed. Sarah's fingers twitched. Her gaze focused on the emerald, and some expression came to her slack face.

"Is it...?" she whispered.

"It's your emerald."

"Oh..." Sarah's fingers caressed it. "I never thought I would see it again."

"It will make you better," Reg said. "You'll be able to go back to normal again."

Reg moved the emerald down, away from Sarah's gaze, drawing it down toward her heart. That was where Sarah needed it the most to begin with. To make her heart strong.

Reg looked over at Jessup, worried that they weren't seeing any miraculous changes. "How long will it take? Is anything happening?"

"I don't know."

"We need another witch. A couple of psychics and a cop aren't the right people for this job. Do you think you could get someone?"

"I'll see who I can reach."

Jessup stepped out of the room to make her phone calls, leaving Reg with Sarah. Reg sat on the edge of the bed, leaning over Sarah, holding the emerald over her heart.

"Come on, Sarah. You can get better. This is what you've been waiting for. Fight for it. Don't give up."

Sarah's mouth formed a single word. "No."

CHAPTER TWENTY-FOUR

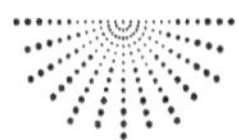

Reg sat with Sarah, waiting, watching for any change or improvement. Marian entered with a tea tray, but she put it on a dresser when she saw that no one was ready for it.

Jessup returned in a few minutes. "Reg…?"

"You couldn't get anyone?"

"No… I did… I just wanted to warn you."

Reg blinked and looked at her, trying to make out her expression in the dimness. Jessup was clearly anxious.

"What is it? What did she say?"

"I tried Letticia, but I couldn't get her."

"But you got someone? Who?"

"Hunter. He's on his way over now."

"You called *Corvin?* Why?"

"He's good at what he does. He'll know what to do, if there's anything that can be done."

Reg pressed her lips together, not happy with this development. "You'd better go wait at the door and let him in, then."

Jessup nodded and left without another word. Reg sat watching Sarah breathe. At least she was breathing. The rise and fall of her chest was more pronounced than it had been. Marian stood by, watching and saying nothing.

"Do you want some tea?" she asked, after some minutes had ticked by.

Reg shook her head. "No. Thanks."

"There just wasn't time," Marian said. "You did your best, she just didn't have enough time."

"Don't say that. I got her the emerald." Reg still had it clasped between her hand and Sarah's, held over Sarah's heart. "It's not over."

Marian shrugged and looked down at her feet.

Reg felt Corvin arrive. She felt his presence before she heard the quick rap at the door. Jessup let him in, the two of them murmuring quietly as they walked to the bedroom. Reg looked up at him as he walked in the door, then back at Sarah. Sarah had a little more color. She wasn't quite as ivory white as she had been when Reg and Jessup got there.

Or maybe it was just wishful thinking.

"Regina," Corvin's greeting was barely a whisper. Out of respect for the woman who lay there on the edge of death? Or because he was embarrassed about what had happened at the hearing?

He walked around to the opposite side of the bed and held his hands out over Sarah. He closed his eyes. No one in the room breathed but Sarah.

Corvin opened his eyes. He looked at Reg's hand, the long gold chain extending from it in a loop. How he must have coveted that precious artifact.

"What can I do?" Reg asked, breaking the silence.

Corvin sighed. When he spoke, his voice was strong and calm. "Focus your energy on the stone. Don't have anxious feelings about Sarah, stay positive and strong. I'm going to build up her strength while you do that."

It could all just be nonsense. It could just be words designed to make her think there was hope and something she could actually do to help Sarah. But Reg had to believe he was telling her the truth and that he thought there might be hope for Sarah. Reg focused on the emerald pressed between their hands. It was Sarah's emerald. The one that had kept her alive for however long she had survived. The precious family heirloom. It felt warm and alive. Just like Sarah. She was still alive, so there was hope.

Reg watched Corvin hold his hands just over Sarah's face, not quite touching her. Reg remembered how he had done the same for her when she had been depleted and faint. She remembered the warm surge of energy and vitality that had flowed from him. That's what he was doing for Sarah now.

Sarah's head turned to the side. Corvin held steady, not moving. Time crept by. Reg wondered if he was still strengthening her, or just waiting to see if there was a response. She refocused her thoughts on the emerald. She had a job to do too; she wasn't there to analyze Corvin's actions.

Sarah moved. Reg blinked and looked at the woman's face. It had a definite pink hue that hadn't been there before. Sarah opened her eyes and smiled. Reg was sure that Sarah was seeing her this time. She smiled back, trying to look reassuring.

"Hey. Did you have a nice nap?"

Sarah's hand tightened around the emerald. She closed her fingers, enclosing it so that it was no longer touching Reg's hand. Reg felt unaccountably disappointed and resentful. She had brought the emerald back to Sarah. Had protected it and her. Didn't that give Reg some rights over it too? Make it partly hers?

"It's back." Sarah took a deep breath and let it out again. "How did you find it?"

"Do you remember the woman you let in the other day?" Reg asked. "You brought her to the cottage when she showed up at your door looking for me?"

Sarah shook her head, but Reg thought she detected some memory in her eyes.

"Did you bring her through your house?"

"I don't know. I don't remember that."

"You wouldn't have gone outside with her, would you? If you brought her back to the cottage instead of just sending her around by the sidewalk, you wouldn't have walked her all the way around the house, would you? You would have walked her through the house from the front door to the back."

Sarah nodded. "Of course."

"She was a pixie, and I guess she sensed the emerald when she walked into the house. She left something here, so that she could come back for it later and get past your wards."

"Oh…" Sarah's eyes showed understanding. "Tricksie pixie. They are so cunning sometimes."

"Yes. I'm still worried that she might have left something else in the house and they might come back looking for it." Reg looked at Corvin. "Is there any way to check for that? To see if a pixie left something here?"

"I'll try a reveal spell. You might try looking around yourself… you might be able to sense something pixie-ish."

Sarah's eyes went to Corvin. "Oh. Hello, Corvin."

"Oh, hello," Corvin echoed, smiling sardonically. "That's all I get when I bring you back from the brink of death?"

"Was that you?"

"Who else?"

Sarah made experimental movements, pushing her hands down to sit herself up. Reg and Corvin both moved in as if choreographed to help her to sit up and get comfortable with a few pillows supporting her.

"I'm feeling much better," Sarah said.

"That's good." Reg forced a smile. Sarah was more energetic and talking to them, but her face was still deeply wrinkled and her body shrunken. The emerald might have been able to arrest the effects of age, but what about rewinding them? Was there any way for her to go back to the sixty-year-old body she'd had just a week before?

"Would you like some tea?" Marian offered. She didn't wait for an answer, but began to prepare a cup for Sarah immediately.

"Oh, Marian. You've been so good to me through all of this. Thank you for being there."

She hadn't thanked either Reg or Corvin, only Marian, who hadn't actually done anything but to sit with her throughout her illness. Reg suppressed a grunt of disgust. She looked at Corvin.

"I need to get back to my cottage. Starlight will be hungry and it's been a long day. Maybe we should check for any pixie leftovers and leave Sarah and Marian alone."

Corvin eyed the necklace, the jewel hidden in Sarah's grip. He was clearly reluctant to leave such a great treasure behind.

"Let's go, Hunter," Jessup agreed, her voice stern. She always seemed to be stern with him, like a parent who knew she couldn't give her child an inch or he'd take a mile. Which, knowing Corvin, was perfectly apt.

Corvin swept the room with a look, then nodded. "Okay. Get me out of here."

Jessup motioned Corvin ahead of her. Reg trailed behind, leaving Sarah and Marian with their tea. They took their time, wandering into the various bedrooms and other rooms to check for anything that was out of place or might have resonated of pixies. Eventually, they were at the front door.

"I don't think there's anything else here," Corvin said. "I'm not sensing anything. You?"

"No."

"You did a good thing, Reg."

Reg looked at him, feeling as sulky as a teenager. "I didn't do it for the thanks… but it would have been nice."

"I'm sure she'll tell you thank you a hundred times over the next few weeks," Jessup said. "She's still finding her feet right now. She was right on the brink of death, don't expect her to bounce right back to normal."

"I suppose. But she's not going to go back to the way she was, is she?"

Jessup looked at Corvin, raising her eyebrows in a question. He gave a wide shrug. "Hard to tell where she'll end up after a few days. All we can do is wait and see."

He leaned against the doorframe, and for the first time Reg

noticed how tired he looked. It had been a long day for him too. Maybe even longer than Reg's. Her life and happiness didn't rest in the hands of a tribunal.

"Are you okay?"

"I might have overdone it a bit on the strengthening."

Reg was alarmed. She hadn't realized that giving others strength drained his own reserves. But of course it did, he couldn't just create energy out of thin air. She'd only ever seen him transfer strength for a few seconds at a time before, and just that was enough to revive someone who couldn't stand on their own. He'd given Sarah a lot of strength. She'd been perilously close to death. "Is there something we can do?"

Corvin shrugged. He gave his head a little shake while leaning against the doorframe to recover his strength. "You could give me some of yours."

He'd done it for her previously, so it seemed only right to reciprocate. She couldn't let him drive home on his own when he was so weak.

"What do I do?" she asked, feeling a little awkward. She didn't know whether she should hold her hands over his body, or whether he'd hold his over her.

"No way, Reg," Jessup said strongly. "After all you know, you're going to put your power in his hands?"

"Well, no... I just thought that if he needed physical strength, because he's depleted himself giving to Sarah..."

"You know how a bird pretends to have a broken wing to lead you away from its babies...?"

"Yeah." Reg looked at Corvin, staring hard. "Are you telling me he's just faking?"

"Not necessarily, but if you think you can give him physical strength without releasing your powers to him..."

"Sort of a package deal, huh?" Reg asked.

Corvin didn't deny it.

"Then no, you're not getting anything from me."

He pushed himself away from the doorframe, standing

without support. "Sometimes," he said, looking at Jessup, "you really are a wet blanket."

"I brought you here; that doesn't mean I have to let you do whatever you want. And whatever your issue is with Reg… you need to get over it. You're not getting her powers."

"Seems like she's got too much these days to be able to handle." Corvin raised his eyebrows at Reg. "I could help with that."

She could feel the heat coming off of him.

"I don't have to take it all, you know. But I could… relieve a little of the pressure. So you're not walking around blowing things up when you lose that red-headed temper of yours."

Reg stared at him. She took the heat he was sending her direction and imagined herself reflecting it back toward him, focusing it like a magnifying glass at the middle of his chest.

Corvin swore and swiped at the spot on his chest she was staring at. "Cut that out!"

"You know I just can't control myself. It's your own energy, I'm just returning it to you. If you want it to stop, then turn off the taps."

He opened the door and stalked off without looking back. Jessup laughed. "You're learning."

"Maybe. But I would have fallen for the 'fainting from overexertion' thing."

"Don't ever offer to give him anything. Whether it's his idea or you think it's yours. Don't do it."

"Roger that," Reg agreed. She sighed. "I need to get home and feed the cat."

"You can tell him he's been cleared in the theft of Sarah's emerald."

"And me?"

"It's looking that way, but we'll have to see how it all plays out."

CHAPTER TWENTY-FIVE

Starlight was stalking back and forth when Reg finally made it back to the cottage and opened the door. He stopped and sat back on his haunches, staring at her, waiting for an explanation.

"It was a pixie," Reg explained. "That pixie that came here for a reading to look for her sister. She got into Sarah's house and she's the one who stole the necklace. I have returned it to its rightful owner, and Sarah... she's okay, but I don't know how much she will recover."

Starlight's tail switched back and forth as he considered this news.

"Sorry, it's been a long day. Or I would have told you what was going on and been back sooner."

With a sigh, Reg went to the kitchen and made herself a sandwich. She put half a can of tuna into Starlight's bowl. He conceded to eat, and afterward seemed a little warmer toward Reg. He jumped up on the windowsill in her bedroom and looked out as she got changed for bed.

"I saw your friend earlier. Is he there now?"

Starlight stared out into the gathering darkness.

* * *

Reg slept heavily. It had been a long few days. It was the first time that she could really relax, knowing that Sarah was not going to die. Now that she had the emerald, she at least had a chance of a happy life, a few more years to enjoy herself and choose her own departure.

When she awoke in the morning, Reg opened her eyes to find Starlight staring down at her, his green and brown eyes unblinking. When she didn't say anything or get up, he tapped her on the nose with a soft paw. Reg wondered how many times he had done that already, waiting for her to wake up.

"Okay, I'm awake," she told him. "Just give me a few minutes and I'll get up."

He continued to stare at her.

"You're kind of a pain, you know that?"

Eventually, Reg rubbed her eyes and sat up.

"Ugh. I told you, I'm up. Just a few more minutes."

She went through her usual morning ablutions and wandered out to the kitchen to scavenge something for breakfast. She hadn't had actual meals the day before and she was hungry even though it was early.

She put on the kettle and started pulling anything that looked appetizing out of the fridge. As she placed them on the island, she startled and gave a little yell.

"What are you doing here?"

Karol Blackmoor was sitting on the living room couch, watching Reg's preparations. She looked small and childish sitting there, with her knees drawn up to her chest and her feet on the couch in front of her. Not like a threat.

"You have not called Alicorn," Karol said, as if that should clear everything up.

"No, I haven't," Reg agreed. "Why would I? You stole from my friend. You nearly killed her. I don't have any reason to help you, and I'm not sure I could do anything, even if I wanted to."

Starlight had followed Reg into the kitchen and gave a little chirp of agreement.

Karol's ice blue eyes stared back at her. "You must call her."

"No. There's no reason I should."

"I cannot find her."

Reg felt a little stab of sympathy. The pixie had, it appeared, been diligently looking for her sister, hoping to bring her home again. Or at least to make contact and know that she was okay. Reg knew what it was like to wonder what had happened to a family member, to wonder if they were okay.

"I get that, but I can't help you. How did you get in here?"

Karol picked up a keychain pendant from the coffee table. Reg recognized the little crystal on a chain. She'd found it and assumed that it had been accidentally broken and left behind by one of her clients. She had set it to the side in case someone called looking for it later. But it had been a ruse. Karol had intentionally left it so that she could get past Sarah's wards on the cottage and enter at will.

"You broke into my home," Reg said. "That's not cool. You expect me to help you when you do something like that?"

Karol looked at her blankly, not seeming to understand.

Reg let out her breath. The kettle started to whistle, so she turned to grab it and pour the boiling water into her teacup. Karol watched her, eyes intent.

"You want a cup?" Reg asked, angry at the girl but unable to ignore her hollow cheeks and dirty appearance. Reg had been on the streets. She knew what it was like to have nothing, not even hot water.

"You show hospitality to pixies?" Karol seemed surprised by this idea. "I have nothing to pay you."

On her previous visit, she had produced a few crumpled bills to pay for her session. It had probably been the only money Karol had.

"You don't need to pay me for tea." Reg prepared and poured a second cup, and took it over to Karol on a tray with sugar and creamer. "Look… I don't know why you think I can help you, but I don't think there's anything I can do for you. Why don't you go back to your family? Were you kicked out? Did you run away?"

Karol mixed so much sugar into the hot tea that Reg was sure there'd be a thick sludge of undissolved sugar at the bottom when Karol was done. Maybe pixies had a sweet tooth. Or maybe Karol didn't know where her next meal was coming from and would take her calories however she could get them.

"I was… I need to find Alicorn."

"And she ran away?"

Karol nodded. "After she was changed."

"Maybe she doesn't want to be found."

"She doesn't know about the emerald. I could change her back."

"You don't have the emerald anymore. And you're not getting it back from Sarah."

"If you call her, she will come here. I can use the power of the emerald."

Reg wasn't sure how the pixie thought she was going to manage that, but she didn't challenge the statement. She took her cup of tea and sat down.

"Tell me about Alicorn and why you think I can call her for you. I've never… I don't know how to call."

Karol sipped the tea, wrapping her hands around the cup to absorb the warmth from the beverage. "She is in place after me and before the other children."

"She's your little sister."

Karol frowned uncertainly. "She is in size larger but in place smaller…"

"Bigger than you, but younger," Reg interpreted.

Karol nodded. "Yes. She was taken long ago."

"Taken by who? Kidnapped?" Reg didn't think that the pixies had any kind of social services that would take a child away from unfit parents. Karol had to mean Alicorn was taken by an outsider.

"Infant-napped."

"By who? Do you know?"

"By fairies."

"Like Calliopia."

Karol's eyes widened. "Calliopia," she repeated. "Beautiful voice. Yes. My Alicorn."

Reg was having trouble following Karol's train of thought. When she had been interviewed for the TV spot, Karol had been clear and concise, but she had probably been prepped and rehearsed a script for that to make sure the producers would have something they could use.

"What was that?"

"Alicorn is Calliopia."

"Alicorn…" Reg repeated faintly.

Karol held the teacup in both hands at chin level. She stared back at Reg without blinking, reminding Reg of Starlight.

"You are connected," Karol said.

"Well… maybe." Reg's connection with Calliopia had been strong since the first time she had reached out to her for Detective Jessup. Reg had believed that the connection would fade once the job was done and Calliopia was returned to her family. She hadn't expected to see Calliopia in her crystal after that, as she had when the girl had run away to be with Ruan, a pixie who might have been her brother or who might have been closer than a brother. They were a little unclear on the actual relationship.

"You are connected," Karol insisted. "So you can call her."

"If Calliopia is your sister, then you don't want her back," Reg said. "She's been turned into a fairy. She can't return to the pixie realm."

Karol shook her head impatiently, as if trying to explain something to a stubborn child. "I can return her."

"It can't be reversed. Once she is a fairy, there's nothing we can do. She has come into her powers." She wondered if Karol didn't understand just how changed Calliopia was.

"The emerald," Karol insisted.

"Which you don't have."

"Call her!"

"I don't even know how. How would I do that?"

Karol put down her teacup. "You must use your powers and connection to reach out to her. Tell her to come here."

"Calliopia is long gone. She and Ruan left by car. They could be all the way across the country."

"It matters not."

"This is too weird. If you want… I could look into the crystal ball and see if I can see her. Maybe you can use your magic to see her too."

Karol surprised Reg by accepting this with a nod. "Look in your crystal."

Reg wasn't confident that she would be able to see Calliopia. Even though they were connected, Reg hadn't been able to find anything since Calliopia had healed her. And that was probably exactly why. Because Calliopia didn't want her to be able to.

She blew out her breath and touched her crystal ball, trying to get into the right place mentally. She was connected with Calliopia. It wouldn't be hard.

Starlight walked over and sat down out of Reg's reach. Karol's eyes darted over to the cat and her lip curled in an involuntary snarl. Cats and pixies did not get along. Reg patted her lap for Starlight to jump up on her, but Starlight didn't move. He just sat there and stared at her.

"Fine," Reg murmured. "I don't need your help."

She touched the crystal again briefly, then focused her gaze and her powers into it. Unlike when she had tried to find the knife or the emerald, Reg felt like she fell right into the crystal and she was there with Calliopia, as the girl laughed and spoke with Ruan. They were sitting on a blanket under some trees, maybe having a picnic. The breeze was pleasant and it was a clear, sunny day. Ruan was protected from the sun, hidden beneath a dark hoodie, sunglasses, and a ball cap. He too was smiling, his apple cheeks pink.

Calliopia stopped laughing, startled by Reg's presence. She turned and looked at Reg. She couldn't have seen Reg there, because Reg *wasn't* there, yet Calliopia was aware of Reg's presence and looked right at her.

"What is it, sweet?" Ruan's boyish voice inquired.

"Call her," Karol's voice insisted.

Reg tried to stay focused on Calliopia, not on the competing voices. Could she call Calliopia as Karol suggested?

"Are you Alicorn?" Reg asked Calliopia, communicating directly with her mind, as Reg had when she was in the shadow world and no one could see or hear her with their physical eyes and ears.

"Alicorn?" Calliopia echoed, frowning.

"Your sister is looking for you. Your pixie sister."

Calliopia reached out and grabbed Ruan's hand.

The healing cut on Reg's hand pulsed with warmth. It didn't hurt and split open like it had before Calliopia had healed her, but it clearly indicated that her connection to Calliopia was still strong. Calliopia's blood had mingled with hers.

"Call her!"

Reg stilled the competing voices in her head, trying to focus only on one message.

"Come to me."

CHAPTER TWENTY-SIX

There was a dizzying whirl of images. Reg tried to keep her balance. She didn't want to faint and hit her head. The vertigo only strengthened. The voices in her head roared. She felt like she was sliding through time and space, but she wasn't the one moving, it was Calliopia.

There was a sensation like hitting a wall, and time and space were again constant and solid.

"Alicorn."

Reg tried to push herself back into being present. She blinked and tried to take in the sights and sounds around her.

She was no longer alone with Karol. Calliopia stood in her living room, with Ruan's hand in her own. Both she and Ruan looked uncertain at the sudden change in their situation. Karol looked both delighted and smug.

"You could call," she told Reg. "I knew you could call her."

Calliopia turned to look at Reg. "Why did you bring me here? You should not have this power!"

Reg shook her head. "Things have been… a little out of control lately. Maybe because you brought me back from the shadow world. I don't know. But I can do things I couldn't do before, and can't do things I should be able to do."

Calliopia kept looking at Karol, seeming puzzled, and then back at Ruan for reassurance.

"Who are you?"

"Karol. Your sister."

It was obvious Calliopia couldn't remember her, but Karol didn't seem perturbed by this. Calliopia had been a baby when she was stolen from the pixies.

"My sister?" Calliopia asked Ruan.

Ruan nodded. "First in place. Before you, before me."

Calliopia stepped closer to Karol, but still held on to Ruan. She nodded shyly. "A sister. Okay. My new sister."

Karol got to her feet. She was significantly shorter than Calliopia. But then, so was Ruan. Calliopia had grown up on fairy food and had been changed by their spells into a fairy herself, tall and slim, growing in beauty daily. The pixies were like children next to her, but she didn't seem to care.

"My pixie family," Calliopia said with a little laugh, bending down to give Karol a friendly hug.

"I will make you a piskie again," Karol said.

Calliopia looked at her, then at Ruan. "No."

Karol's eyes widened. She had obviously never anticipated this response to her mission. "I can," she insisted. "That human being," she motioned to the main house, "she has a powerful gem. I will turn back your time. Make you piskie again."

Calliopia shook her head. "No."

Karol appealed to Ruan. "You want her to be piskie. Tell her I can do it."

Ruan's normally cheerful face was serious. "She is changed. She does not want to be piskie."

Karol's face took on a thunderous appearance. "I will change you! I searched many years for you and for this gem! Now I can restore you. You will be whole. The family will be whole again."

Calliopia's mouth was a hard, straight line. Her beautiful, haughty face held as much stubbornness as Karol's. She was equally determined to stand her ground. "I am a fairy. Full fairy with full powers and I will not go underground again. I will live in sunlight and not crawl in the earth."

Reg was ready to dive behind the furniture if the two of them started a physical or magical fight. Why did the confrontation have to take place in the middle of her living room?

Karol held her palm out, directed toward the main house, and Reg could feel the electrical charge that gathered around the pixie. She looked at Calliopia, her blue eyes glowing.

"No," Calliopia repeated.

A buzzing noise filled the room. Reg stepped away from Karol, trying to distance herself from the power the pixie was channeling. No one had ever told her that pixie magic could be so strong. She had assumed that they were limited to protecting their colony, breaking into houses, or committing acts of mischief. Domestic magic, nothing like the power Karol was gathering. She'd had no idea that the emerald could be used over a distance, knowing Sarah needed it to be close by for it to have any efficacy. It seemed from Karol's vibration and glow that it was more like a power source that could be accessed from some distance away. Reg again thought of how valuable such an object would be for Corvin. Maybe if he had it, he would never have to feed on the powers of other humans again.

Calliopia fought back against what Karol was doing. She raised her hands only slightly, but her aura changed color from the silvery glow that normally surrounded her to red like a brilliant sunset. Reg put her hands up to her eyes to shield them from the brilliance of the light.

Ruan did not jump to the aid of either of his sisters, but stood watching them, eyes alert with interest and intelligence, waiting to see how it would all work out.

After a minute or two, Reg could see Karol weakening. She had clearly not expected to meet any resistance. The buzzing started to recede. Calliopia took a step forward and brought both hands up to push the energy from the emerald back.

"I will turn back your days," Karol insisted, her voice trembling with the exertion or her emotion. "You will be piskie. You will come back to the family, back in thy place."

"No."

One had to admire Calliopia's brevity. No needless explanations or excuses. No pleading or whining or discussion of her unhappy childhood caught between the pixie and fairy worlds. Just one word, repeated as necessary, an answer that was full and complete in itself.

Karol growled deep her in chest. Trying to push the energy of the emerald onto Calliopia was clearly a huge effort. Her face and body were rigid. The tone of the vibration went up another note and Reg again took a step back, hoping to avoid any backlash. Karol started to shake. She still hung on gamely, funneling the energy into the room, but Calliopia kept pushing it back without apparent effort.

Karol gave a cry and fell to her knees. The buzzing and the glow were cut off. Calliopia let her hands fall back to her sides. Ruan looked at Calliopia, and then went to Karol.

"She does not want," he told her.

Silent tears dripped down Karol's cheeks. Ruan held his hand out to her, and with her head bowed, Karol allowed him to raise her back to her feet. He walked her a couple of steps back and sat her down on the couch. Karol sniffled and wiped at the tears on her face.

"She is our sister," she told Ruan. "She was piskie."

He nodded. "No longer."

"She does not want."

Ruan nodded again. Karol didn't speak directly to Calliopia. Callie let out a sigh and looked around the room.

"Your house?" she asked Reg, who was still doing her best to be invisible.

"Yes. My house. Or Sarah's. I rent it from her." Reg had no idea whether renting was something a fairy would understand.

"You are her subject," Calliopia suggested.

Reg laughed. If Sarah was the lady of the manor and Reg was

living in the little cottage at her will, then Reg imagined she was, in fact, Sarah's subject. "Yes, something like that."

Calliopia noticed Starlight sitting nearby watching them. He had retreated to the kitchen during the battle of wills and was peeking out at them from behind the island where he was protected.

"Cat!" Calliopia made a hissing sound at Starlight. Starlight responded by raising his hackles and hissing back.

"Oh, leave him alone," Reg said crossly. "He has more right to be here than you do. He's not hurting anyone."

"I have the right to be here."

Reg hesitated. She didn't actually want the pixies and the fairy in her house, and the sooner she could send them on their way, the better.

"You called me," Calliopia reminded her.

"Well, yes, I guess I did. I didn't know it would work, though. Karol kept asking me to call you… so I tried it. But I didn't think you would actually come."

"You are a powerful wizard."

"No!" Reg laughed. "Just a psychic. No magical powers, just a few mind tricks…"

Calliopia raised her brows and shook her head. "A powerful wizard can do a call. You called me here."

"You are connected," Ruan said, looking back and forth between them. His eyes lingered on Calliopia for longer. "You did not tell me you were joined."

Calliopia made a face. "Unintended. She was tainted with my blood."

It wasn't until then that Reg noticed the belt with a sheath around Calliopia's waist. There was a knife in the sheath.

"You have your dagger," she said in surprise. "How did you get it? I thought Corvin had it!"

"It is my knife," Calliopia said simply.

"I know. But I thought it was in the car when we left your

house that day. I thought Corvin had taken it from the car later, or one of those people from his club."

Calliopia shrugged. Obviously, she had taken it from the car without their realizing it. It was evidence and was supposed to go back to the police department for use in the case against Hawthorne-Rose, but had mysteriously disappeared before it could be returned, a fact that still rankled Detective Jessup, whose custody it had been in at the time. Reg suspected that Jessup blamed her for the disappearance of the weapon, since she was the one who had wanted to see it and compare it to the one in her vision of Calliopia.

"If it is an unintended joining, you should sever it," Ruan suggested.

Calliopia nodded. Reg's stomach clenched. She had no idea what severing the link between them would involve, but she suspected she wasn't going to like it. Calliopia made a regal gesture for Reg to approach her. Reg wasn't in the habit of being ordered around by fairies, but she thought it might be a good idea to listen to what Calliopia had to say. If the two of them were magically joined or linked, Reg might continue to be harassed by magical folk who wanted to use that connection for one thing or another. Some, like Karol, would mean no harm, but Reg could imagine up several scenarios where people's intentions might not be so pure. She took a tentative step toward Calliopia.

"You two are... done...?" she asked tentatively, making a motion to include Calliopia and Karol.

"Here," Calliopia ordered, indicating the floor immediately in front of her. "Bring thyself here."

Reg rolled her eyes. She didn't have anyone to speak to about how ridiculous Calliopia's order was, but it deserved some kind of sarcastic comment that could be appreciated by a third party.

"You're not queen here," she muttered. "Before I do anything, I want to know that the two of you are done."

Calliopia said nothing. Reg looked at Karol, looking for some kind of response.

"She is fairy," Karol said dully. "She does not want."

"Okay. So you're done with your fight. Do you know anything about this joining…? Or unjoining?"

Karol shrugged, not answering. With Calliopia's refusal to be turned back into a pixie, she seemed uninterested in anything else. Maybe she was just exhausted after the effort to use the emerald to change Calliopia.

"Come," Calliopia ordered, pointing again to the floor in front of her.

"I called you here," Reg reminded her. "This is my home not yours. You can't give me orders here."

"We will sever the connection."

"Are you sure you want to do that? Do we need to do that?"

"Fairy and human should not be joined."

"Or what?"

"It is not natural. We shall sever the connection."

"What all is involved in severing the connection? Can I ask that?"

Calliopia sighed. She shook her head as if Reg were a stubborn child, refusing to do what she was told and asking too many questions. Reg didn't know how many years old Calliopia actually was; the fairies didn't age as quickly as humans, so there was no telling whether her apparent sixteen years of age might actually be sixty or six hundred. So to her, Reg might have been considered to be a child, just as Lord Bernier had referred to her.

"I will show you," Calliopia said.

Reg took another couple of steps forward until she was in front of Calliopia. But not exactly where she had pointed. Reg knew she had a stubborn streak a mile long. The fact had been pointed out to her many times. One of the things she could not stand was being ordered around and treated as a child. Even when she had been a child. It wasn't fair that adults should know what was going on, while keeping children in the dark. If there was one thing she had hated when she was a child, it was to be told, "you're too young to understand."

So she knew she was just being stubborn and rebellious when she refused to stand exactly there Calliopia said she should.

She waited for the next step, getting the distinct impression that Calliopia had expected her to go down on her knees. Calliopia stared at Reg for a minute, considering the situation, and then reached for her belt and drew the knife.

Reg took a step back, bringing her hand up in self-defense. "Whoa, whoa, whoa! Hang on, there!"

"We will sever the connection."

"How? If this involves cutting me again, I'm not on board. No more cutting."

"It is not a physical cut."

"What does that mean?"

Calliopia reached out and grabbed Reg by her injured hand. It was healing nicely, and Reg didn't like Calliopia assuming that she could just do whatever she wanted to. She resisted, pulling back.

"Tell me," Reg insisted. "I didn't ask you to show me. I want you to tell me with words."

Ignoring her, Calliopia held Reg's hand firmly and brought the knife closer.

"No," Reg tried to pull back.

Calliopia started to chant, her own fairy language that Reg couldn't understand. The least she could do was repeat the incantation in English, so Reg would know what to expect.

Calliopia ran the knife down Reg's forearm and hand. Not cutting into her with the point or the side of the blade, but skimming over the surface with the blade held parallel with Reg's hand and arm, as if cutting away invisible cobwebs. She might have shaved a few hairs, but she certainly didn't do any damage. When Calliopia was above the healing cut that had been inflicted with the knife in her hand, she paused, still chanting, but examining the condition of Reg's hand, studying the wound with a professional air.

"It's healing," Reg commented.

Calliopia ran the knife over the spot several times. That was where Reg felt their connection, so it made sense for Calliopia to focus her attention on it.

While it seemed ridiculous to the old, cynical Reg that a knife could actually have lasting magical connections that needed to be cleared away with a chant and ceremonial severing, the new Reg accepted that this was so. Even if she didn't understand it, she knew that there was some kind of connection between her and Calliopia. She wasn't sure she wanted it severed, but if Ruan and Calliopia thought that was for the best, then Reg was willing to give it a try. Especially if it meant her psychic abilities would go back to normal so that she would stop damaging things and could perform a find if she wanted to track something down.

Calliopia's chanting wound down. She pressed the handle of the knife into Reg's injured hand, wrapping her fingers around Reg's to tighten Reg's grip on the instrument. Reg gripped it, letting the roughness of the handle press against her hand.

After a few seconds holding it, with the chant still echoing in her ears, Calliopia released her hold on Reg, and pulled the knife back out of her hand. She ran a thumb over the cut on Reg's hand.

"This was an evil wound," she observed.

"It wasn't any fun, that's for sure," Reg replied flippantly. She paused. "So is it better now? Our connection is gone?"

Calliopia made a face. Reg had no idea what that meant. That it was gone and Calliopia was sad about it? That she hadn't been able to sever it? Or was it an expression with another cultural meaning that another fairy would have understood?

"The knife is contaminated," Ruan said.

Calliopia looked down at it.

"Show it to me," Ruan ordered.

Calliopia didn't seem offended by his terseness. She held it out closer to him. Ruan didn't take the knife from her hand, but just looked down at it.

He shook his head slowly.

"What's that supposed to mean?" Reg asked.

"It is not just your blood," Ruan told Calliopia.

She looked down at it. "Mine from the blood spell. And yours."

"And hers," Ruan nodded toward Reg. "And other piskies."

"It's my knife."

"It should be unmade."

"No."

"If it were to fall into the wrong hands…"

"It will not. It's my own." Calliopia slid it back into her sheath and looked at Ruan stubbornly.

"This is an evil thing," Ruan warned. "It will bring you both pain."

"It's already brought me pain," Reg said. "Hopefully, that is done."

"You have psychic power?" Ruan asked. "Look at it. Is it done?"

A rush of images flooded through Reg's head. She tried to grasp them, but could not hold on to any of them. It had been so quick, she hadn't been able to get a sense of what the future held for the knife, but she knew that what both of them said was true. It was an evil blade, and it would cause the both more pain before it was finished.

CHAPTER TWENTY-SEVEN

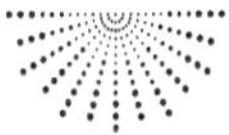

Karol was the first to leave. She got up from the couch and headed to the door without a word.

"Fare thee well," Calliopia offered.

"Good bye," Reg added, not sure what to say to this pixie who had barged into her home. She was glad to see Karol go, but sorry to see that she was so unhappy about not getting her sister back. Unlike Ruan, she didn't seem to be happy about seeing Calliopia and being able to know her as a fairy. She wanted everything to be as it was supposed to be, with Calliopia the fairy turned back into Alicorn the pixie, taking her place in the family.

Ruan said nothing by way of goodbyes. Maybe male pixies weren't that voluble. Ruan had never had a lot to say, keeping his counsel if he didn't have something to impart.

"She didn't leave anything here, did she?" Reg asked, looking around the coffee table top and feeling under the cushion where Karol had sat. "I don't want her to be able to come back in without permission."

Calliopia looked around and shook her head. "I think not. She will not want to return here."

"She's not going to come back for the emerald? She stole it once, you know."

Calliopia gave an unconcerned shrug. "The gem was important to her… but I do not think she will come for it again."

"Sarah will die if it gets taken away. She just about died this time."

"Humans are short-lived," Callie observed.

"Well… yes, usually we are, but that doesn't mean our lives aren't worth anything or that we don't want to prolong them when we can, when the person has good quality of life…"

Ruan stared at Reg inscrutably. Calliopia made no indication that she had even heard the comment.

"She will yet live," Ruan said.

Calliopia took him by the hand again. They looked like mother and child, Calliopia so much taller and Ruan with his boyish pixie face. They walked out the door without any farewells.

Reg looked at the closed door after they were gone. She wondered how they would get back to their car and their picnic.

"Well… good riddance, I suppose. I didn't actually want them here, and now they are gone."

Starlight made a couple of meows of agreement. Reg went over to him and scratched his ears.

"You just never know what's going to happen around here, do you? Every time I think I'm getting a handle on what's going on, something new pops up."

Starlight purred and rubbed against Reg.

"At least now I know you're not going around burglarizing houses and stealing jewelry."

Thinking about Sarah and her emerald, Reg decided she should go over to the main house and see how Sarah was faring. Hopefully, she was recovering her strength and would be out of bed. Reg wasn't sure how much longer Sarah would have to live, but hopefully she could have good quality of life for at least a couple more years. Reg didn't want to lose her.

She knocked at the door and waited. She felt heavy and tired after the strange events of the morning. Dueling magic was not something she wanted to get in the way of.

The door opened and it was not Marian, but Sarah. Not the Sarah that Reg had left in bed the day before. She was bright-eyed, dressed and made up for the day. The dark, hollow eyes and deep wrinkles were gone. If anything, she looked younger than she had when Reg had first met her. Reg stood there with her mouth open, unable to find the words.

"Well, don't just stand there catching flies," Sarah laughed. "Come in, Reg."

Reg followed her into the kitchen, and Sarah motioned for her to sit down, going over to the stove to stir something she had bubbling on the back burner. Reg shook her head in disbelief.

"I don't understand. I thought... everybody kept saying that the emerald couldn't make you younger, it could only stop or slow the aging process..."

"I'm really not sure what happened," Sarah said slowly. "It's never done that before. I was just sitting in my bedroom, trying to get up the energy to get out of bed and get myself dressed, and the emerald started to vibrate. I was holding on to it, and it nearly writhed right out of my hand. It started to glow and pulsate and kept buzzing..." Sarah shook her head. "The whole room was glowing. I felt like it was going to burst. And when it eventually stopped... I didn't have any trouble getting up to get ready. I had the energy, and my knees didn't hurt..." She gave a little laugh. "Nothing hurt! It's been a long time since I could say that."

"You look amazing."

"I feel amazing. But I can't explain what happened. I wasn't aware of any power the emerald had to reverse the aging process. I don't know what I did to trigger the reaction..."

"I might know something about that."

"You?"

Reg motioned for Sarah to sit down, then told her about waking up to find the pixie in her living room, and the encounter with Calliopia and the dueling magical powers.

"So Karol was trying to use the emerald to reverse Calliopia's change, and Calliopia was pushing it back," Sarah said slowly. "Reflecting that magic right back to me."

"I guess." Reg shrugged helplessly. "I can't say I understand how it all works. Every day, I learn something new. You've had the emerald for years, and you never knew it could do that?"

"It may be something that only pixies can access. They have an affinity for gemstones. Things that come out of the ground…"

Reg leaned back in her chair. "What a rollercoaster this has all been."

* * *

After Jessup's stubborn refusal to believe that Reg hadn't been involved in the theft of the emerald, Reg wasn't in much of a mood to call her. If they were going to be friends, or if Reg were at least going to consult on future cases, then Jessup should believe her and not the wild stories told by Corvin or anyone else.

But Reg had been retained to try to find the knife before the whole emerald affair had begun, so she felt some responsibility to report back to Jessup the details of what had happened. Jessup suggested The Crystal Bowl for dinner, and since Reg hadn't had a real meal in a couple of days, she agreed, so long as it was on Jessup's tab.

They looked at each other across the table warily. It was too bad, when Reg could be so useful to Jessup and could have used another friend, that they had to be separated by their respective associations with the law, Jessup in law enforcement and Reg… frequently on the other side of the fence.

"You had something to tell me?" Jessup asked, brushing back a lock of hair that had escaped her sleek police bun.

"It's about the knife. Hawthorne-Rose's knife."

"What about it?"

"Calliopia has it."

Jessup's brows went up in surprise. "Calliopia? Are you sure? I was sure it was Hunter."

"Nope, I guess we were both wrong. I remember her asking for it at the castle… she got her hands on it somehow. Maybe the butler retrieved it, or Callie called it with some spell."

"How do you know? You had a vision?"

"Better than that. She came to my house. She did this ceremonial thing, severing the link between us with the knife. I held it my hand, for part of the ceremony."

"You shouldn't have given it back. Or you should have called me."

"I already tried to wrestle an emerald away from a pixie. I don't think I'm about to tackle a fairy and a pixie for a knife. I'd end up with it in my throat."

"Most knife fights lead to—" Jessup stopped, reconsidering sharing this tidbit. "You're probably right, but I wish you would have at least called me."

"Things happened pretty fast. I don't think I could have. And then even if you got there before they had left…"

"I might not have been able to get it back, but at least I could file a report saying that I'd seen it and knew whose possession it was in."

"Would that do you any good with the department?"

Jessup sighed. "No. Probably not. Best to just let them forget about it at this point. If I keep bringing it up, they'll just keep extending my probationary period."

"You're on probation?"

"You can't get around losing important evidence without repercussions. Now there's the emerald too. But I think they're happy if they can just sweep that one under the rug without any physical evidence being logged. Seeing as they lost the accused."

When their meals arrived, Reg expanded on the story and gave Jessup the details of the encounter with Calliopia, Ruan, and Karol.

"Wait a minute." Jessup held up her hand to stop Reg while she finished chewing a big bite of her burger. "You *called* Calliopia?"

"Not like on the phone. And I didn't know I could do it. Karol kept telling me that was what I had to do, so I gave it a try."

"That is super complex magic. I don't know of anyone in the community who can do a call."

"Really?"

"Moving a person over time and space. What do you think?"

"Two people. Her and Ruan."

Jessup shook her head. "That's incredible."

"I don't know if I could do it with anyone else. I think with Calliopia… since we were connected, it was easier for me to do."

"Probably, but it's still pretty amazing."

Reg shrugged, not sure how to respond to this. Since she had arrived at Black Sands, she'd been told that her powers were unusual. Her ignorance of the magical world meant that she didn't have anything to measure herself against. Before coming to Black Sands, she hadn't even known that she actually had psychic powers.

They ate in silence for a few minutes, each thinking through the details.

"It riles me that she stole the knife," Jessup said.

"I'm sure she didn't think of it as stealing. It was her knife, she was just taking back what was hers."

"Just like Karol feeling entitled to the emerald because pixies claim everything formed underground. I get it, but it burns my butt. Without the knife… we still have a case against Hawthorne-Rose, but the loss of physical evidence makes it that much harder, gives the defense a crack to pry at. I don't like cracks."

Bill approached their table, a towel thrown over his shoulder. "Evening Reg, Detective Jessup."

Reg nodded a greeting.

Bill flourished a scroll. "Message for you." He kept it just out of reach of Reg's fingertips. "Maybe you could read it outside."

"Why should I read it outside?"

"If it's bad news… I don't want any broken glassware."

"Broken…? Why would it be bad news, did something—"

Reg suddenly had an idea of where the scroll had come from. She swore. "Is this some kind of official notification? Like from Corvin's tribunal?"

He gave her a shrug that was also an affirmation that she had guessed correctly. "Like I say, it may be better if you read it outside, away from the breakables."

"I'll control myself."

He sighed and handed it to her. Reg didn't open the scroll right away. She looked at Jessup.

"Is this going to be really bad?"

"I don't know. I haven't heard anything."

Reg laid it beside her plate and took a couple more bites of her dinner. "They're not going to bind him. I already know that."

Jessup nodded. "That's only done in rare cases where harm has been done and the subject continues to put others in danger or threatens the community with exposure."

"So what are the other options? They put it on his permanent record and don't let him be prom king?"

"That would be a censure, which is a possibility. They could go all the way in his favor and say that he didn't do anything wrong. That he didn't break any of the rules of the coven."

Reg made a face. She pictured Davyn Smithy and remembered the way she had felt under examination by the tribunal. They would love to put all of the blame for the incident on her and say that Corvin had followed all of the restrictions that were placed on him. They could say that he was right and it was against the constitution of the coven to restrict him from doing what he was naturally born to do. Feeding his hunger was a physical need. If he didn't feed, she knew what kind of agony he would be in. Whether it would eventually kill him like starving would, she didn't know, but feeling his pain had certainly affected *her* physically.

"They as much as told me I was asking for it," she told Jessup, trying to get the bitter taste out of her mouth. "I knew what he could do. I had doubts about whether he could control himself. I ended up alone with him. Therefore…"

She shook her head and took a drink.

Jessup reached across the table and picked up the scroll.

"Hey!" Reg protested, trying to snatch it back.

Jessup kept it out of her reach. She broke the wax seal and unrolled the scroll. "You're just torturing yourself. You'll be happier a lot sooner if you read it."

"Not if they let him off!"

"You're making yourself miserable thinking that they did. You're not going to be any worse if you know for sure."

"That's my scroll! Isn't interfering with mail a federal crime?"

"It's not federal post. It's a hand-delivered message. It might not be ethical, but it's not illegal. And in this case, I'm doing it to help you." Jessup dropped her eyes to the scroll and read it. She turned it around and showed it to Reg, holding it open.

Reg scowled. "I told Davyn I can't read his stupid old-fashioned writing!"

"They've shunned him."

"Is that the same as censuring?" Reg didn't know why they couldn't just speak plain English. They were as enamored with their old-fashioned words as with the unreadable script and archaic attitudes.

"No. It means that no one in his coven can talk to him or have anything to do with him for the length of the sentence. He's basically kicked out of the community."

Reg was surprised. She hadn't been expecting anything as severe as that. "For how long?"

Jessup looked at the scroll as she dropped it on the table in front of Reg. "Indefinitely." She looked up. "I've never seen that before. Ever. He's shunned from the community until he can prove that he can be a worthy member again."

Reg's stomach felt like it was filled with lead. "Really? That's… they really are punishing him, aren't they?"

"Yes. Hunter is a strong warlock and he has an incredible store of knowledge. They're sacrificing those assets in order to discipline him."

Reg was embarrassed about having made accusations that the tribunal was just going to let Corvin get off scot-free. She looked down at the scroll, her heart thumping.

"So what does that mean to Corvin? He can't talk to anyone in his coven, but he can still practice…?"

"Yes. He can still support himself. They haven't cut off his livelihood. But no one will refer business to him. No one will talk to him. He won't be able to go to any of their gatherings."

"But he can go to other stuff. As long as it's not his coven."

"Yes."

"And he can still talk to anyone he wants to."

"Yes."

Reg took a couple more bites, but she was no longer hungry. She poked at her dinner. "I keep going back and forth between feeling sorry for him and being so angry with him that I could—"

She saw Jessup's look of alarm and felt the people around her tense. Reg took a breath and tried to keep her voice calm and reasonable. There was no point in making people think she was going to start blowing things up. Hopefully, now that Calliopia had severed her connection with Reg, there would be no more incidents.

"I don't know how I'm supposed to feel about him," she said in a more reasonable voice. "Am I supposed to be mad? Or feel bad? Or not care?"

"I don't think there's any one way you're 'supposed to' feel. You feel how you feel, and if that's ambivalent, then that's fine. That's just how you feel."

"But what am I supposed to do with that? Should I go the other direction when I run into him? Should I 'shun' him too? Or do I pretend that I don't know what happened or that it's not my fault? I know I'm going to run into him again. So what do I do?"

Jessup studied her for a few long seconds. Then she gave a small, slow smile. "WWRRD?"

"What?"

"What would Reg Rawlins do? The Reg Rawlins I know doesn't concern herself with what other people think. She has her own opinions. Why make a choice based on what someone else thinks you should feel or do?"

Reg felt herself flush. "Well… yeah. Why should I?" She considered. "I'm getting so wrapped up in how different things are here that I think I need to follow some set of rules to get along. But when have I ever fit in? Why start now? I am what I am."

Jessup nodded. "Exactly. I'd still recommend following the local laws, but as far as who you choose to talk to or be friends with… you should make your own choices, not follow everyone else's rules."

Reg felt a rush of warmth confirming that it was the right path for her. The accusations of the warlocks at the tribunal had thrown her off balance and made her question her own decisions, but no more. She would do what she wanted and be friends with who she wanted, no matter what anyone else thought.

"So does that mean Hunter is in your crosshairs or that he'll live to fight another day?" Jessup asked.

* * *

It was a relief to step out of the hot sun into the cool shelter. Ruan lowered his hood and took off his dark glasses, smiling at Calliopia.

"I am handling it better, don't you think?"

Calliopia gave him an arch look, eyebrows raised. "You do very well for a pixie."

"I can stay in the sun almost all day."

She reached out a long, slender finger and touched his cheek. "I love you for you, not whether you can stay in the sun."

"But you like the sun, so I like the sun."

"You don't have to like it."

"But I do."

Calliopia gave Ruan a long look, and he knew that she understood his words were not true. But he had not said them to be believed.

"I remember how I hated the sun when I was a pixie," Calliopia said, her musical voice amused. "It burned my skin and hurt my eyes. I had thick dark curtains in my room. I would keep them shut all day. I would crawl under my covers and pretend I was in a burrow underground."

Ruan's heart went to the tunnels he had grown up in. He would have done almost anything to be able to return there or to be able to dig even a small burrow of his own. It was instinctual. Unable to return to a burrow of her own, Calliopia had approximated one the best she could until she had turned. Once she was a fairy, she no longer wanted to escape the sun, but to bask in it. Now the mere thought of returning to the underground realm made her shudder.

Ruan would have done almost anything to be able to go underground, far out of reach of the sun's rays.

Anything but give up Calliopia.

Calliopia stroked Ruan's face again. "So far away, my boy."

"Just thinking." Ruan caught her fingers and kissed them. He tugged her closer and she bent down to kiss him. Ruan felt the dagger in its sheath at her waist. He pulled back from her, his hand hovering over it. He again felt its dark presence, the menace that the blade held toward them.

"You must unmake the blade," he urged her yet again. "It has peril in it."

Calliopia's hand dropped to the sheathed knife and she stroked the length of it.

"No. It will be safe as long as it is with me."

CHAPTER TWENTY-EIGHT

*R*eg turned over, tangled in the sheets. Her mind wandered restlessly through half-formed dreams. There was an ominous presence that seemed to follow her from one place to another.

It was familiar.

She could remember it from when she was young, from her earliest memories. That threat had followed her from one place to another, making it impossible for her to sleep soundly, impossible to trust anyone, and impossible to do anything without fear.

She wasn't sure when it had gone away. Maybe there had been one good thing about foster care, and that was that in her movement from home to home, she had eventually lost the presence. In her later years, she had been able to live a relatively normal life, without the constant anxiety that something terrible was going to happen.

Reg struggled to pull herself into consciousness. She needed to wake up so she could leave the nightmares behind once more.

She awoke with a deep gasp, like a drowning man rising for air. Then she lay there for a few minutes, waiting for her heart to stop racing. She pushed the sweat-soaked sheets away from her and got up. After the bathroom, she walked into the kitchen and looked for something to eat. She stood at the counter, taking another deep breath and waiting for the feeling of impending doom to fade.

Like it always did.

Only this time, it didn't.

**Did you enjoy this book? Reviews and recommendations are
vital to making a book successful.**

**Please leave a review at your favorite book store or review site
and share it with your friends.**

Don't miss the following bonus material:
Sign up for mailing list to get a free ebook
Read a sneak preview chapter
Other books by P.D. Workman
Learn more about the author

Sign up for my mailing list at pdworkman.com and get Gluten-Free Murder for free!

PREVIEW OF NIGHT OF NINE TAILS

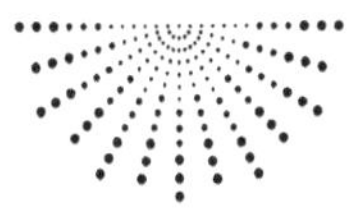

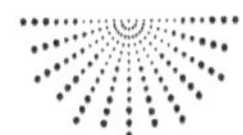

Reg climbed out of bed, the dread from her nightmare still squeezing her heart so tightly it hurt. It had been a long time since she had felt that anxious without knowing what it was she had to fear. She was keenly attuned to the possible dangers in her life, always staying one step ahead of the authorities or anyone who might have figured out her latest scam, but the heart-squeezing dread was different. It wasn't connected to any specific risk she could identify.

She could write it off as the vestiges of her nightmare, but she didn't want to ignore the warning. It could be something that her subconscious was trying to warn her about. If something was bothering her, she needed to know what it was to address it. If it was time to leave Black Sands… she didn't want to, but if it were the only way to stay safe, then she would.

Starlight was sitting in the window looking out at the back garden. He looked over at Reg and let out a low, mournful howl. Reg went over to him and petted him and let her tuxedo cat rub the top of his head against her chin and neck.

"What's the matter, Star? Did you have a nightmare too?"

He sat back and started to wash, giving her the cold shoulder. She felt his rebuff keenly. She knew very well that he wasn't unhappy because he'd been having a nightmare. She was being silly, but in doing so, she had made light of his problem, which, as far as he was concerned, was far more important than her petty human problems.

"Okay, I'm sorry." She stroked him again. "What is it?"

She peered out the window. She could see Sarah working in the garden, something that lifted her heart just a little. Not so long ago, she had been worried that she was going to lose Sarah for good. Suffering the effects of losing her powerful emerald amulet, Sarah had been on the brink of death. It had been a hard-won battle to bring her back. Seeing her puttering around in the garden was something that Reg had never expected to see again and it warmed her heart.

She kneaded the back of Starlight's neck. "Are you looking for your friend?"

This time he didn't rebuff her. She could feel the warmth of his confirmation, but also the emptiness and longing that the other cat had left behind.

Reg had only seen the black cat he watched for twice. Then, Reg's mind had been on more important things; finding the emerald and proving that she wasn't the one who had stolen it. It wasn't easy for someone with a past like Reg's to prove her innocence. While no one in Black Sands knew her full history, both Corvin and Detective Jessup had a pretty good idea that she had stolen and fenced jewelry and other valuable goods before.

"I'll ask Sarah if she's seen any sign of him," Reg told Starlight, kissing his velvety black ears.

He stared at her reproachfully with his mismatched green and blue eyes. Reg coughed and corrected herself.

"I'll ask Sarah if she's seen *her*."

She chuckled as she grabbed a housecoat to pull on over her shorts and t-shirt and walked out to the kitchen. Starlight remained in the window watching for any sign of the black cat rather than following Reg into the kitchen and demanding breakfast. He really was worried about the black cat.

Reg turned on the coffee machine. She looked at her phone for any new mail or messages while she waited for it to brew a pot of coffee, trying to immerse herself in something other than the tightness around her heart. If she just ignored the feeling, it would go away. If it was just general anxiety, then distracting herself with something else should help.

But even before she filled her first cup of coffee, she knew that it wasn't going away. It wasn't just the vestiges of a bad dream, brought on by imagination or watching TV too late into the night.

Something was really wrong.

She just didn't know what it was.

* * *

Reg slipped on a pair of pink flip-flops and went around the cottage to the garden, where Sarah was standing, hands on well-padded hips, looking at the bent and broken plants, shaking her head. She glanced at Reg and shook her gray head.

"It looks like a hurricane was through here."

Reg sipped her coffee, which was really still too hot to drink.

"I'm sorry," she acknowledged. She wasn't apologizing for something she had done wrong, just saying that she felt sorry for the state of things. She was sorry that Sarah was feeling bad.

It was, in fact, not Reg or a hurricane that was responsible for all of the beaten-down plants in the garden. The damage had been done by Sarah herself, in a demented frenzy as she had tried to chase off the black cat that Starlight was looking for as he sat in the window. Reg hadn't seen it—hadn't seen her —since.

"I half-remember doing it," Sarah said, her forehead wrinkling into frown lines, "but it's like it happened a long time ago to someone else. I know I was angry, uncontrollably angry, but I can't remember feeling that way. Not... really."

"You were not well. But now you're feeling better... and I bet it won't be long before you have everything whipped back into shape again."

"I think it's taken a bad enough beating already. I need to remove all of the detritus and tie up some of the plants until they are strong enough… a lot of them won't bloom again this year. It's such a meaningless loss. It didn't have to happen at all…"

Reg tried another sip of coffee. "Do you want a cup?" she offered Sarah. "I just brewed a pot."

"No, dear. I have found that since my… reanimation… caffeine just puts me over the top. I have more energy than I know what to do with."

"I could make you some tea."

"I'm fine. I've had my breakfast and I don't need anything else. I just need to figure out how to get started here." Sarah sighed. "You're up early. Do you have an appointment?"

"No. I'm just having nightmares. I thought I might as well get up."

Sarah nodded. "I could make you a potion to help with nightmares."

Reg shook her head. She assumed that Sarah just meant some herbal remedy with valerian and whatever other brain-calming herbs she could think of, but Reg wasn't about to swallow anything called a potion. She wasn't that far gone yet.

"It's okay. I'm sure they'll pass in a few days."

"You need to make sure you get a good sleep. It can affect your productivity. Especially your psychic abilities."

Uncomfortable, Reg changed the subject. "So, I was wondering if you saw that cat around here again."

"Which cat?" Sarah frowned and motioned to her wrecked garden. "The one that caused all of this?"

It certainly hadn't been the cat's fault that Sarah had freaked out, trying to beat it with a broom and flattening most of the garden.

"Uh, yes. The black cat."

"It's a stray," Sarah said dismissively. "It will be in someone else's yard."

"Well, probably," Reg agreed. "I'm just looking for it… Starlight is looking for it. Her." She looked at the cottage window. "He's sitting there watching for her. But I haven't seen her since that day."

"I don't want another cat wandering around here. Starlight is inside, and that's fine; I don't want a cat out in the garden chasing away my birds."

"I know. But Starlight is very… convincing. He really wants me to look for her."

"You're not going to become the neighborhood cat lady, taking in all of the strays in the neighborhood. Not while you're living in my guest cottage."

"I don't want more than one cat."

"Then what are you going to do when you find it?"

"I don't know." Reg just knew that Starlight wanted her to look for his new amour. "I guess… maybe I would find a good home for her, and I could take Starlight there sometime to visit with her?" She rolled her eyes. "I don't really know anything about cat relationships. Do you?"

"No. Nor do I want to."

"So, you haven't seen her around anywhere?"

"No, I haven't. And if I do, I'll chase her away again."

Reg nodded. When Sarah said that she didn't like cats, she had meant it. Even though she was polite to Starlight and would even feed him when she came to see Reg, she was still not a cat person and didn't want them anywhere near her birds.

There was a loud crash, and Reg whirled around, putting her hands up, ready to defend herself. But there was no imminent attack. Just the rattle of a truck as it continued to drive down the street in front of Sarah's house. It had hit a bump or a pothole along the way, that was all. Sarah raised her brows at Reg, amused.

"A little jumpy today?"

"I just thought…" Reg trailed off. "Yeah, I guess I'm a little jumpy today. I don't know what is going on with me… I'm feeling anxious all the time… like something is going to happen. Something is wrong."

Sarah picked up a ball of twine, finally deciding where to start on her garden refurbishment.

"Well, you could help me with the garden. It's a very relaxing hobby."

"I'm not really looking for a hobby. I need to stay focused on my business if I'm going to support myself."

"Are you worried about failing? I thought that your psychic services business had been going quite well."

"It is. I can't complain about that. You've been a real help to me with all of your contacts and I'm always getting new clients. It's just that… I don't think this anxiety is related to my business; it's something else."

"But you don't know what it is?"

"No."

Reg watched Sarah as she approached a droopy, bent-over plant and lifted its branches tentatively as if trying to gauge whether it were still alive or beyond repair. She started to tie it to a nearby stake.

"Maybe you're picking up someone else's anxiety, then. Maybe it's not even your own."

Reg still had a hard time believing she actually had a psychic gift. She was good at reading people, that much was certain, but all of the other odd things that had happened since she had moved to Black Sands seemed like magic tricks. Someone using sleight of hand to gaslight her into thinking that she really did have unexplained powers. But she couldn't think of a way to explain everything that had happened using science or illusion.

She couldn't deny that she was often influenced by others' moods, though. Maybe that's all that Sarah was saying. She had recently met with someone or been around someone who had been very anxious, and she had just taken on those emotions herself without realizing it.

"Yeah. Maybe that's it."

"Have you had a client recently who was worried about the future?" Sarah suggested. "I imagine that a lot of the people who hire you are concerned about the future. That's what tends to worry humans the most. Not knowing where they are going."

"I can't think of anyone offhand, but there must have been. That must be what I'm doing. I'm just… empathetic."

"Exactly," Sarah agreed. "Maybe have a nice, calming cup of tea instead of caffeine in the morning, take some time to meditate and center yourself. I'm sure it will help to smooth away your anxiety. And if not… I do know some recipes. Or I could help you to find a healer who could help you if you don't trust my skills."

"Oh, it isn't that. I'm just not used to… magical solutions." Reg tried to explain it in a way that wouldn't offend Sarah. "I'm sure that your potions are just as good as the other charms and protection spells around the property. You're very good at what you do."

Sarah sighed, tying up another branch. "I think I'm going to have to find someone who can fix gardens. It's going to take forever to repair one plant at a time, and then to wait to see how they respond. I need a spellcaster who is good with flora."

Reg couldn't offer much help in that direction. "Maybe… Letticia would know someone."

"I'm sure I have a name in my Rolodex. I'll just have to take a look. It's been a long time since I needed to hire someone to do this." She put her hands on her hips again, surveying the minuscule amount of work she had done. "I really don't want to be tied to my garden all day. I want to be out, having a good time."

For a woman who, according to Jessup, was several centuries old, Sarah had a remarkable level of vigor, which had grown with her recent healing.

If Reg hadn't known that taking the emerald away would kill Sarah in short order, she might have been tempted to have it for her own.

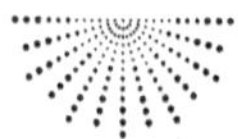

*O*nce Sarah decided to get someone else to come and help her to put her garden in order, she headed back to the big house, and Reg returned to the rental cottage to report to Starlight on her non-progress.

The cat made a snorting noise that suggested to Reg that she wasn't trying hard enough and finally left his perch on the windowsill to yowl around his bowl, insisting that Reg find something better than the stale kitty kibble that remained in his bowl. He rubbed against Reg's legs and then the fridge to encourage her to make the connection between the cat and his need to eat something tasty and nourishing from the fridge.

"I'm not that stupid," Reg said, "I actually do know what you want."

He sat back and looked at her, his gaze steady. If she knew what he wanted, then why did it take her so long to comply with his requests? How hard was it to go to the fridge and use her huge paws with their opposable thumbs to get him something good to eat?

Reg sighed, shook her head, and did as she was told, poking through the leftover fast food boxes and Tupperware containing offerings from Sarah. She found some beef stew that she needed to get rid of one way or another. She spooned some into Starlight's dish, and he pushed his head in to start eating before she had even finished dishing it up.

Reg watched him chow down noisily for a few seconds, then picked up her coffee and watched the house, feeling for Sarah. She knew without having to see that Sarah was going out again. Since her miraculous healing, she had been going out nearly every day. She was meeting with this friend or that new beau or somebody else who Reg had never heard of. Having decided that she wasn't going to do the garden work herself, she was now free to go gallivanting off yet again.

It was pretty sad that a centuries-old woman had a better social life than Reg. Reg didn't have a boyfriend, though she wasn't sure that she wanted one. And she didn't have very many people she could actually call friends. There was Sarah, of course, but she and Reg didn't see each other socially unless Reg happened to be eating at The Crystal Bowl, which was where Sarah usually ate, or they were both at a community event together. There was Detective Jessup, but Reg was not happy with her, primarily due to the fact that Marta Jessup had considered Reg the prime suspect in the investigation of Sarah's missing emerald. It was true that multiple witnesses and Reg's past had all made her look guilty, but she *wasn't* guilty, and if Jessup had been a friend, she would have known that.

But that was fine, because it wasn't a good idea for Reg to have a friend who was a cop. She knew that there were a lot of cons and cops who were close friends, but she had never understood how it worked, and she couldn't see herself fully trusting anyone who had anything to do with law enforcement. Back in Bald Eagle Falls, her foster sister Erin's boyfriend was a cop. But Erin had a legitimate business baking gluten-free products now. The fact that she kept finding bodies or getting involved in police investigations didn't help matters, but in spite of all of that, she seemed to have a pretty good relationship with Officer Handsome.

Reg needed to find some new friends. She was usually good at making friends quickly. She had been moved around a lot as a kid, so she'd had to develop some good social skills if she wanted to play with anyone other than her imaginary friends.

Corvin had suggested that Reg's imaginary friends hadn't been invented, but ghostly, but Reg thought he was either pulling her leg or he was mistaken. She hadn't learned until later in life that she could pretend to talk to dead people and get money for it. As a child, she had just been entertaining herself by peopling her surroundings with interesting characters, like a writer writing a book. The psychologists had always said that she had a vivid imagination, if they could just get her to put it to good use.

Which was precisely what Reg was doing.

* * *

After Corvin's hearing, a security guard had walked Reg out to her car. He hadn't been an unattractive guy and had shown an interest in her. He had given her his card, but she couldn't remember what she had done with it. She tried to remember what she had been wearing that day. It was probably still in her pocket or her purse. She wouldn't have thrown it out.

She tried her purse first, but it was the sort of cavernous bag where miscellany went to die. Who knew what kind of crud had collected in the bottom of it. She was always putting little things in there for an emergency or to put to good use later, and could never find them again when she wanted them.

She looked through the top few layers, including pulling out her wallet and checking to see if she had put the card into one of the slots, but there was no sign of it. She didn't want to dig all the way to the bottom or to dump it out, so she decided to try her pockets instead. She always put her clothes back in her dresser or closet if they didn't need washing. She couldn't see the point of washing an item every time you wore it if you didn't sweat or spill and it still looked fresh and unwrinkled. Her wardrobe was pretty small, and she didn't want to have to do the laundry every two or three days.

She was pretty sure she had been wearing pants, not one of her gypsy skirts when she went to the trial. She had driven to Letticia's house that day, and it was a long way through the woods. She hadn't known whether she was going to end up having to hike up a trail or something else requiring a full range of movement, so she had worn pants rather than a skirt.

Reg went through the pockets of a couple of pairs of pants. She hated how women's clothing so seldom had pockets and refused to buy any without pockets. It was easy to sew pockets into a skirt, but tailored pants were another story. It was much easier to hide things quickly if one had proper pockets. What else was she going to do, stuff something down her bra? While that might work for smaller items, something larger would end up looking odd.

In the second pair of pants, her fingers touched a card. Reg pulled it out, feeling a warm rush of satisfaction over having found it. She turned the card over to look at the name on it. Damon Knight. She didn't know much about him, but it sounded like a magical name. He had appeared to have some magic the day of the trial, able to put out a small fire with his powers without even turning a hair. And he hadn't escorted Reg to her car because she was causing trouble or because he wanted to protect her from an ugly mob. He'd walked her to her car because he wanted a chance to spend a few minutes alone with her and to give her his number.

Reg left her bedroom and walked over to the wicker couch. She had left her phone on the coffee table in front of it. She didn't have any appointments in the next couple of hours, so the time was hers to use as she liked. She sat down on the couch and curled her feet up beneath her, trying to get comfy. The wicker couch always seemed to be lumpy or poky somewhere. But it was a piece of furniture that she hadn't had to buy herself, so what did she have to complain about?

"Come on over, Starlight."

The cat was washing in a bright sunbeam. He stopped and looked at Reg as if he couldn't believe that she had interrupted his ablutions.

"Come on." Reg patted the cushion next to her. "I'll scratch your ears."

He looked at her for another minute, then consented to join her. He jumped up beside her and accepted the pets and cuddles and ear scratches. She touched the white spot on his forehead, the star that gave him his name. His third eye, Sarah called it.

"What do you think?" she asked him thoughtfully. "Think Damon will answer the phone, or will it go to voicemail? He might be working. I don't know if he works regular hours or only special events. He could be an accountant or something boring the rest of the time."

Starlight rubbed against her hand, purring, lapping up the attention. Reg focused on him for a few more minutes before picking up her phone to call Damon.

"Here, lay down now and cuddle," she encouraged, patting the couch to encourage him to lie down. Starlight continued to rub and bump against her. She rolled her eyes and tapped Damon's number into her phone.

It only rang once or twice before a click told Reg it had connected. It was so fast that she was sure it had gone to voicemail and she was trying to think of what she wanted to say in her message. Did she even want to leave a message, or should she try him again another time so that they could actually talk to each other and judge each other's temperature?

"Damon," he said.

Reg waited for the rest of the recording, then realized that was it. She wasn't talking to a machine; she was talking to the warlock himself.

"Oh, hi, Damon. I don't know if you remember me, but I met you at Corvin Hunter's hearing…"

"Reg Rawlins," Damon said, a smile in his voice.

Reg smiled back. "Yes. That's right. You do remember."

"I was hoping you would call."

"Well… I did." Reg rolled her eyes at her response. How quickly the conversation was dwindling to something she was likely to have had in sixth grade.

"How are you?" Damon asked politely. "Did you hear the verdict about Hunter?"

"Yes, I did. I got a delivery."

"Good. They're supposed to notify all of the concerned parties, but sometimes someone gets missed. Whether by accident or on purpose…"

"So they decided to shun him."

"Yes."

"Are you… part of Corvin's coven?" Reg asked tentatively. She didn't know how big the magical community was and whether there were multiple covens or just the one. Were all warlocks automatically admitted to the coven, or did they have to qualify to get in? Or did they have a choice as to what coven they wanted to go to?

"No." Damon gave a low chuckle. "I'm more of a lone wolf. Which is one of the reasons that I can work security at something like that. You couldn't do security if the warlock on trial was someone from your own coven. Too close of a relationship."

"So the two of you are not friends?"

"No. I don't have anything to do with Hunter. Not because I have anything against him… he was just never my type. You know. The kind of guy that I would associate with."

"What kind of guy do you associate with?"

"Well, as I say, I'm sort of a lone wolf. So… not a lot of people. I have a couple of close friends, but other than that… my circle is pretty small."

"Mine too," Reg admitted. "I need to make some new friends."

"Old ones just not holding up?" he teased.

"No." Reg let out a sigh that was all too real. "I need someone I can hang out with. I haven't had a lot of luck in making friends here. I mean… I haven't made enemies, but I'd like to get to know some people who are… more like me."

"Psychics?" Damon suggested.

"No way," Reg said immediately. She had only associated with one other psychic so far, and Marian was not the kind of person she wanted to be around. She didn't want to be around anyone who was going to try to read her or to influence her feelings. Marian was good at manipulating people, and Reg wanted to stay in full control of her own thoughts and feelings.

"No way?" Damon repeated, laughing. "You sound pretty adamant about that!"

"Have you ever been in a room where everyone is trying to read everyone else?" Reg asked. "I'd go crazy. I'll keep my thoughts to myself."

"That makes sense." Damon didn't say anything for a moment, and Reg tried to figure out how to take control of the conversation and steer it in the direction she wanted to go. "So did you decide to take me up on my offer?"

Reg frowned, trying to remember the conversation. What offer had he made?

"Umm… I…"

"I offered to take you out to dinner, show you around town. I didn't hear from you right away, so I thought maybe you weren't interested."

"Things have just been a little crazy with me lately. Well, forget lately, they've been a little crazy ever since I hit town. But yeah, I would be interested in getting out… getting to know Black Sands a little better."

"Excellent. Are you free tonight?"

"Let me take a look at my appointment book. Hang on. I should have done that before I called you, but I forgot."

"Sure."

Reg went to the kitchen, where her appointment book was lying on the island. She kept it out where Sarah could access it so that if Sarah happened to make an appointment for her, she would not be surprised. She opened the calendar and quickly found the day.

"Yeah, it looks like I'm free tonight. About seven onward?"

"Seven it is," Damon agreed. "Can I pick you up at your house?"

"No, you don't need to do that. Why don't we meet somewhere?"

* * *

Night of Nine Tails, Book #4 of the Reg Rawlins, Psychic Investigator series by P.D. Workman can be purchased at pdworkman.com

ABOUT THE AUTHOR

Award-winning and USA Today bestselling author P.D. (Pamela) Workman writes riveting mystery/suspense and young adult books dealing with mental illness, addiction, abuse, and other real-life issues. For as long as she can remember, the blank page has held an incredible allure and from a very young age she was trying to write her own books.

Workman wrote her first complete novel at the age of twelve and continued to write as a hobby for many years. She started publishing in 2013. She has won several literary awards from Library Services for Youth in Custody for her young adult fiction. She currently has over 60 published titles and can be found at pdworkman.com.

Born and raised in Alberta, Workman has been married for over 25 years and has one son.

* * *

Please visit P.D. Workman at pdworkman.com to see what else she is working on, to join her mailing list, and to link to her social networks.

* * *

If you enjoyed this book, please take the time to recommend it to other purchasers with a review or star rating and share it with your friends!

facebook.com/pdworkmanauthor

twitter.com/pdworkmanauthor

instagram.com/pdworkmanauthor

amazon.com/author/pdworkman

bookbub.com/authors/p-d-workman

goodreads.com/pdworkman

linkedin.com/in/pdworkman

pinterest.com/pdworkmanauthor

youtube.com/pdworkman